TICKETS

by
Richard P. Brickner

SIMON AND SCHUSTER
NEW YORK

Published by Simon and Schuster
A Division of Gulf & Western Corporation
Simon & Schuster Building
Rockefeller Center
1230 Avenue of the Americas
New York, New York 10020

SIMON AND SCHUSTER
and colophon are trademarks of Simon & Schuster
Designed by Eve Kirch
Manufactured in the United States of America

3   5   7   9   10   8   6   4   2

Library of Congress Cataloging in Publication Data

Brickner, Richard P.
Tickets.
I. Title.
PS3552.R45T5   813'.54   80-22683

ISBN 0-671-41209-4

Excerpt from *The Ring of Nibelung* by Richard Wagner,
copyright © 1960 by Stewart Robb, is
reprinted by permission of the publisher, E. P. Dutton.

PART
ONE

1

In the lobby of the Met, Alan leaned like a proprietor against the wall by the Ezio Pinza memorial drinking fountain, trying to draw from the intermission gathering a familiar face—a friend, a former friend, a friend-to-be. Only the crowd itself was familiar. He lifted his arms (as if his jacket were tight), transforming the opera-goers into a chorus and the lobby into a stage set of a lobby. The chorus sang, in Alan's improvised libretto English, to a waltz tune his mind doodled:

We are smoking, talking, strolling,
Gaily praising, all excited.
Ah, such music! The conducting!
By this evening we're delighted!

He, the lead tenor, steps out of his corner for an aria . . . in praise of his new black cashmere double-breasted blazer, his black-and-white-striped shirt, his scarlet silk tie, the gray silk pocket handkerchief with fine scarlet stripes tamped to a low bulge at the edge of his breast pocket. Pearl-gray slacks. Black lisle socks. Shoes of Italian tenderness. Bravo!

9

With Carla in the ladies' room, he was having such a cozy time surveying the lobby, belonging to the lobby, clothes buyer, holder of admired job, ticket-rich (and, though forty, still boyish-looking, they told him), that he wished Carla would never come out of the ladies' room. A man raising his head from the drinking fountain nodded at Alan and smiled in his light-brown beard as if he knew him and would chat with him in a moment. The man turned away. The back of his blue pinstripe, monumental and immaculate, made Alan feel junior. Ah, that was who, behind the tawny beard. Ring. Lawyer on the good side. Curtis Ring. Alan tapped Ring's shoulder, feeling as if he were knocking on a great door. The man turned around, disclosing a small woman in a pantsuit of wine velvet. She was bent over, drinking. "Alan Hoffman," Alan said. "From *Newsworthy*. I interviewed you, four or five years ago, after the *Curious Yellow* case. Curtis Ring?" "That's right," Ring said. "That was a good interview, too." Another smile broke his beard. "You'd done your homework." Ring's gray necktie made Alan think of chain mail. "Dear—this is Mr. Hoffman. My wife, Betsy." Ring's voice was a suave baritone, with a light boom of amiability to it.

"Alan Hoffman." He stuck out his hand. She took the edges of his fingers and let them go, smiling somewhat politely. She was wearing a creamy ruffled blouse. Cherubino. Alan thought of city winters, going to the opera as a boy. She glanced at his nose, jumping her eyes then to the loose bunch of curls on the right side of his forehead. She looked at her husband. Ring said, "Mr. Hoffman interviewed me after *Curious Yellow* for *Newsworthy*." "I eavesdropped while I was drinking," she said. Her voice sounded recently cleaned. Her dark hair hung straight and close; it stopped at the base of her neck. Her face seemed to show what she had looked like when she was ten and what she would look like at seventy. Nose, mouth, and chin were brief. "Are you still with *Newsworthy?*" Ring asked.

"Very much, yes. What do you do?" Alan asked Betsy.

"My wife has her first novel coming out in a few months."

"Called?" Alan asked her.

She pinkened and looked at him as if the title were a distasteful thing to say. *"Ecuador."*

"Historical novel?" He sounded too surprised, he felt.

"No." She smiled at him quickly and shook her head in a little flurry.

"Well. If you'd like, have them send me a copy. They'll probably send one to us anyway, but have it sent to my attention. Who's the publisher?"

"Wynn, Marcovici. Thanks, I'd like to. I appreciate it." And she nodded, and smiled again.

"How are you enjoying the performance, Alan?" asked Curtis, who had been standing by like a chief of protocol.

"I've heard far worse. And there's always the music. What about you?"

"Fine, just fine. Though I must say the story makes me think of Gilbert and Sullivan. The gypsy mixing up the babies is a bonkers Little Buttercup."

"They behave as if their lives depend on it," Betsy said. "No matter what they're doing." She bent forward at the waist a little, and looked down, sideways, as if listening instead of talking. Her posture seemed to conceal energy; she might have been beating time with her foot.

"Their lives do depend on it," Alan said. "That's exactly it." She had stood that way, he imagined, from adolescence on, half in, half out of, groups.

"Do you go a lot?" she asked, lifting her head, letting it drop.

"All the time." No one was saying anything, so he added, "I go three or four nights a week, here or at the State Theater or somewhere else. Or concerts." He smiled. "Sometimes more."

She looked. "Are you kidding?"

"It's true." He felt as if his boast were a rosebush growing out of his shoulder. He shrugged, as if there were nothing there.

"Does your life depend on it?" she asked him.

"I don't know." He laughed. "I haven't tried doing without

11

it for years." The gongs, like a busybody, warned that intermission was beginning to end.

Betsy said, with a frown of involvement, "I think that is certainly—"

Carla squeezed his arm, and his arm jumped. "Here's—Carla List. Curtis Ring. And Betsy Ring."

The Rings murmured.

"Hi, Curtis, Betsy. Hi, darling. Sorry I was so long. Incredible mob in there. Glad to be back." Carla laughed, pressing her cheek to his shoulder.

Curtis said, "It was a pleasant surprise to run into you, old man."

"My goodness, I haven't even heard what you're up to."

"Same old law, same old law," Curtis said, giving a double pat to Alan's other shoulder. And he said to his wife, "We'd better start off."

Betsy Ring looked at Alan, entertained. "Your ears must be very rich."

"I neglected to tell you that I'm stone deaf. Listen." He looked at Curtis. "Why don't you folks join us for a drink after, across the street at O'Neals'?"

Curtis looked down at his wife, then at his watch. "Maybe we should do it another time. I have to be in court tomorrow morning."

"The last act's quite short," Alan said.

"We have to get up early, too, darling," Carla said.

"I truly don't want to put anyone out. It was just a suggestion, a terrible suggestion."

"Oh, don't mind if I do," Carla said. "Whither thou goest." She grinned her winklike grin.

"A drink," Betsy said. "Of course, we could all line up here afterward at the Ezio Pinza and have a drink."

"What the hell," Curtis said. "Just a quick one. Where'll we meet?"

The three-minute gongs sounded. "*Andiam*," Alan said. "Let's meet at the doors. Where are you sitting?" The four

12

moved in the crowd across the lobby toward the same aisle. Carla took possession of his hand. Betsy was at his other side in the slow-moving mass, Curtis behind her. Alan inhaled an enormous breath. He glanced at Betsy. "Pedestrian traffic jam," she said, not looking at him. "Isn't it," he said. They were strangers. They could have had that exchange without being introduced. He wanted to enfold her. He would kiss her delicately, showing her how delicate he could be. First, the shyness of her lips would be the excitement, then the lips would moisten, slide. He imagined letting go of Carla's hand and taking hers. Who *was* she? She seemed to remind him of someone he didn't remember. He would never know her better. They would have a drink, but why? What had he done? The prick sang, the brain sang. Just the way it happened on the stage inside. Opera lovers had only to lay eyes on each other—Manrico, Leonora. Faust, Marguerite. Octavian, Sophie. Rodolfo, Mimi. Siegfried, Brünnhilde. Alfredo, Violetta. Manon, Des Grieux. They barely saw each other before they were in love. The brain sang a serenade. The serenade miraculously became a duet. One glance, one instant, changed lives. It was out of your control.

The singers received tame ovations at their final bows, when they appeared like jeweled pins against the white gold of the curtain. At the opera, blocs of the audience must sing back to the singers. Thus, there are always ovations, but often they are not ripe. On occasion, though, the audience joins at the throat, and a roar like a stadium roar erupts, world-ending, too large, it seems, for the auditorium to contain. These dangerous-sounding ovations were among the moments in Alan's life he valued most; they could make him weep with awe and gratitude. More often than not, he was unable to participate in them; they took his breath away. But he was thrilled to be clobbered by such violent unison. It was as if, between the audience's ferocity and what had happened on the stage to provoke it, he was a victim of assault. If he tried to rise, or to shout, he would get clobbered again, and continue to sob. Caught in the legitimate, the genuine, ovation, the roar, the tantrum-like foot-drumming, he became the audience's audience. He loved the audience when it couldn't help itself.

Tonight, respectfully out of his seat, he applauded with polite force over the heads of the many hurrying to leave, their backs turned to the stage as if the bowing singers had not sung, or were not bowing. Carla, though standing too, was unable to see the stage steadily beyond the risen and shifting crowd. Alan named the singers for her as they appeared and reappeared, and finally the young conductor. The house lights came on like a chill. He had pushed for the drink. What would they all talk about? How was he going to be able to talk with Betsy? He could have phoned her in the morning if, in the morning, he'd wanted to. He had absolutely arranged for awkwardness. He looked at Carla's pert, always unexpectedly wholesome face. "You okay?" he asked. "I miss you," she said, with a warm pout. "I'm right here," he said, then made a little kiss at her. Abruptly, she tilted toward his ear. Her hands embraced it. "I'm dying for you to make love to me," she whispered. She nicked his ear, licked the nick, and drew away. She glowed at him. "What can I do?" he asked. "I'd feel asinine calling it off now." They entered the aisle.

"What did you want to have a drink with them for, anyway?" She jiggled his arm. They moved sluggishly with the congestion toward the lobby.

"Carla, it's too late to do anything about. Unless they've left."

"You could lie. You could tell them you're sick with desire. Who are the Rings? Her suit's incredible."

"You didn't like it?"

"I want it, are you kidding?"

"He's a lawyer I interviewed once. She's evidently a writer. She's just written a novel about Ecuador." What a strange thing to have pulled off. Ecuador. She was peculiar yet elegant. Extraordinarily shy but so alert. She would not think him smart enough for her.

"Has she written a novel or published a novel? There's a difference. If I could afford a suit like that, I'd be rich enough to write the screenplay."

This, it had turned out, was a main theme of Carla's. If only she didn't have to be a textbook editor, she'd be writing screenplays; also articles for *New York*, *The New Yorker*, *The New York Review*, *The New York Times Magazine*. She had all these ideas, but no time! Ten days ago he'd liked her too much not to agree. Now he didn't care enough to disagree. "Suggest it to her, the screenplay. Ask. The novel is coming out this winter. Curtis is interesting. Talk to him, too. You'll like him."

"Don't direct me, darling, okay?" She looked at him with a frown supported by raised eyebrows.

"Huh?" The tiny wires behind his forehead heated fast to orange and began a delicate buzzing and curling. "Come on, Carla. I'm not directing."

"Listen. Really. I don't feel much like company. I'll get myself a cab and go home. It's best." She nodded agreeably, agreeing with herself.

He stopped with her at the bottom of the stairs to the outer lobby. If the Rings were up there, he couldn't let Carla leave alone. He would have to insist that she stay, or else leave with her. "Carla, I'm sorry. I didn't mean to be directorial. I guess I'm tense because I got us into this silliness." His words tired him. "It would be embarrassing now for everyone if you left. Or if we left." Though coy, she was right. She should go home, alone.

"I've had better invitations." Again her forehead flew the pennant of injury.

With his next breath, he tried to suck back the time this talk was taking. "Okay. I'll take you home."

"I don't want you to if you don't want to."

"It's best. Let's end this. No more discussion." And he felt a little better, warmer.

"I don't want to go home with you in this mood." Her knees

15

touched his legs. She caressed his wrist bone. Her knuckles bumped his thigh.

"Let's talk about that when we get there," he said.

"You're not mad?"

He would call Betsy in the morning. "I will be if we don't go." Only set to music could this dialogue pass.

"Let's have a drink with them first. It's easier. We'll feel better. It'll be fine. You'll see."

Alan glared at her. He would have liked to tear her in two. One of the disadvantages of not being married was that you didn't get enough chance to express outright dislike. "Let's go, Carla. I'm taking you home."

She looked, now, disappointed. Alan made a noise like a dreamer whimpering. "What do you *want?*"

"I want to be with you happy, not mad."

He pressed his hands to his cheeks. "Okay? Jesus! I'll be happy! But let's go!"

"You're humiliating me, Alan. I can't deal with that."

"Aw, shit, Carla, then don't deal with it. Okay?"

Her jaw tensed toward him. And then she turned and was trotting up the stairs. He stared after, as if not realizing she was leaving, this woman in a black coat. But she continued away, hurrying now across the floor of the lobby, and he sprang after her as though he had discovered she'd picked his pocket. He saw the Rings, actually waiting. Carla was talking to them. Alan wondered if she might be crazy. He arrived at the glass doors to see her skittering down the shallow steps to the plaza; she appeared to him to be fluttering from a great height. "I'll be back in a second," Alan said to the Rings (Betsy was showing that oddly supercilious look of someone trying to ignore a scene), and started out. "Hold off, old man," Curtis said, pressing Alan's elbow. "Your friend said to tell you not to worry, she'd be fine, she just wants to be alone. She'll call you tomorrow, she said. Come have a drink with us."

Alan had lost Carla in the darkness, the crowd, or the distance. "She's on her office track team, and practices at odd moments." The Rings smiled but did not laugh. "Excuse my suavity. This is very embarrassing. It's very kind of you, the drink, but really we don't have to." He looked at each of them, as if he were telling a joke and carefully dividing it among his listeners. Betsy was wearing a Russian-length brown suede coat, braid-trimmed.

"I demand a drink," Curtis said.

"Do you handle breakups in your firm?" Alan asked him.

"A drink," Betsy said. "A drink sounds to me tonight like a new thing in the world everyone's talking about." She opened a door with her shoulder.

It was chilly enough so that they hurried along the plaza. "*Fuggi, fuggi,*" Alan muttered.

"*Fuggi?* Cold is *freddo,* isn't it?" Betsy asked.

"*Fuggi* is flee. I mean *fuggi means* flee."

"Flee association," Betsy said. "I once saw a graffiti, graffito, in Harlem that said, 'Free Huey,' and it took me a minute to realize that someone wasn't giving away something called Huey. Why did you say *fuggi, fuggi?*"

"I don't know, it's an opera cliché, someone is always admonishing someone to flee or wanting to flee with someone, *fuggiam,* and here we are fleeing across the plaza, the three of us, and I thought of it. It's like a tic with me, these clichés."

"How strange."

"*È strano.*"

"Stop it!"

"I will. You have my word."

At O'Neals' they found a table in the noise. They got out of their coats, Curtis helping Betsy with hers, Alan handing his to Curtis, who laid it on the banquette. They sat down, Curtis and Betsy facing out, Alan facing them. She was wearing the same suit, the same blouse, of an hour ago. She was the same person, but there seemed to be more of her. In the fuller light of the restaurant, Alan noticed that her eyes were brown and much bigger, fatter, than they had seemed in the lobby. Though she was not smiling, her cheekbones, her little wedge of jaw, her

17

thin lips, gave off an entertained air. Her eyes covered the room in a swift, wheeling gaze. Curtis tried to snag a waitress and missed. "So," Curtis said.

"If she was going to run off that way," Alan blurted, "why didn't she just do it? Why does it have to be such a *scene?* So histrionic?" Of course, even the fight had been histrionic. Carla was public in private.

"If you're apologizing for involving us, forget it," Curtis said. "I deal in scenes all day long. Often it's calculated, for bargaining. It can be bullying. It can be silence. It's not so terrible. Mostly it's just a game. You learn tactics to handle it."

Alan laughed. "You do?"

"Interesting," Betsy said. "Maybe it's always a kind of bargaining. Some people don't think they're going to be believed unless they inflate what they feel. Or maybe they can't feel. Do you know many histrionic people?" Her entertained quality, unchanged, seemed now to suggest that she expected him to avoid the hook of her question with ease.

"I don't know," he said, feeling bored or full. "I know people, and especially women, to tell you the truth, who seem to act their most intense emotions. And it doesn't seem at all calculated"—he appealed to Curtis—"or a game. It's as if they were acting with*out* knowing they were acting. I mean, Carla—" He could not tell them. "It's so *insulting.*"

"Very complicated," Curtis said, appearing to lose a few grains of interest in the matter.

"Why do you love the opera so much?" Betsy asked.

Alan chuckled. "Look, opera singers are *supposed* to be singing. They're licensed. Opera doesn't suggest fakery to me, but the opposite. As we said in the lobby, their lives depend on it."

"I gather you're not married, old man," Curtis said.

"No. I'm only forty, after all." Alan gave a big smile to the waitress, who, cheerful and rushed, dealt them menus and ran off, saying, "Back in a minute. Better have your minds made up."

"They read their menus. "Onion soup and cognac," Alan said.

18

"That's two drinks," Betsy said, still studying.

"One of the many ways in which my wife is charming is by being rather literal at times. What a good idea! Soup and a drink."

" 'There's a certain grain of stupidity that the writer of fiction can hardly do without,' " Betsy said. " 'And that's the quality of having to stare, of not getting the point at once.' Flannery O'Connor. I'd like Irish coffee. I haven't had that for years."

"That won't keep you awake?" Alan asked, hoping he sounded nosy.

"Maybe hot chocolate. I'll have hot chocolate. Though usually my insomnia happens when I am awake. I mean in the daytime, when I'm not trying to sleep. That's when I feel insomniac. Cognac certainly keeps me awake."

"Me too. But that's all right, since I don't like to go to sleep," Alan said. "I love to sleep, but not to go to sleep." Would Carla arrive now, all smoothed?

"Only decide before the waitress comes back, Bets," Curtis said.

"I have a habit of restaurant indecision." She was still looking at the menu.

Curtis stood. "Excuse me, folks. I'll be right back. When the waitress comes, I'd like an onion soup and a Cutty Sark on the rocks." Curtis sidestepped out. Alan followed Betsy's eyes following Curtis, then he watched the door of the men's room close on Curtis's back. Freedom and suspense brightened in him.

Betsy said, "What do you want to say? We only have a moment."

"What did you say?" He looked at her. He laughed. "Oh, you're kidding." He laughed some more. "Why did you say that?"

"It just popped out. It's not really my kind of joking. It must be you."

"Do I find you less shy than I thought you were in the lobby?"

"I'm shy about my book. I'm shy about people being inter-

19

ested in me. But I like talking about myself. It's unreasonable of me. About fifty percent of me doesn't want my book published."

"Is that true? Why?"

"Failure, success. All that. Reviews, no reviews. The problem of appearance, mainly. It's not a novel about me, it really isn't, but because there's less to hide when it's not about you, I seem to have ended up putting in more to hide. I'm in there all over the place, upside down, inside out, inside others, an arm here, a leg there. It's embarrassing. It's a way of asking to be found out, no doubt." She talked fast once she got going.

"Well, I'd love to read it, I promise you, but I don't want to pry."

"I'll manage. I want you to read it. I want everyone to read it. I'll escape to Ecuador."

"Did you go to Ecuador when you were writing it? I haven't been to Ecuador."

"No. It's not literally so much about the actual country. A few years ago I dreamed just the words 'Quito' and 'Ecuador,' Quito's the capital, as you know, and I was so excited at having had a dream of two words that I began imagining a novel around the words. The dream seemed to be telling me to do that. When I began imagining the novel was when I started having insomnia in the daytime. I have never been so excited. I started without knowing anything about the country, but I did a lot of research. I'd like to go. I'd like to see how much like entering my mind's eye it would be. I might go, actually, during publication."

"I've truly never been given a better interview."

"This isn't an interview."

"Kidding."

She smiled for less than half a second.

"I envy you, dreaming two words that become a novel."

"Now I envy myself. I guess it's not the sort of thing that's supposed to happen more than once in a lifetime."

The waitress pulled up. Betsy ordered the Irish coffee, Alan the two onion soups, a Cutty Sark, a Hennessey with soda on the side. The waitress scribbled and left.

" 'Quito' is 'key-toe'?" Alan asked. " 'Key to'?"

"Yes. Also 'quit.' Also, in Italian, *qui* is 'here.' You of all people know that. And *chi*—'who.' And French *qui*, 'who.' And the book is all about here and who. Here comes Curtis."

Alan didn't want her to go to Ecuador. She was more extraordinary by the minute. Where were her deficiencies?

Curtis reappeared and sat down. "Well, where were we?"

"The waitress has just been and gone, with orders," Alan reported.

"I decided," Betsy said to Curtis. Curtis patted her arm urbanely.

Did they have children? Alan wondered. They must have children. "Are you starting another book? I'm told that's the healthy thing to be doing at publication."

"I'm fiddling. Now I have a question. Do you always dress so carefully?"

"I believe you mean foppishly?"

"It's almost like a costume."

"Dear—" Curtis said.

"I don't mind," Alan said to them both. "I like to dress up."

"Do you wish you were an opera singer?" Betsy asked. "I am interested in knowing about this obsession."

"I have a chorus voice. I sing in amateur choruses sometimes. No, I don't want to have been an opera singer. I don't much like singers when they're not singing. I wanted to talk about you here," he said to Curtis. The waitress was serving them. "Enjoy it, folks," she said.

"What's the difference?" Curtis said. "We can talk about me. We were talking about you. I have no obsessions, except for my wife." The remark sounded more *galant* than literal, yet Alan found himself warm in the cheekbones.

"You've forgotten the Knicks," Betsy said.

"Not your work?" Alan asked.

"Sometimes, sure. I wouldn't want to be anything but a lawyer. But there are cases I take defending people I find rather unsavory. On the other hand, I was involved on behalf of a publishers' group before the Supreme Court in an obscenity matter earlier this year. We lost the case, but my heart was in that one. That would be close to an obsession."

"That was the local control of obscenity standards?"

"That's right. That decision is going to ruin some harmless sinner some day."

"I hadn't known you were involved. I would have gladly interviewed you again. Had you been interested." Alan took a spoonful of soup, to be natural.

"*Newsworthy* is doing well?"

"We are. About the time I last met you, we were dipping some, but circulation's almost two million now. We added a Natural Resources section last month. It's amazing to me. It's always amazing when something you have something to do with succeeds."

"What are you there?"

"A so-called Senior Interviewer. In effect, an interviewer-at-large. The honor of that is that I'm restricted to no section of the magazine."

"Going to operas and concerts as often as you do, don't tickets cost you a fortune?" Betsy asked. "Do you get in for free?"

"Not often enough to make a big difference. I spend an awful lot on tickets. That's why I work—to feed my ravenous obsession. Not really." He swallowed some cognac. "Opera is *about* laws," he said to Curtis. "Rules, breaking rules, or about having to choose between rebelling and submitting. Obedience, disobedience. Punishment. It's politically extreme, domestically, emotionally extreme. Duty versus emotion." He didn't know what he was going to say next. Betsy was looking at him with her head tipped, as though she were thinking more than listening. He talked mostly to his soup. "People complain that operas are unbelievable. I think that what operas are *about* is believable, even though the librettos are overly convenient, you might say. Characters so often show up in the right place at the wrongest time. At the beginning of *La Forza del Destino,* a man shoots the father of his beloved while throwing *away* his gun in order to show he has no intention of killing him. The gun fires fatally from the floor. Accidents will happen. But divided loyalty, for example, is believable. Immense sacrifice for love. The hard road of love." Adultery. "Very few operas are not about love. Or death, of course. I mean, is *Oedipus Rex* unbelievable? In reality—" he smiled at Curtis—"you'd be likely to recognize your mother if you found yourself in bed with her. I hope I'm not being offensive." Still smiling, he drank more cognac.

"Perfectly all right," Curtis said.

Betsy laughed, evidently delighted.

"Even if you hadn't seen her since you were a child. You'd know something was wrong. But in reality also, don't you fear" —he looked at them both; he did not recall ever having noticed how difficult it was to talk to two people at once—"not seeing what you're doing until after you've done it? In some way not watching or knowing what you're doing? Or that you're not going to remember the name of an old friend? I've run into people—not my mother, but people I thought I had remembered well physically, who hadn't aged or changed at all, but who didn't fit my memory of them, who might as well have been strangers. *Oedipus Rex* is more about memory, about being aware, than about incest. No one laughs at the idea that Oedipus doesn't know Jocasta's his mother. Opera's no more farfetched, is the point. In tonight's opera, we had love at first sight and we had two brothers not knowing they're brothers, both in love with the same woman. It's a small world. Or as a friend of mine once said, 'Of course it's a small world. There are only ten thousand people in it.' People are living out operatic situations all the time. They just don't think of it that way, but it's all part of our lives—uncontrollable passion, dreams coming true, what we want turning out to cause what we don't want, unbelievable coincidences, heavily ironic, fateful deaths, the heavy but quick hand of fate. All that. The point is that life is full of significant unexpectedness." Significant unexpectedness! Betsy must be making his tongue flap with this elegance. "We *live* farfetched." He finished off his cognac and looked around unsuccessfully for the waitress.

23

"Actually, you're talking about melodrama," Betsy said.

"I guess so, but I think of it as operatic."

"We'll have to be going when we've finished this, I'm afraid," Curtis said.

"I might stay for a little while."

"Just sit here?" Betsy asked.

"Have a nightcap, look on. It's pleasant. You have to understand"—he talked directly to her now, with relief—"that no one who loves opera would think of denying that it's full of grotesque stupidities—loose ends and ludicrous staging and gestures that make no sense. Pop singers make those gestures, too, of course. I assure you, it still drives me nuts when a singer is on the stage looking for someone, and craning around on tiptoe as if there were a high wall blocking the view. Or entrances will be staged through no doors when there are doors. Or choruses having to be townsfolk in the square, lolling, flirting, all that atmosphere crap. And that's the least of it. The point is that there's so much that has to work if the whole thing's going to work that when it does work I feel so grateful that I think I must feel that I become part of the perfection. I love my own admiration. What we're always after, anyway, is intelligence over heavy odds, isn't it? That's what opera is when it works."

Betsy shook her head with the slightest slow swinging. "I have no doubt that opera needs no defending when it works. It's the four times a week you go I'm curious about. Nothing you've said explains that."

Curtis said, "Dear, I'm sorry, it's twelve-thirty."

"Look at the orchestra pit sometime," Alan said to Betsy. "It happened tonight once or twice. There's a glow of light like stove gas under a pot. The music gets going—a tricky pizzicato bass with a gutsy melody sailing in over it, and the singers are in a trio, say—it's as if the orchestra were cooking the stage, as if everything were boiling in complete control. Just think of the intelligence. A three-hundred-pound soprano weighs a hundred and twenty when she's singing beautifully. We're talking about people doing something beautiful and crucial, overcoming fantastic risks. Why isn't that—? It seems to me that's worth hoping for, time after time."

Curtis had stood, and Betsy stood, putting on the coat her husband held for her. "I'll have to figure out what bothers me about it," Betsy said. "Anyway, it was interesting. So." She looked at Curtis. Curtis laid a ten-dollar bill on the table. "Will you let me take it?" Alan said, standing too. "Otherwise, I'll feel you were paying for a lecture." He picked up the ten and handed it to Curtis.

Curtis laughed and pocketed the money. "Irresistible offer. Thank you. But I learned a lot, and I didn't feel lectured, either."

"Goodbye," Betsy said. Alan shook the hand she stuck out. She held her shoulders back. Her chin was up. She looked suspicious, or disdainful, in some way suddenly aloof. The look struck him as inappropriate to her face. He wondered if he could hate her. He had let go of her hand quickly, and was sorry. "Glad to have met you," he said. He did not want her to know that he was miffed at her disapproval, and he didn't want her to think he was uninterested in her hand. "I'll look for your novel."

"Early January. I just hope you'll be able to find it."

The two of them had had such a wonderful talk before, Alan thought. It seemed wasted now.

"Good night, old man. Thanks again. We'll see you." They went off, Betsy rustling her fingers in the briefest wave. Alan took her seat, surrounded by a faint ambience of perfume and coat. Betsy departing looked like a boy, a Juilliard student, the brushlike bottom of her chestnut hair spread on her collar. She was taking the conversation with her. Was she rude? And Curtis polite because she was rude? Could someone be so interested and still be rude? Was her interest rude? Would he feel like calling her in the morning to find out? He would. Raising his hand as if for a cab, he slowed down the waitress long enough to ask for another brandy. He felt vigorous because something had happened, something might happen, and he looked over

25

his surroundings feeling cheerful. Betsy was standing to his left.

"Curtis thinks I was hostile. I don't think he's right, but if he is, you have my apology."

"Can you sit?"

"I can sit in a cab. Curtis is getting a cab. This is meant to be a five-second conversation."

"I don't know if you were being hostile. My question would be, Why does what I was saying concern you? I mean, it seems to irritate you."

"I don't know. With all the enthusiasm and intelligence you have, it seems so lonely."

"I'm not so lonely. Aren't you lonely? I'm sure there's more to it, the opera-going. But in any case, after all, I don't keep on going to the opera because I don't like it. So everything's all right. You were fascinating about your book. You do fascinate me, I must say."

"I liked the talk. Particularly. Perhaps you'll come to dinner some night. Or do you just grab a bite during intermission?"

"Very funny. I'd love to come to dinner."

"We'll call you."

"I may call you tomorrow. Or in a day or two. Is that okay?"

She bounced her head left, right. "We're listed. Who knows if it's okay? Curtis has probably gone off in the cab. Good night."

"I loved your suit."

"It's yours." She again gave her minimal wave, and she hurried out.

Alan had a shallow appetite for his second cognac. Everyone nearby was engrossed in food or talk. The wrangle with Carla —Carla herself—had come back to him full force. He wanted to clear the air between them, or he wanted to clear the air of her. It was ten minutes to one. Should he surprise her? Appear there? Risky. Either it would infuriate her or she would like it too much. He traipsed to the phone booth and dialed her easy number. Her hello sounded ambiguous as to sleepiness.

"Hi. It's Alan. How you feeling?"

"Oh, hi, darling. I'm fine. Where are you? What time is it?"

"Sorry if I've awakened you."

"That's all right. I've only just dozed off."

"And sorry about before."

"Listen, I was greedy. I wanted you. Aren't you with Betsy and Curtis?"

"They've left. Went home."

"And what will you do? Are you at O'Neals'? Sounds like a party."

"No party. Guess I'll go home."

"Okay, darling."

"Do you want me to come over?"

She laughed gently. "I did."

He could not turn away from the sound of grievance. What he had hoped for, he realized, was that when she'd run from the opera house she'd run all the way to a dignified-sounding decision against their seeing any more of each other, to which he would agree with a reluctance that, while recognizably respectful, did not give her time to change her mind. He tested for seriousness of intention: "I don't want any hard feelings."

"Come to me, my demon lover." She attached a humming purr.

Now, did she mean, or in general? He'd had trouble all along figuring out how much she meant what she said. It was often difficult to tell her glibness from her intensity. "You sure?"

"As sure as a girl can be who was yelled at in the lobby of the Met an hour and a half ago. Is that sure enough for you?"

"I'll be right over. Fifteen minutes."

The Redundancy East, she'd called her apartment house ten days ago (on their way to it from the restaurant they'd gone to from the party where he'd met her), convincing him that on top of her cheerful sexiness, her healthy ambition, and her natural chic, she was witty, an original, a find. Leaving her salmon-and-turquoise elevator, he turned the corner on the eighteenth floor and started off along the road of movie-theater rug. He'd reach her door by dawn: 18-Y.

27

Carla, however, was not going to rank among those women of his experience who had once been, for a brief time, everything to him. Janet Lawrence, whose book on modern American men contained three paragraphs devoted to Alan (called "Ian" in the book), had said to him while he was packing his disappointment after seven weeks of affair, "You're the only person I've ever known who believes that love is best at the beginning and therefore isn't worth maintaining." The poise and reach of this epitaph were so impressive, not to say surprising, to him that he hurriedly recollected the difficulties Janet had been contributing and asking him to tolerate: she was often silent, and never happy when silent. When she talked, much of the time that she did not spend pleading for his attention or solace she spent asking to be forgiven for her impossible neediness.

It confused his understanding of his life with women that its uncountable endings were almost never clearly the fault of his evident bent for endings, or of his lust for gorgeous beginnings of his own confection. None of the loves since Roz had lasted; none should have lasted. He had loved Roz for years, but it was, already, almost twenty years since then. Now, as if *instead* of loving enduringly, he had learned to try to break off with women in a friendly manner. He preferred to thank them for their trouble rather than blame them for their cooperation. Most of them knew, should have known, that even those relationships not begun as if they were supposed to last a lifetime usually had in them only enough goodwill and interest for a week or two, or a month or two. But most people were not prepared to admit, near the beginning, the possibility of an ending. He himself had felt the energy drain from his heart when a woman would say to him something like, "But how can I tell you how I'll feel next week? Please don't be so serious. And please come to bed." He never said things like that.

All in all, pressing Carla's doorbell, he felt nearly tender. The door opened right away. She said "Hi" shyly from behind it. Alan stepped in and turned to watch her as, naked, she flipped and slid bolts. She stood, then, with her arms out to him as if to receive long-stemmed flowers, benevolence on her face. He smiled as cordially as he could and took her wrist, swinging her arm back and forth, not knowing what else to do.

"Silly," she said, and came to him with her pretty breasts, putting her arms over his shoulders. He smelled Jean Naté. "I'm sorry if I was overemotional, darling. Let's put it behind us, okay?"

"Absolutely. Let's talk."

She didn't let go. "Mmmmm. Your coat's still on. I can feel its buttons against me."

"I'll take it off. Here."

"Let me." Staying close, she undid the buttons and pushed open the coat. She snuggled. Her arms were low on his waist. "Mmmmm." He eased her away by her elbows and stepped back, kissing her left hand. He didn't know what to say if he couldn't say the things—and the one thing above all—that he shouldn't say. He needed her help. "Are you still mad, darling?" she asked.

"No, of course not. But I'd like to talk." He gestured them down the hall. "Into the drawing room for brandy and cigars?" she said. "Right," he said, smiling just a little, even though she wasn't looking at him. They passed the Steinberg exhibition poster, the low bookshelf of contemporania—Nin, Fowles, Vonnegut, Hesse, Greer, Millet, Toffler, Sexton, Plath, Mailer —with Carla's collection of glass, ceramic, and wooden penguins spread along its top. In her room, the spindly orange enamel floor-lamp was on. Alan shifted out of his overcoat and plopped into the black director's chair, folding his coat on his lap.

"Can't make it any farther?"

He let his head fall back as far as it would go and closed his eyes.

"Am I keeping you up?"

"No. No. I just want to sit."

"Gee, I guess I shouldn't have called you so late. I think I'll slip into something a little less comfortable."

29

These were lines such as he feared she would put into her screenplay. He brought his head forward an inch, opened his eyes an undetectable degree, saw Carla going around the corner of the alcove occupied by the double bed with its sporty print sheets. She came back tying the belt of her little yellow terry-cloth robe. He opened his eyes fully, smiled again. She sat down on a fluffy black throw rug, just beneath him, cross-legged. "You may be wondering why I've asked us all here," she said.

"Or I may be wondering. Are the British coming, the British coming?"

"We have not been bringing out the best in each other over the past five days, I think. I don't know what's happened, but I feel that."

"I agree. But didn't your mommy ever tell you that relationships need work?" An encouraging grin.

"I get the feeling I'm always letting you down, or about to."

Her smile was cast like soft light at her knee, and it looked nostalgic. "I wish I could disagree with you. You've hurt me. I've tried three times to set up dates for us to have drinks or dinner with Nyssa and Patrick, who are eager to meet you, to say the least—God, she writes good poetry. I've met at least four of your friends. I'd like you to meet two of mine. I'd like just one night not to go to something musical but to a lousy movie with you, a plain fun movie, and hold hands and eat popcorn. Everything with you is so planned, all your tickets. They're like a fence around you, Alan, don't you see that?"

He shoved his hand into his pants pockets to feel for the past evening's stubs. "Yes. You need tickets to get *in,* Carla. That's the way it works."

"Why can't we go for a weekend in the country, find a homey old inn? Breathe the air. Spend the night under a quilt on a down mattress. I love old quilts."

"Fine!"

"I just have the sense that you take me for granted, I'll be around to do what you want to do. That's what wounds me. I'm

30

an independent cuss, Alan, as you may find out. Oh—and you got so irritated at me the afternoon, Monday, when it was pouring and I asked you very sweetly if you could pick me up at the office in a cab on your way home, if you were going home." She looked ready to forgive if she possibly could.

"I was just going out on a job, as I told you. And it was pouring, as you say. I was late and already through the door."

"All you had to do was say no nicely."

"I'm sorry about that. We've been to a first-rate movie, which you loved. Nyssa and Patrick couldn't go to dinner on a night we wanted to. And it seems to me you and I have had a number of excellent dinners without Nyssa and Patrick."

"I'm not a gold digger, Alan. Just underpaid. My love can't be bought."

The wires behind his forehead writhed. "Who threw that one in? I'm only saying it's not accurate to say I take you for granted. Not that you're a gold digger, for God's sake. I've liked taking you to dinner."

She was looking exhaustedly at the floor. "I don't want to fight. You called me. What did you want?"

"I just think we should cool off for a few days, separately. I don't really agree with your charges, but I can see how I might not be being good for you."

"How?" Her expression was bewildered and pleading.

"I—I've just lost it, I guess. I don't know."

"In ten days?"

"I'm not proud of it, Carla."

"Do you remember what you said to me our first night? In the restaurant?"

"Yes, I do."

"You said I had everything. *Everything,* Alan."

"I remember."

"You should be careful. You might hurt someone someday."

"Look." He got up, placed his coat on the seat of the director's chair, and squatted beside her, his arms lightly around her, his cheek in her neck. "Sometimes people find out they're not

31

right for each other. You have to start in order to find out. People take chances."

"I've never had anyone come on to me so strong. Your eyes pinned me to the wall like a butterfly at that ghastly cocktail party."

"I get excited. It's wrong, I know. It's something I have been learning to try to stop. I hadn't done it for some time. But you were—you are—exciting. I want it all to be true, you know. I want too much. And I think you're terrific. It's just that maybe we're not right for each other."

"But maybe we are." She clutched his back. "We could improve. We're so incredible together in so many ways. We both love music, the arts, reading. I could teach you more about film. You could certainly teach me more about music. It's so good making love. We fit so well, Alan . . . so well." She pushed her face across to his lips and kissed him committingly. He pulled away a little from the pressure, but his left hand was in her crotch and his other hand was shoving her robe off her shoulder. He kissed the side of her neck.

"Mmmmm. I'm wet for you, my darling mahn."

"I know. I feel it."

"You have all those clothes on." Her left foot had found his erection and was wiggling against it.

"Okay." He helped her up.

"We're going to be all right, darling, I know." She was unbuttoning his shirt. "No one touches me like you."

"I'll do it." He got out of his clothes as if he were alone, and rapidly, thinking he would have to put them back on. When he looked at her again, she unbelted her robe and let it drop. "Hold me, love," she said. He embraced her. "Oh, Alan, I feel you."

"I know."

"Let's get on the bed, love."

They walked to the alcove, her arm across his buttocks. She sat, eyes on him, and lay, eyes on him, smiling as if all along she had known what was best for them. He lay beside her and shut his eyes. He began.

32

"My darling, you're stroking my breasts," Carla crooned. "My nipples are hard."

"Right." He asked himself once more, did she *know* she did this? Should he tell her? Had anyone ever told her? Had someone once told her to *do* it? He licked rapidly, like a clumsy version of a drinking cat.

"You're licking me, Alan, sweetness. Your tongue on my nipples. God—touch me."

He touched her.

"Your hand is on me, baby. Your fingers. Wet. Oh, beloved, I'm bursting."

Ciel! He climbed over her leg and planted himself within her.

"Oh, you're inside me, Alan, so big, darling Alan." They moved. "We're moving. Together. You're fucking me." They speeded up. "Alan and Carla are fucking. Carla and Alan."

Mi sento morir! Fuggi, fuggi, fuggi, fuggi, fuggi, fuggi, fuggi, fuggi. He laughed aloud.

"I'm coming, Alan, darling, I'm going to come. Are you? Come. Let's come together."

Io tremo! Vieni.

"Oh, beloved, we came." She gazed at him as if she'd just given birth to him. "Thank you, I heard your joy, your passion."

He smiled at her as if shyly. "I heard yours, too." *Addio, addio,* Carla. *Addio. Addio per sempre.* He slid out of her, through the noiseless pop of separation.

2

When the bed sank and rose with Curtis's getting up, Betsy saw the tail fin of a dream vanish. "As if their lives depend on it," she was thinking. What was that? Was it the dream or the dream's message? Something else? Nothing? She poked for hidden lobster meat: depend. Deep end, Pee-dend. Peedenda. Pudenda. Addenda. *Nada*. Alan Hoffman had said it—she had said it to Alan Hoffman. In the lobby. At the opera. She had met a problem last night. Without having opened her eyes, she closed them against the problem. When she heard the shower go on, she flipped over and read Curtis's bed-table clock. She flipped again, and went instantly back to sleep. Betsy felt it was positively unfair to Curtis to let his shower wake her for the day. Curtis was quiet in the morning—quietest during those phases when he was paying the least attention to her, she had learned—but there was nothing he could do about the shower. Out of consideration, she had taught herself to sleep right through it.

When she woke again, first she thought it was still the shower, but it was the buzzer grinding at the end of the hall. The clock said ten-twenty-seven. How could she write with such a late start? With nothing to write? The buzzer tried again. Such an unpleasant noise to announce a surprise. She ran to the bathroom door, yanking her brown velour robe from the hook and shoving into it. Of course, not everything unexpected could be classified as a surprise. It could be a mistake, for instance. The buzzer, this time, repeated itself in long throbs. "Say please!" she said, hurrying head-down to the intercom. She lifted the earpiece. "Who is it?" Alan Hoffman.

"Messenger!" a quavering male voice berated her. "I have an envelope here for a Mrs. Betsy Ring."

Something from Larry Turnbull. My God, the book? "Sorry. Come up, please. Turn right at the top of the stairs." She pressed the button to unlock the entrance door below. She belted the robe over her white flannel nightgown and opened the door. A small man became visible through the upper banister slats, bobbing. He wore a brown leather helmet. He bobbed around the corner and continued to bob, limping strenuously, as he approached her. He appeared to be in his early nineties. Whatever this was, it had better be good. She was going to move to an elevator building. Let Curtis keep his precious brownstone floor. The man's arm, as he handed her the manila envelope, was quivering. *Newsworthy,* the envelope said. The envelope was very light. "MS. BETSY RING" and her address. "BY MESSENGER." Above the *Newsworthy,* "Ah!" had been typed. The man, the monkey, handed her a pencil almost as short as he was. Betsy scribbled her name on his pad. "Thank you," the man said cheerily. "And good day." "Thank you very much," Betsy said, swallowing her desire to explain that she was not responsible for this delivery. She closed the door so gently there was no sound of wood, only the lock's click. Alone with the envelope, she felt her arms and chest emptying, felt herself a vacuum. The envelope hanging from her fingertips, she walked across the living room into the yellow kitchen. Curtis had left the coffeepot plugged in for her, optimistic fellow, and a note slouched against her mug. She laid the manila envelope on the tiny table, unplugged the coffeepot, placed the note face down on the envelope. She passed again through the living room, went down the hall, into the bedroom, the bathroom. When she reappeared, her robe was off. She came back down the hall, through the living room, into the kitchen. The apartment was to her this morning a boat on which she alone lived. She filled her gray-and-violet-striped mug two-thirds up with coffee, flipped in not quite a spoonful of sugar, and another incomplete spoonful, and got out milk. She poured the milk carefully, watching it bloom. She stirred the milk until the coffee became a pale, flat beige. She swallowed some off, then took the mug, the note, and the envelope to the dining table in the living room, sitting down facing the windows. The clear, gray light in the room, her nightgown, the oak table, the tan envelope, the white note, the milky coffee, the colors of her mug—everything seemed to her subtly chosen for a scene.

Dear B for Beautiful, Brilliant, and soon-to-be Best-known novelist in her early thirties in New York ("Best Bet" Betsy). I won't be in office 'til at least 3. If I don't call by 4, call Cathy. Should be able to meet you at restaurant by 7. Hope you have your breakthrough today, but wish you'd recognize magazine possibilities. The public doesn't deserve to be deprived of you. You deserve to be famous.
C for Crazy about you
Pick restaurant. Café des Artistes? Or cancel Monroes and stay home? Great idea.

She reread the note, and this time the words didn't reach her eyes. She had begun asking herself if his crazy persistence wasn't, after all, a tactic for getting rid of her. He nagged her to be famous, he nagged her to have a baby (or now—his gift of a compromise—to adopt a baby), as if he were deaf to her, or teasing her, or enjoying being obtuse, or as if she weren't there at all. He had turned sadistically silly. Whatever he intended, she was losing him. She cuffed the note away as if it were trivial, but noticed herself gulping down a clump of anger that burned her next breath.

She swallowed some of her coffee and reexamined the manila

envelope, the "Ah!" the "MS. BETSY RING," the "BY MES-
SENGER." He had calculated the delivery for well into the
morning, a most probable Curtis-avoiding time. She remembered now that Curtis had said in front of Hoffman that he had
to be in court in the morning. It must have seemed to Hoffman
as if Curtis were clearing the way. She turned the envelope over
and raised the wing clasps. She took one more swallow of coffee, then fingered open the sealed flap. Her finger against his
dried saliva. Only she in the world had thoughts like that. She
reached her hand into the envelope with the sense that she was
putting her hand in a man's pants pocket while the man was
wearing the pants; she slid out three stapled sheets of bond
typing paper. Lots of typing. No salutation. She lifted the first
two sheets from the lower left-hand corner. He had signed his
name on the third page beneath a handwritten paragraph of
which she allowed herself only, "The scene goes on some, but
I'll spare you the rest," at the beginning, and "Yours" at the
end. She let down the sheets and began to read.

Wednesday, October 24
3 A.M.

ACT THREE

The summit of a rocky mountain

*To the right, a forest of fir trees. Left, the
entrance to a cave.*

He'd written her the last act of a play, or a play called *Act
Three,* at three in the morning? Set in a cave—where they lived
together in bliss?

*Above this the rock rises high. At back the view is uninterrupted.
Rocks of various sizes form an embankment to the precipice.
Occasional clouds fly past the summit, storm-swept. Gerhilde,
Ortlinde, Waltraute and Schwertleite are ensconced on the rocky
peak above the cave. They are in full armor.*

Betsy's mouth spread by smooth degrees into a full smile, the
process giving her the sensation of a cool spreading of pleasure.
She settled in to read, her flanneled forearms embracing the

37

manuscript, her face the face of someone dreaming something funny.

GERHILDE
(higher placed than the rest, calls toward the back)

Ho-yo-to-ho! Ho-yo-to-ho!
Hi-ya-ha! Hi-ya-ha!
Helmwige, here!
Hie here with your horse!

HELMWIGE'S VOICE

Ho-yo-to-ho! Ho-yo-to-ho!
Hi-ya-ha!
(A flash of lightning breaks through a passing cloud: a Valkyrie on horseback is visible in it: over her saddle hangs a slain warrior.)

Valkyrie meant Wagner. Voggner.

GERHILDE, WALTRAUTE & SCHWERTLEITE

Hi-ya-ha! Hi-ya-ha!
(The cloud with the apparition disappears behind a fir tree on the right.)

ORTLINDE *(shouting in the direction of the fir tree)*

Your stallion should be by
Ortlinde's mare.
My Gray is glad to
graze with your Brownie.

Betsy giggled.

WALTRAUTE

Who hangs from your saddle?

HELMWIGE
(stepping from the fir trees)

Sintolt the Hegeling.

SCHWERTLEITE

Lead off your Brownie
far from my gray one.

38

Ortlinde's mare now
bears Wittig, the Irming!

She shook her head, smiling with benign astonishment, like someone reading a wonderful letter from home.

GERHILDE

As foemen I saw just
Sintolt and Wittig.

ORTLINDE

Hi-ya-ha! Hi-ya-ha! Your horse
is butting my mare!

SCHWERTLEITE & GERHILDE
(laughing)

The warriors' strife
makes foes of the horses.

HELMWIGE
(into the trees)

Quiet, Brownie!
Peaceful does it!

With the ringing of the telephone behind her, Betsy banged her fist on the table, quietly but tensely, as if she'd been interrupted in her own work. She bounced from her chair and took long steps to the kitchen and grabbed the receiver of the wall phone. She could hear the cordial rise of her hello flatten into exasperation.

"What have I taken you from?"

"Why do you sound so amused?"

"You sounded so peeved. Are you working?"

"Yes. Trying. How come you're not in court?"

"There's a delay. I just wanted to see how you were. When did you get up?"

"About nine."

"I really called to suggest that we spend the evening alone."

"I'm very fond of the Monroes, as you know."

"I consider myself lucky for that. But I have to work tomorrow night and we're busy Friday and Saturday."

39

"Is something specific bothering you?"

"Am I a patient? I just want to talk. Did you read my note?"

"Yes. I am not still in bed."

"That's not what I was suggesting," Curtis said, in a tone of light admonition. "I'm concerned about you, frankly. Got to go. think about tonight. I'll speak to you later." He hung up.

He thought she thought too much. She wouldn't think. Betsy returned to her chair and found her place at the bottom of page two. The first few days of Curtis's attentive periods were the heaviest, she reminded herself. Keep calm.

WALTRAUTE
(who has taken the place of Gerhilde at the top of the peak)

Ho-yo-ho! Ho-yo-ho!
Siegrune, here!
Where were you so long?

(Siegrune rides by in the direction of the fir tree.)

SIEGRUNE'S VOICE

Work to do!
Are the others all here?

These women certainly lacked malaise.

SCHWERTLEITE, WALTRAUTE & GERHILDE

Ho-yo-to-ho! Ho-yo-to-ho!
Hi-ya-ha!

(Siegrune disappears behind the firs. Two voices are heard from the depths.)

GRIMGERDE & ROSSWEISSE

Ho-yo-to-ho! Ho-yo-to-ho!
Hi-ya-ha! Hi-ya-ha!

Hey, muth'-fuckuh, gimme five. Ho-yo-to-ho!

WALTRAUTE

Rossweisse and Grimgerde!

GERHILDE

They ride as a pair.

40

(Grimgerde and Rossweisse, on horseback, appear in a glowing thundercloud which ascends from the depths and vanishes behind a fir tree. Each carries a slain warrior at her saddlebow.)

ORTLINDE, HELMWIGE & SIEGRUNE

Hello, you travelers!
Rossweisse and Grimgerde!

ALL THE OTHER VALKYRIES

Ho-yo-to-ho! Ho-yo-to-ho!
Hi-ya-ha! Hi-ya-ha!

That was it. She could have read these *Ho-yo-to-ho*'s indefinitely. It was their persistence that was funny. Tireless greetings. The energy of the women was like people walking in early movies. To read the note, Betsy drew her head back; her mouth and eyes tightened.

The scene goes on some, but I'll spare you the rest. Wagner lacks the wit of Oscar Wilde or even Neil Simon, but you can see from this that he is underpraised as a humorist. Yet, change the language back into German, cover it up with music, keep the stage dark, and you have an effective scene. Why am I typing at this time of night to send you this bit of Act Three, Scene One, *Die Walküre?* I am sending you this so that . . . why? I am sending you this because . . . damn it! Yes? Ah! I am sending this to you . . . because . . . because I wanted to make you laugh! That was it, after all. I was too serious. You were too serious. Opera is not sickness. I wish I could say everything I had to say to you. Also, I wish I knew what it was I had to say to you.

Yours,
Alan

Her heart thumped harshly, as if its treble had been turned way up. An intimate minnowy wriggle invaded her. She read the note again. She gave it an A minus, then a B plus, for calculation. Surely he had done things like this before. What, now, was she supposed to do with the thing? What did he expect her to do with it? He didn't think that far ahead. "Yours." Whose? Share my daring, he was saying. I am sending you a message behind enemy lines. Be bold enough to receive it, otherwise I'm endangered by my foolishness and presumption. Or:

I am sending my heart out to you by itself. Please meet its plane and adopt it. I know you'll learn to love it. And he couldn't stand histrionic women. No wonder he couldn't stand histrionic women. She could throw the whole thing away, or cut off the note. But cutting off the note was as telltale as keeping it. She saw the pages she had just read rolled up like a diploma in Curtis's hand, Curtis handing them to her, his smile at an angle of suave bitterness. She stood abruptly, as if she'd just come to a decision: she'd made no decision. She wanted to call Hoffman before he called her. The thought of calling him made her squeamish. She felt he was going to call at any moment. She didn't want him to call. It would be perfect if she never had anything else to do with him, as if he were a stranger who'd given her a lift in a cab at rush hour and never asked her name. Then she would always love what he'd done. Someone like him would not understand that. She was someone like him. She shoved the pages into the envelope, again feeling as if she were in a scene. At what point in the scene? She heard, she thought she heard, a tiny splash of telephone ring. Nothing more. With the envelope, she returned to the bedroom. She stood at the foot of the unmade bed. She saw herself and Hoffman meet in the middle of the bed like opposing waves. She felt that she had thought of him a dozen times since last night—the strangely careful clothes, the longish nose and drooping curls, the mouth both full and small, his face an early-nineteenth-century face, a poet or composer, someone she'd seen in a book as a child— but to the best of her recollection she had not thought, or dreamed, of their screwing. Sex was the answer to nothing, Hoffman! If you were a writer and you weren't writing, writing was the only answer. Curtis was more interested in her "career"—in his ambition for her—than he was in her work. It should have been as obvious to him that having a child would only make everything worse as it should have been obvious that *Ecuador* could not be "promoted" into fame. She must ask him tonight, was it a famous mother that he felt she deserved to be? By the time you were thirty-three, you learned that nothing beat work for making you feel good. Nothing could make you feel as good for as long as work could. Nothing was safer than work. Other happiness depended on work. She was standing in her bedroom at eleven in the morning, doing nothing but watching herself doing nothing. She had this stranger's envelope in her left hand. She would put it in her file drawer. Then she thought, Leave it out. If Curtis sees it, he sees it. I didn't write to Hoffman. Hoffman wrote to me. Hoffman signed his note "Yours," he didn't address me as "Mine."

She went into the tiny room that was her study, which she would not call her study but called the study. (For the same reason that she called her novel "my novel" and not "the novel.") She took a quick, cranky look out the window to her right, at the lusterless trees and the remnant of garden, and sat down, dropping Hoffman's envelope on top of her typewriter. She looked at her opened notebook, feeling as if she were raking a bare floor.

Bay of Fundy (dream, July 28) Bay-Fun-dee. So? Cast eel. Cast steel. Snare Andalusian (dream? Aug 15–16)
Novel about lawyer who wants to be novelist
Novel about woman lawyer
Novel story nory stovel snorey tovel Mazel tovel
"Teledu" sighted in dictionary Oct. 15! "Stinking badger of Sumatra" (novel from Teledu's point of view?)
When I was a child, I told my father in the middle of the night that I wanted my heart and his and mother's never to stop beating. He told me that it would be so long before I died that I couldn't even imagine how long, and I would be so old and tired that I wouldn't care. I did not remind him of this, of course, when mother died at 41, or when he was dying, age 61, and told me straight out that he did not want to die (embarrassed to tell me this, not because he could have remembered his reassurance when I was a terrified child but as if not wanting to die were something to be ashamed of. He looked half away from me, like a child admitting something). And he died the next day. May be a story here if I give the terrified child, when grown, a child of her own, whom she is trying to reassure about death while her (the mother's) father is dying and not wanting to. What does the mother say? Child asks, Is Grandpa dying? Is Grandpa scared? Will I be scared? Mother must say no to all child's questions and doesn't know how she herself will feel near death. She

cannot say to child, Nobody knows what it will be like or when it will happen. Any time, any place. Tomorrow. Never.

She added beneath: *Oct 23–24—As if their lives depend on it,* and closed the notebook. The typewriter keys were grimy at their base. She took the pack of Q-tips from the desk's center drawer and started toward the kitchen for the Fantastik. The phone rang. She stopped in the hallway to hear if it would continue to ring, and when it did, she went back into the bedroom, sitting down at Curtis's side of the bed as she picked up the receiver. She did not say hello. She was not clear as to why. While waiting for the caller to speak, she thought that she had never done such a thing in her life. The caller hung up. Betsy lifted the Manhattan book from the bottom drawer of Curtis's bed table, looked up *Newsworthy,* dialed, and asked for Alan Hoffman.

"Hoffman."

"Alan Hoffman?"

"Yes. Hi," he said.

"This is Betsy Ring. Betstraute. Did you know that?"

"Yup."

"Thanks for the strange pages. I really enjoyed the dialogue. I'm sorry it doesn't fit in with our publishing plans at this time. Did you just call?"

There was a conspicuous pause. "Yes."

"Why didn't you say who you were?"

"I should have. That's not a fair question. Why didn't you?"

"I was just getting to the typewriter. I guess I was preoccupied."

"I see. That probably means you can't have lunch with me."

"If I hadn't guessed it was you and hadn't called you back, would you have sent another of your sprightly messengers with the lunch invitation?"

"I wasn't sure I'd gotten the right number when I called you."

"Uh-huh."

"Why did you call me back?"

"To thank you for your valkyries. *Walkures. Wa-alküres.*
Probably we shouldn't see each other at all."

"You yourself said last night you wanted to invite me to dinner."

"Dinner isn't lunch. You know what I mean."

"You don't know what I want."

"Do you have your own office?"

"Yes, of course I have my own office. Do you mean am I alone?"

"Yes."

"I'm alone. Let me tell you, I don't want to have an affair with you. I did not sleep last night. I have got to tell you who you *are,* what you *are.*"

"My God, I wish you would!"

"I mean why I want to know you. I just want to talk."

Was it not Curtis, her husband, who had said just that fifteen minutes before? Surrounded by men who wanted only one thing. "I don't talk all that easily. I talked easily with you last night. Your just wanting to talk, so-called, doesn't make things any easier for me."

"You are the most intelligent woman I've ever met."

"What do you mean, 'most intelligent woman'?"

"I mean—Christ. I mean it's not as important to me whether men are intelligent or not. So it's men I condescend to when I say that, you see, not women."

"Quick work."

"Will you be working all day?"

"I just might go to the movies later."

"What movie?"

"I don't know. Almost anything. Have you ever been to a movie?"

"Not since a woman named Sophia Loomis said to me that cinema was really the only viable medium."

"What did you say to Sophia Loomis?"

"I smiled, I think, and backed away."

"What happened to your friend Carla, by the way? Did you ever find out?"

"Yes, I found her hanging from her lobby chandelier. She's all right. I'd love to go to a movie. I haven't been to a movie in months."

"And we'll neck. Don't you have to work?"

"If you did go, when would you go?"

"At any minute, without warning." She stood. "Okay." She sat again. "I don't quite understand what I'm about to say here. And after I say it, I'm going to say goodbye. I don't want to make too much of anything, and I don't want to be rude. But I would like you not to call me again. I'll call you in a few days. When I've figured out what's sensible, if there is such a thing. It's barely twelve hours ago that I met you. Maybe I didn't even meet you. You'll have to let me think, or whatever that is. My brain needs time to revolve."

"Do you have children?"

"Curtis has a son who lives with his mother. Little Curtis. Why?"

"I don't know."

"What opera will you be catching tonight?"

"Nothing, as a matter of fact."

"I thought maybe you could join us. We're eating with some friends, out."

"Rather go to the movies with you this afternoon, if we can't have lunch."

"Well, I'm going to try not to go to the movies. But I'm going to get off the phone. So farewell. Take care. I'll call you."

"I have *got* to have one long conversation with you before the day I die. I have too many questions to ask you."

"Before the day you die? What's the rush? There's more time after. It's your urgency that's the problem. Goodbye. I'll speak to you." She hung up. She pulled her nightgown over her head. The phone rang, startling her neck. She disengaged the receiver as if she were tranquil. "Yes."

"It must be my urgency that you *like*," he said.

She cleared her throat with an almost sleeplike refinement. "I may like your zeal, or your energy. But I don't understand

46

the urgency—or rather, I do understand it and that's why I don't like it. Take it easy, okay? You'll feel better, too.''

''All right, all right.''

''Goodbye again. Thank you again. You have a beguiling imagination. Save your questions.''

''Yes. It's very difficult.''

''Just imagine how much more difficult it would be if we knew each other. Goodbye. Goodbye? Hang up.''

''*Addio.* I mean, of course, goodbye. *Scusi. Perdono.*'' He hung up.

Betsy supposed she had removed her nightgown in order to take her shower, not to clean her typewriter keys. She was evidently already on her way to *Blume in Love* and *Get to Know Your Rabbit.* Washing herself, drying herself, dressing—green corduroy pants, brown turtleneck, black boots—she felt unexpectedly elated, without any reason she could identify for the elation. Two and a half months until publication meant two and a half months still in the bank—time she could spend. It also meant that she had finished *Ecuador* almost a year ago. Three stories since then had died beneath her hand, as if, writing them, she had been killing them. She had admitted to herself months ago that she was giving up to restlessness. Her concentration felt enfeebled. Her father on his deathbed was the beginning of a workable idea; but she didn't want it. It was as if she were full, though in fact she was empty. Or it was as if she wanted to stay empty until publication, as if purified in expectation of judgment. But publication was not, after all, life or death. It just felt as if it were going to be. No matter what happened to the book, there was no law against her getting an original, workable idea after publication, or going back to teaching, or doing something else—living. But it was as if, if she got bad reviews, or no reviews, she would disappear off a cliff into a winter ocean and drown, not by jumping or being pushed but through the complete vanishing of safe land, land that her novel itself had spread beneath her, the land of her novel, land she had discovered, some of which she had still not finished understanding and might not ever understand. Her novel was as if it were real earth. As

47

if became actuality. Writing was as if. Metaphors were as if, and metaphors were everything, the explanation of reality. Alan Hoffman went to the opera as if opera were food. The singers sang for their lives, as if their lives depended on it. They sang as if people sang in life, in rooms, on streets, and Alan Hoffman believed opera was life—no more farfetched, he had said. Curtis didn't work the way he did only to make his money or to satisfy his standards or because of his convictions but because to win the cases, the important ones, was as if to succeed in not dying. Important failure was a version of death. Why else would anyone work so hard, care so much? She had not needed to write her novel in order to survive, but it was as if writing it allowed her to survive, gave her a chance to avoid dying, a reason to avoid dying. Her novel was itself something to survive. Curtis hadn't died when the Knicks lost the playoffs last year. Probably he wouldn't live forever because they'd won them this year. Or last year. She mixed them up. Even the players didn't die when they lost. But when they lost, it was "all over." Curtis cared about their losing as if he were the loser. He watched the games on TV as if he were watching life against death, as if he were life against death. She had silently but visibly thought it silly. Even when he'd shoved the set off the stand. Just a game. But nothing was just a game. She had been brought up contemptuous of both competition and failure. Maybe what people did was to act imperiled, choose to act imperiled, as if acting imperiled might enable them to avoid being imperiled. Her childhood terror had been as if to prevent her and her parents from ever dying. It hadn't done anything for either of her parents. Why would it save her? The evidence stank. Still, as if sounded secondary but it wasn't. As if was what counted. She was tempted to call Alan Hoffman and tell him—it all came from their conversation in the lobby—but she couldn't. If she did, she would be behaving like him. He would understand too well what she was talking about. It would be as if she were approving of him.

In the kitchen, she ate most of a cup of blueberry yogurt, leaning her shoulder blades against the refrigerator door. If she went to the first show, she would be back by three-thirty, when she would call Curtis, who in any case would have called her while she was out—buying groceries. She took the grocery list from the pad under the telephone. She'd pick up the mail downstairs before leaving, she decided. She went back to the bedroom for the keys. The study door was open. Hoffman's envelope. *Hoffman's Envelope,* a story. She slid it between two folders of unpublished stories, in the rear of the file drawer. She nudged the drawer with her thumb and watched it slide shut. With the envelope in the drawer, was she in the envelope? Had she sealed her fate? Little did she know that with this one small act she had set in motion a chain of events that was to alter her life irrevocably? Not likely. Did Curtis own her? Yes, he did, damn near. But then he also owned the secrets in her head, which were much more dangerous to him than the envelope in the drawer.

She took her keys and her brown corduroy bag from the top of her bureau and left her bedroom. At the end of the hall, she dropped her bag by the closet and let herself out, locking the door. Running like a drumroll down the steps, she saw a shape in the foyer through the frosted-glass door and above her heard the muted ringing of the buzzer. She pulled open the door. Her shoulders and heart jumped. "My," she said. He was wearing, today, a gray tweed overcoat. At his throat, a robin's-egg-blue muffler was folded ascot-fashion. He was holding a black attaché case.

"What are *you* doing here?" he said, then grimaced disarmingly, as if anticipating her anger.

"I've learned that if I keep my right foot against the door, I can just barely reach my mailbox from here without the door closing behind me." She stretched her left leg and torso forward as if she were stepping over a stream, unlocked the mailbox, and pulled out Curtis's *New York Review of Books,* his *Scientific American,* and a batch of envelopes. She locked the mailbox and drew her body back. "Are you dangerous?" she asked, quickly examining the envelopes. Common Cause, Planned Parenthood, dentist, Yale Law School, Wildlife Preservation. "How did you get up here so fast?"

"It didn't seem that fast. I was sure you'd be gone. Anyway, please forgive me. I'm sure you think I'm nuts. I'm not nuts. And I'm not dangerous." He looked at the names above the buzzers. "In fact, I've come to visit H. and L. Lupini."

"If you make me late for the movies, I'll never want to speak to you again. The most intelligent woman you've ever known is going to the noon show of *Blume in Love* and *Get to Know Your Rabbit*. So please tell me what you want. And please don't tell me you're in love with me."

"I am not in love with you."

She was relieved that he wasn't smiling. "You're not really here to see the Lupinis, are you? No one sees the Lupinis."

"No."

Now she wished he weren't looking so serious. "Why are you acting as if you're in love with me? I'm married. Do you care that I'm married? I care that I'm married. My husband cares that I'm married. Look, for all I know you're perfectly capable of calling me at two in the morning to tell me that you're not nuts and not in love with me but you've got to see me immediately. If you wanted to, you could ruin any desire I might have to get to know you."

"But you're interested in me."

"That's my business, not yours. I don't know what I am. I don't know you. You are interesting. That's not the same as my being interested. But I can tell you that if I were, the more you pushed me, the less interested I would be."

"I understand that perfectly. I can't *stand* women who rush me. I can't stand myself when I do it. You will have reason to trust me. I do not seem trustworthy, but I will be. You remind me of the reserve of which I am secretly capable. I didn't want to tell you before because I thought it would relieve you too much and you would forget about me, but I am going to Europe tonight for a week. I wanted to see your face again. I will not be calling you from over there. I won't even *think* about you. So you can think about me. Okay?"

She smiled squintily at him. "What are you doing in Europe?"

"For interviews on the Saturday Night Massacre, Agnew's downfall, all this eventful mess. Yom Kippur War, the oil boycott. It's been an extravagant month for news. I'm going to see government people, politicians, man in the street, woman in the street, *via, rue, strasse*. Also going to some opera. It was all just resolved this morning. So I'm out of your hair. Wonderful? Not that I'm in it. You keep it very trim, anyway. And you look like a chic elf today."

"While you reconsider that, I'll go back up to get my coat."

"I'd love to see where you live, as long as I'm here."

"I'll be late." Why wouldn't it be better, she wondered, to spend the afternoon with him? Let him be the movies? "Okay. Come on. But very quickly. You'll have to run through the place. It's quite small. The bed's unmade, too."

She opened the door and let him by. "Go ahead. After you." Wishing he were moving faster, she followed his overcoat, attaché case, fawn trouser legs, up the stairs. At the top, she preceded him to the door. "Where do you live?" She unlocked.

"I live across from Lincoln Center. I've lived there from before the time anyone knew there was going to be a Lincoln Center. An old West Side boy."

Betsy pulled her pea coat out of the closet and put it on. She picked up her bag.

"Are you taking your mail to the movies?"

"No. That goes in here. This is the living room. And dining room. Plants, chairs, walls, windows." She placed the mail at the end of the dining table. "This is where I read your funny pages before."

"This is such a serene room. You could cure a headache in here. Are you keeping my valkyries?"

"I guess I am, for the time being. Yes."

"May I see the rest? I'll hurry."

"Let me get the bed." The man she had imagined in bed with her less than an hour before was following her to the bedroom. She heaved the bedding in one haul over the empty sheet. "And this is where I just hung up the phone."

"What's in here?"

51

She opened the study door. "Want the place?"

"Are you moving? I love my place, thanks. What's wrong with this place?"

"I don't know, it's both compact and inconvenient." Curtis's eye for the sneakily pretentious. "You have to do an awful lot of walking to get not very far and back."

"This is where you wrote your book?"

"This is where I write and where I don't write."

"Where did you put my envelope?"

"I ate it."

"Where, really? I'm just interested."

"Here." She opened the drawer.

"Where?"

She pulled up the envelope and pushed it back down. "See?"

"What else is in there?"

"Stories. Mostly unpublished."

"You've published stories?"

"Four. In ten years. But I was working—I was teaching then."

"Where?"

"Prentiss."

"I went there!"

"I am not a bit surprised."

"Why do you say that?"

"You know. The way you are, or are not, of this world. Your evident sense of optimism that everything will go your way, or that at least it's meant to."

"Ah. I am certainly hoping you're going to give me the chance to prove how wrong you are. Why did you stop teaching?"

She looked at her watch.

"Your movies."

"I won't make it." She dropped into her desk chair. She looked out the window, away from him. He was leaning against the narrow white wall.

"I hate to make you late. Why can't you catch the beginning at the other end?" she heard him say.

"I stopped teaching because at about the same time I married Curtis I started this novel and he could support the time it was going to take." She felt as if she'd swallowed a chicken bone; she began to cry so smoothly that she was sure he'd have no way of knowing. But wet was wet. Either she wiped her eyes or she'd have to face him with a wet face. She made a pass with one hand, as if she were pushing at her hair. She got up and walked past him into the bedroom, to the Kleenex on the bed table. She wiped her face with her back to him and threw the Kleenex into the wastebasket. "Let's go." Turning back to him matter-of-factly, she feared she looked either angry or sorry for herself.

"Go where?" His lips were slightly open; he seemed both concerned and fascinated.

"Interrupt the movie, go to a different movie. I don't want to stay here. Don't you have to go back to your office?"

"I'm going to my house to pack." He picked up his case. "I'm terribly sorry if I upset you." He came from the wall toward her with very slow, heavy-looking steps.

She held up her hand and rapidly shook her head, looking at his eyes. "Nothing, don't," she said, with the tiniest smile.

He touched his palm to hers. "I hadn't intended to." He took his hand away, and she let hers fall. She thought how easy it would have been to put her cheek against his muffler. How hard it was to do such easy things. "So." She started out ahead of him, down the hall. "You needn't have apologized for upsetting me. It's mostly because I'm not working."

He was behind her at her side. "Sometimes when I'm nosy, I forget that questions can be like shovels. I don't imagine the consequences. It's not like interviewing."

She opened her front door and held it open, facing him, as if she were leaving his apartment.

"Are we going?" he asked.

"Aren't we?"

"Where? Want to come watch me pack?"

"Sure."

"You do?"

"Why not?" She felt slightly surprised herself to have said it. "Is it safe?"

"Don't be silly."

"Silly yes or silly no?"

"You shouldn't ask. It's like my apologizing. I would love to have your company. Show you my digs."

"Where you keep your shovels. I have to be home by three."

"Three is hours from now." He walked past her through the door and again she locked it.

On their way to the stairs, Alan turned to Betsy, his forehead strained high with expressiveness, and crooned, " '*Sarebbe cosi dolce restar qui. C'è freddo fuori.*' Then *you* sing, '*Vi starò—*' "

"Shh!" Betsy said, hitting Alan in the chest with the edge of her hand. From the top of the stairs a figure could be seen moving below, beyond the frosted door. Curtis home with a virus, she thought.

"Okay. I'm your typewriter repairman, if plumber's taken. I've just interviewed you for *Newsworthy*. Maybe it's just a burglar."

"It's a tenant." The figure was unlocking the door. Betsy and Alan started down the stairs, her high heartbeat making her queasy. A sour-looking, baby-faced man in a sheepskin jacket came through. He and Betsy nodded. The man smiled with his eyes closed as Betsy and Alan passed him.

"E. Nichols. Fourth floor. Would you mind if we took a taxi?" Outdoors felt dangerous to her; outdoors included taking a bus.

"Of course."

They descended the stoop and walked toward Central Park West, neither of them saying anything.

3

They got a cab. Alan told the driver to leave them at the corner
of Sixty-fifth Street.

"Why the corner?" Betsy asked.

"The traffic goes the wrong way for us there. Nothing to
panic about."

Betsy looked out the window at the Park as they rolled. From
Ninety-fifth Street to Eighty-fourth Street, Alan looked at her
back and the back of her hair, which bulged and splayed against
the collar of her pea coat. He scratched his nose and folded his
hands.

At the red light, Betsy withdrew her face from the window.
"If you had been to interview me, and it had been Curtis coming
through the door, actually he would have been delighted, I
think." She looked at Alan. "You know I don't want to be
interviewed. I would feel like a different person, being interviewed."

"Of course, I thought about this last night. I could give a
nudge at the magazine, but it could easily be turned down. I'm
sure the book will do fine by itself."

55

"The book is going to do poorly. Interviews are beside the point."

"Please. The existence of a book is already doing well. A book by you." He filled with tenderness, as if he knew her, as if he knew the book. Then he thought, Maybe it's no good, the book, maybe it's precious or self-centered. What did a man do if he loved his wife and hated her novel?

At Sixty-fifth Street, when they got out, Alan said, "We have half a block to go. I could hire a closed van, I guess, but I'm assuming you're far enough away from your neighbors and merchants, family, friends, lovers, not to worry at the moment."

She was entertained. "You're remarkably imaginative. I'm sure you've had practice."

"I'm imaginative. There's no such thing as practice. Down here." In the middle of the block they entered a six-story building of deep-raspberry brick, its windows framed in white. Alan stopped for his mail. A small elevator took them slowly to the fifth floor. They stepped into a little hall of green-and-white tile; on each side was a door thickly painted green. She followed him to the left. He let her into a rectangular foyer that gave onto a large white room, a scarlet rug. From where she stood in the foyer, Betsy could see a couch, striped in pale-blue and ivory, against a short wall, and two big, awkward chairs with lions' faces in the knees of the legs, the oval seats and backs a stiff, ancient bronze plush. She glimpsed the prow of a grand piano. Along the base of the long wall opposite her were closed white cabinets, interrupted only by a hallway. Along the top of the cabinets, on each side of the hallway entrance, ran a row of thick, dark-blue volumes or binders. Above these, on the wall to the left of the hallway, hung colored prints, framed in black or gold, of people in costume. Above the blue row to the hallway's right were shelves of books. "I don't know what this room is," Betsy said. "It looks like the office of a retired theatrical producer or something. I've never seen anything I can compare it with."

"I don't spend much time here."

"I want to see your closets. That's why I'm here. To count your clothes."

"Well, here's a closet. Let me have your coat." He opened the closet door to their right.

Betsy looked in. "Three coats plus the one you're wearing. That seems fair enough. A cape? Velvet? Do you wear it?"

"You know, to the dentist sometimes."

"Blazers, trousers. Four, five blazers. Do you get dressed out here?"

"My bedroom closet is full. This is spillover. Will you excuse me?" There wasn't room for him to approach the hangers without touching her. If he touched her, he would seem to have done so intentionally. Touching her would give him a deep shock.

"Excuse me." She stepped out of his way. "You spill over all by yourself. I spill over because I have to share the bedroom closet with Curtis." She went into the living room.

Sliding the hanger into her sleeves, he felt the pea coat to be her, draping him with excitement and sadness. The lapels of his own overcoat covered her shoulders from behind. He exhaled. He would now be showing her a sixth blazer, the new brown double-breasted twill beauty, pale-blue shirt, green tie with tiny dots. He picked up the attaché case and mail. "The rest is this way," he said, heading toward the hallway. She wandered toward him from the direction of the windows. This other person in his living room was like someone of universal fame, a household word. "In these cabinets are my records and tapes, turntable, speakers, deceased wives." He switched on a light as they entered the short hallway. He opened the kitchen door. "No clothes in there." He closed the door. "You're rushing me," she said. "And this I usually use as an office," he said. He snapped another light switch, which turned on a small crystal chandelier. She saw a long table, a typewriter, two piles of books, dining chairs, four against a wall, one at the typewriter, another across from the typewriter. "May I proceed?" she asked.

"Sure. On your left down there is my fabulous collection of personal ticket stubs."

"May I see it for free?" Passing by the dining table, she approached a fish tank nearly the size of a trunk, on the floor at the end of the room, catty-corner. The stubs crammed the glass, the rectangular heap taking up over a third of the tank's height. She turned to him—he remained in the doorway—and said, "Will you donate them to a university?"

He felt unfamiliar with himself. He smiled as if he were eight years old and announcing a death. "Opera, concert, theater, movies. Anything taking place in an auditorium. Twenty-nine years' worth, from the very beginning, except for the first few movies, when I didn't know better."

"Did you ever lose any?" She sat down sidesaddle at the edge of the table. "Is this okay?"

"Fine. The answer is no, not as far as I *know*. I've dreamed of being told that a very few stubs have been missing from the collection for years. I've dreamed of losing the evening's stubs, returning to the opera house—the opera house was in Russia— insisting to the cleaning people that they find them, mine—I had to get an interpreter for this—and having to accept any pair as substitutes. I hope you're not giving this the raised psychiatric eyebrow."

She looked impatient.

"I also dreamed once that the stub collection got into the Stub Hall of Fame, quite apart from me." He placed his hands on top of the chair nearest her—his typewriter chair—and tipped its back toward him. "Anyway, I typed to you in here last night, and then I was thinking I wanted to tell you things, things I knew and didn't know, and wondering why you. Partly it must have had something to do with the way you were talking about your book, a useful way you take yourself seriously. You're not the *end* of yourself. It's a matter of your having something to be serious about other than yourself, and other than getting people interested in you. It's as if your kind of self-involvement were a gift—something that others wanted."

"My. Are you sure?"

"Dreaming Ecuador, Quito, the mystery of the thing, a country that's about you, the key-toe, key-to business, something

58

big coming out of something small, a word, like a clue. You made it time for me to remember things I haven't thought of for years, as if your brain had jarred mine, or something. Things I've digested, take for granted. And your being upset that I go to the opera so often. Usually I ignore that in people, or it irritates me, but today I'm interested in it myself. Partly because your being upset has nothing to do with my inconveniencing you. After a while there's so much in a life, you forget what's in storage. I was sitting here, staring at the tickets in that tank, it must have been close to four this morning, and rolling out of storage comes the scene of my parents taking me to the opera for the first time, when I was eleven." He wanted to sit down now but felt as if he had forgotten how it was done. "We listened together to the broadcasts on Saturday afternoons, usually while they marked their students' papers—they both teach science in the city school system. They and I listened, not my older sister, she was the brain, she's a biochemist now, and she thought operas were silly screaming. She once asked why didn't they broadcast from the Central Park Zoo instead. Anyway, it was my territory. And I heard Milton Cross describe the great golden curtain and the golden horseshoe in his huge way, and I was dying to *go*, to *see* it. I pestered them carefully. They had very little money to spare. I wanted to go so badly that I didn't push. But it made my father happy that I cared so much. I think it impressed him that I meant it, that I wasn't just trying to get in good."

"It didn't make your mother happy?"

"Oh, sure. It made them corporately happy. I always had a sense that my listening with them was good for *them*. I don't know if it's true. Sure it made her happy, but I didn't have to try with her. So finally we went, one Friday night, to *Trovatore*, same as last night, but that's not what made me think of the first time. I've been to dozens of *Trovatores* since the first time. It's you. Were you ever in the old opera house?"

"Yes, but I remember only some ballets there, no operas. I remember wishing I could dance on the wide stairs during intermission. It was like a movie staircase."

"That first night we went, we sat way up at the top, on the side, but it was perfect, because I could see the whole theater. Being *in* the theater, *en*tering the theater, the first sight of that interior, that plush, ruby plush, with a kind of amethyst tinge, and the gold crust on the boxes, it looked so old, but it glowed, it glowed but it was dusky. It was as if I'd never seen *nature* before. It *was* nature—a hanging red garden in deep twilight, or underwater if water were red, or a high cave, a sumptuous cave. It was mystery that was visible. Even in the dark, I spent half the evening looking around me. I couldn't believe what I'd come into. The music just made it better. The *opera* house was the opera. I think now, as I'm telling you this, and I never thought of it this way before, that coming into that theater was like coming on a secret in the woods, in a fairy tale. Everything began for me then. It's as if there had never been any real light before. It was like something that had been waiting for me. It was mine, my *house*. Like walking into the interior of my own body. Or my brain. The tiers of the theater were shelves of my brain. I still don't know why it was so important, but I've never let go. Keeping the stubs from such an occasion seemed perfectly natural. I kept theirs and mine, of course, then it occurred to me to do it forever, with just my own stubs. Only it was very slow at the beginning. My parents and I went twice more when I was a kid. My rich uncle took me once, in a box, but my father and he didn't get along, they still don't, so there was some strain in my going. When I was fourteen I realized I could save my allowance and go by myself occasionally, and I began putting the opera that was on the stage together with going to the opera house."

"If the opera was your house, then your stubs must be keys. Your own key-to."

"Of course." He let the chair stand up, holding on to it. "I don't mean of course, I mean of *course*. That has never, never occurred to me. That's it, you see. You've unlocked me."

"It's the kind of thing another person usually has to tell you, isn't it?"

"Maybe, but who? It's thrilling!"

Her brief smile was distinctly happy for him. "If your parents had so little money to spare, were you on scholarship at Prentiss?"

"That's correct."

"Was that difficult?"

"It's not what was difficult. How long did you teach there?"

"Six years. Seven."

"You're how old now? Do you mind?"

"I mind being thirty-three. You don't have to give up the floor. What happened after fourteen? After twenty?"

"Look. I would like to tell you everything I know about myself. That's the point. Part of it I can see—I thought of it last night also—and some of it's invisible but I know it's there, I know connections are there. The trouble is that the part of it I can see is both very personal and somewhat silly to be telling someone I don't know."

"It's up to you. I'm curious."

He felt as if she had laid her hand on the side of his neck. He leaned the back of the chair into his chest again. "I wish I knew you." He smiled his regret at her.

She nodded at the chair. "You haven't sat down since we got here."

"The tour's not finished. Are you more comfortable in my house than I am? You're not really sitting down, either."

"I'm more comfortable in your house than I was with you in my own. Even discounting your visit before, or paratroop landing, or whatever it was, there's some way in which I prefer visiting to being visited. It's not that I don't like having people to dinner. I like to cook. Curtis cooks sometimes and is an excellent restaurant captain at all times. When I was little, I liked having friends visit. But in high school and college, if a boy was too obviously interested in me, he was like an unwanted visitor. If he was quiet about it, matter-of-fact, that was okay. And it was all right if he could let me indicate that I was interested in him, quietly. But if he was aggressive, or silently

61

nervous and needy, that was too noisy, embarrassing. I didn't want fuss to be made. I wanted to be like a guest who wasn't seen entering or leaving by anyone on the street.''

"What are you telling me?'' Alan sat down in the chair he had been holding. The slender swell of Betsy's green-corduroyed thigh was a forearm away. "How can you stand *me?*'' He made himself smile.

"Well . . .'' She looked down at him. Her expression reminded him of a way she had looked in O'Neals'. Though her mouth and eyes were sober, his sense that her brain was working in her face, like colored beams slipping back and forth in her bones, made her appear to be enjoying something droll. Or it was as if her energy were subduing her self-consciousness. "I had to begin to learn to stop penalizing people, including me, when they showed open interest in me. I am still learning. There's no question that you're an extreme case—I hope. I'm not even sure that *extreme* is an adequate word. So possibly you don't even count in this. You are outside the particular problem, maybe. Or maybe you are so bold that you blow away the problem. No. But the trick is that underneath all that skittishness of mine, the secret really turned out to be that I wanted to be the one to start things. Surprise. I was the aggressive one, a secret aggressor. And this is a very crude version of part of what my novel is about. It is not, however, what I'm doing here. I don't want to start anything with you, or be a secret aggressor or a nonsecret aggressor. But I'm here, so I must want something.'' Her voice suddenly sounded contemplative to the point of misery. She got off the table and strolled away from him and along the other side of the room.

Alan felt so tender and victorious with her unhappiness that he did not dare respond to her last observation. "Did Curtis pursue you noisily? Could you let him.?''

She faced him, smiling a little. "No. In a way, he was a reversion. He was almost ideally pursuable by the earlier me. And of course I was less sneaky by the time I met him than I had been. He absorbed me. Calmly. Aspects of me that had sometimes caused difficulty with other men. I think he was intrigued by my literary obsessiveness. My verbal anxiety amused him, my literalness. He wasn't jealous of my time. He loved it that I was seriously writing a novel. He let me alone. He was proud of where my stories had been published."

"And now?"

"And now what?"

"He's still proud, isn't he? He sounded very proud of you last night."

"I've done nothing to be ashamed of."

"Did he have a beard when you met him?"

She took a step toward the table. "Now that's the kind of question I love! Yes, he did. Why did you ask that?"

"I don't really know. But I'm certainly glad I did. Have you ever asked him to shave it off?"

"No. I've always thought of it as part of his absorbency."

"Does he have a nickname?"

"No, afraid not. Curt sounds rude, and Curtsy would be inappropriate."

"How long have you been married?"

"Why don't I see you taking any of this down? Two and a half years."

"Was he divorced when you met him?"

"Separated. Okey-dokey?"

"Where did you meet him?"

"We met at a party for a magazine that was a client of his."

"Pothole Review?"

"How would you know that?"

"It just makes sense."

"That is possibly an insult. More likely, probably an insult. Why have you never been married? I'm not answering any more questions." She pulled out the chair opposite him and sat down.

He pushed the typewriter to the right. "Did I say I'd never been married?"

"What you said last night was that you weren't married, you were only forty. You didn't say you'd never been married. I'm making an assumption. You don't seem divorced to me."

"Widowed?"

"Sorry. Even less widowed than divorced."

"I haven't been married. I was almost married once."

"You lived with someone."

"I mean we were going to get married and didn't."

"Sophia Loomis?"

"Hardly. It was *the* important woman."

"But there've been lots of others. Histrionic."

He was almost, but not quite, relieved that she was being silly. Silly and snide. "Not all histrionic, no. There've been some good women, good friends. And the histrionic ones aren't only histrionic, either. It's just that if someone is histrionic, that quality usually stains the rest of the personality. So it seems to me."

"Forgive my archness, will you? The circumstances are unusual. I want to know what you want to tell me."

He felt as if she had saved them; it was not her apology for the archness, but her recognition of the archness. She was doubly sympathetic: she had an excuse, and she had found it. "I know. I was being somber, in any case. My solemn self. I'd like you to understand—I promise you, I avoid them, the histrionic types, when I can recognize them. They're not necessarily so easy to tell. They may distract you by telling you cinema is the only viable medium. Or how together they feel since they've joined group vomiting. Or they'll brag about going to bed with Norman Mailer and how he wasn't very good. A feminist told me two weeks ago, as angry as if I had just stepped on her foot, that Homer was a sexist. In any case, I'm not saying everybody turns out to be histrionic. But you see it all over the place. I do. Don't you?"

Betsy bounced her head, left, right, skeptically, as she had last night.

"There are women who enter an apartment as if they're Martha Graham. The Annunciation was not as big a deal. But it always looks *tragic*. They'll gaze at you, lovingly, as if you've just died on them. Mostly what it boils down to is a kind of opportunistically mournful way of living. They look to be gypped. Their TV pilots are stolen. Their political brainstorms are stolen. Or they've been married to thieves and liars, so *they've* been stolen. Being cheated, being *denied,* is their success. That's the point. Preferably by someone famous or important. I knew a woman getting on toward thirty who had a very sweet voice you could barely have heard over a piano in a bar, and the reason she couldn't get an audition at the Met or the City Opera was what she called 'the closed establishment,' right? And you *know* she had some schlocky, withered voice teacher who kept her coming to lessons by encouraging her. That kind of thing. Why are you letting me babble on so intolerantly? It isn't nice of you."

"I'm just waiting for you to get to yourself."

Her cool attentiveness felt like praise. He was about to start to tell her the story he had begun to connect last night with the opera-going, start it where it was least awkward, when the phone, on the floor beside him, softly rang. He had forgotten to worry that it might interrupt them. He decided to forego the obligatory disgusted grimace and reached for the phone, feeling chilly, as if his shirt had been removed. So that Betsy would not feel herself to be the interruption, he gave a receptive "Hello."

"Hi, darling. Are you busy?"

A painless headache flared. He drooped. "Hi. You tried my office?"

"Last night was so precious, Alan."

"Lo and behold, I have to fly to London." Betsy stood up across the table, and he flashed his left arm violently. He rose with the phone, frowning at her. She sat again, her lower lip pushed under her upper, her eyebrows raised, as if she had gagged herself. Alan nodded at her once, firmly. "It was just decided," he explained to Carla. "I'm leaving in a little while."

"I'm glad I caught you. I would have missed saying goodbye."

"No, I was going to call you. May I call you back before I leave for the airport?"

"I turned down an invitation for *A Little Night Music* for tonight, Alan. I was so sure I'd be with you." Her voice was peacefully aggrieved.

"Maybe you can retrieve it. I'm sorry. I should have called, but I just found out."

"On business?"

"Yes."

"Lucky. For how long?"

"A week."

"Is that it?" She sighed, or blew out cigarette smoke.

"Is what what?"

"Goodbye?"

"I'm only going to Europe, Carla."

"I think it's funny that you're the one who's being impatient, Alan. Have a good trip." She was gone.

He laid the receiver into its cradle and sat himself down. He pushed the phone away. He smiled at Betsy sourly and tapped rapidly at the table with a fingernail. "There never seems to be anyone to blame."

"You were very short with her."

"She hung up on me." The phone rang. He picked it up. "Yes."

"I know you're in a hurry, but I just can't let this go, Alan. I have a stake in this, too. I don't really want to do it on the phone. It seems so impersonal."

"Well, we have to."

"To be frank with you, I felt used last night."

"Used."

"When we were making love, if you recall that. I felt that you weren't really there. I was making love for both. It was lonely."

He was silent.

"Are you there?"

"I'm sorry, but I have to go."

"You also had to leave last night, right after, I seem to recall. Leaving seems to be your thing. I have to ask you not to call me on your return."

"I'm sorry about the whole thing. Take care."

"Take care? You mean have a good life?"

"I just mean I'm sorry. Be well."

"Are you going first-class or tourist?"

66

"What?"

"Alan, that is it. I will not be snarled at." This time her receiver sideswiped his ear.

With a bleak little bow, he hung up. "No observations, please," he said to Betsy. "She is the dead end of what I have to tell you. The dead end of dead ends."

"How long have you known her?"

"A week and a half."

"It sounds worse than that."

"A lot can happen in a week and a half."

She looked at him as if to say she knew that. "I need your bathroom."

He stood. Was she having her period? "Will you join me in the kitchen? Some soup?"

"What kind of soup? What time is it?" She looked at her watch as she stood. *"Blume in Love* isn't even over yet. That's nice. I'm not clear when it is you're leaving."

"From here not 'til about six. The bathroom is just opposite the bedroom."

Betsy went out ahead of him, holding her bag. From the kitchen door, he asked, "Have you a preference in soups?"

She stopped with her hand on the knob of the bathroom door, her back to him. "Could we talk about it in roughly half a minute? I need time to think. Clam chowder, maybe. See you."

He hung his blazer over the rounded back of the kitchen chair and undid his necktie and his collar button. He hurried leftover Fontina and Jarlsberg onto the table, the jar of pickled beets, the stoned wheat thins, two white plates, silverware, paper napkins. He got a second chair from the dining room and settled it at right angles to his. He reviewed the soup cans at the back of the counter without finding chowder. He folded his necktie into a side pocket of his jacket. He rolled up his sleeves and washed his hands and face. With his hands on his face, he recognized that, despite his rushing, his anticipation was calm, distributed evenly over him by his wish to be careful of her, to leave her importance to her. His hands stayed on his face. To leave her importance alone. To let it speak for itself when it chose to

67

speak. He dried himself slowly with a paper towel and stared at the window. It still happened at parties—it had happened meeting Carla—that leaving a conversation for the bathroom, he could not wait to get back to the woman, or the group with the woman in it, to her importance, to his scotch and water, to the subject they were discussing. Time would run out, everything would be over before he got back. You could not speed up urinating. At college, curfews had been like death. If he was with someone important, or someone becoming important, he would try to spend those college evenings, grim with beer, in as much darkness as could be found, so that time could not find him and the face beside his. He had, since then, become his own curfew. It was as if he always started off drunk with a woman and always sobered up. What he needed to do was start off sober and let himself get drunk. The flushing of the toilet sent him back to the row of soups. Still no chowder. As she came in, he turned to her, holding out a Black Bean and a Tomato. "Chowder's fresh out, but I can easily get some at the corner." She approached him with a smooth directness that looked to him like caution and tapped the Black Bean can. "Then you just sit right down and I'll have this ready in a jiff," he said. They separated for different corners of the room.

Betsy said, "I was thinking in there that histrionic men tend to be histrionic physically. And there are lots of them. They want to be heroic in storms, carry heavy things for people who can't. An excess of Ping-Pong will do. Sweating is a form of boasting. It looks like suffering. Most men simply don't need as much love melodrama or career melodrama as women do."

"Very clever," Alan said from the stove. "I admitted I was being intolerant before. In fact, I don't tend to fall into the physical histrionics, but this summer I broke up a mugging and got stabbed."

"A perfect example. Stabbed where?"

"In the arm. Lost a beautiful amount of blood. Passed out in the emergency room of Roosevelt Hospital. *And* I was with a woman. My friends called me stupid. I had to stop telling the story. But the cops got the mugger."

"Were you wearing your cape?"

"Too hot. But in fact, I'm always seeing city scenes as opera scenes. The metropolitan opera. It's very easy to do. The Hudson River, in almost any weather, at almost any hour, looks like an opera river. Particularly in winter twilights."

"I would have been furious and not hidden it well. The woman you were with loved you for it, no doubt."

Alan looked quickly over his shoulder to see her lowering a slice of cheese into her mouth. "I'm just mushing this glop. I'll be there in a minute. Help yourself to the pickled beets. I think they're open."

"The question is only, Why haven't you found anyone for yourself? Someone who could last."

"How long is the longest you've loved someone?"

"Two years, three. But I'm younger than you."

"I want to tell you something. Just a minute. I can't talk this way."

"Where are the bowls?"

"In the cabinet above you. I forgot the bowls?" He was excited now; he had a way to begin his story. Finally, he was able to bring the pot to the table. He poured the soup, took the pot to the sink, blasted water into it, and sat down beside Betsy. He had not been closer to her since they'd come into the apartment. She had sliced some of each cheese for them. His knees felt as if they were breathing hers.

She placed her spoon in the soup and regarded it. "There is a Spanish proverb, 'Only the spoon knows what's in the soup.' "

He smiled quickly. "That's not much help to *us,* is it? The name of the woman I was with when I broke up the mugging was Penny Long. I'm spilling my beans here. At the bottom of this is everything, I think. Including the reason I'm so glad to be sitting here talking to you. Penny Long was absolute perfection. I met her at the house of a couple that plays chamber music. She was the violist that night. She played so beautifully, she was so accomplished, physically so angelic, wearing blue jeans, a blue pullover or something, she looked fifteen, with the most winsome imaginable face. I wept. I cry a lot at the opera,

69

but this took me absolutely by surprise. I have this *thing*—the perfect moment, the perfectly sung note. Her face was the perfectly sung note, held permanently. Anyway. Miracle. We left together, and the next day she left her boyfriend. It was amazingly gorgeous. And she was the real thing. Juilliard graduate. Had good orchestra jobs around the city. She of course loved going to the operas and the concerts with me. She taught me a lot. But she knew nothing about anything but music. She had no opinions beyond believing there should be no wars. If we would all just spend our time emphasizing the good in each other, there would be no wars. 'Celebrating life,' was the phrase she used. She was twenty-nine years old. I was very careful. I warned myself that I would never know a lovelier, more loving, more musical woman. She was truly decent. She wouldn't have known how to *spell* histrionic. And she had absolutely no self outside her music and this violetlike loveliness. She and I lasted two months. Where do you go in this world to find someone who will last? I've *always* wanted things to last. Forever, in fact. In a way, that's the whole problem.''

Betsy's gaze hadn't shifted from her soup. She smiled to herself, but not privately. "I would say it's a problem. Is this what's too personal and somewhat silly to be telling someone you don't know?''

"No, not quite, but it seemed to be a transition. Are you disappointed? It sounded silly enough to me. Aren't you going to eat some soup? The spoon isn't going to tell you all that much, not unless you talk to it, nicely, bring it up, nice and slow, don't spill.''

Betsy laughed through her nose and lowered the soup-filled spoon from her mouth. "You're a big help.''

He imagined kissing her, imagined her putting down her watchful reserve and facing him, totally serious, ready to love him. Her sweater was loose, her breasts inconspicuous. The most opulent women in the world could so lack mystery that they might as well be made of rubber. Everything about Betsy seemed to him magically secret and unique, untouchably intimate, crushingly crushable. "Look. I plan to finish my story, if

70

I can find it all. I want to. But I think I hope to hear more from you."

"I understand." She gave him no more than a glance; then she looked at him. "I'm sorry. It's really as if I'm trying to find out why I'm here in the first place by what you tell me about yourself. I don't trust my motives, in any direction. I don't know what they are. I'm not even confused. I don't know how dangerous you are. I'm susceptible to something. I have to find out what it is."

Alan's heart dropped. "What happens when you find out? You get shots?"

"Easy!" She laughed, embarrassed. "There's your scar, I see."

He rolled down his left sleeve and buttoned it. He laid a hand in the sweatered crook of her elbow and took it immediately away. "I think if I tell you the rest, I'll seem less dangerous." Gloom entered his lungs, surprising him.

"Or dangerous in a different way."

"How am I dangerous? Do you think you're not dangerous?"

"I'm not accusing you of anything."

"I *feel* like an *idiot*. An idiot. It is ridiculous to have told you about Penny Long; it is ridiculous to have fallen in love with someone like that, in that way, at forty. I seem to want to tell you all this, as if I were throwing myself on your mercy or something."

"Just a little too much opera, that's all. I do think it's good you have a full-time job. Anyway, who are you to think you're such an idiot? You're embarrassed, but I'm being nosy. Which is worse? You're unusual and interesting, which is not all that common a combination."

"Aren't you sounding just a bit detached?"

"If you had your way, how exactly would I be? At this point." She seemed about half amused and half irritable. "If detached is what I am."

Her face could never look stupid. Possibly too smart, but not stupid. "I don't know, I'm in my own way here." He gobbled a piece of Fontina on a wheat thin. He started his soup. "Tell me this. Where were you when I was fifteen? And what were you wearing?" What had her bedroom been like? Had she ever played doctor? Who with? "And where did you go to school?"

"When you were fifteen? I was eight? We lived at Five-forty-five West End. I attended fashionable Hunter Elementary School. And I was wearing a plaid jumper and a red sweater. Nineteen-forty-eight."

"Is your real name Betsy? What was your last name, maiden name?"

"Our last name was Harris. I was born Betsy."

"Did you mind that?"

"Betsy? For a while, around eleven or twelve, I gave myself smokier names, of the Valerie or Simone type. Then it just got used to itself, like other things."

"Is your novel going to be under Harris or Ring?"

"Harris. My stories were all published under Harris. My father was a radio news producer. Ted Harris. My mother was an editor at *Life*. I thought we were very spiffy, in communications."

"No brother or sister?"

"Not a one. Just Bea and Ted and Betsy."

"Where are Bea and Ted?"

"Dead."

"Oh." He raised his eyebrows. "When? Together?"

She appeared to be amused by the number of his questions."My mother in fifty-six, my father last year."

"You were sixteen when your mother died?"

"That's right."

"She had to have been very young. My God. What did that do to you? I shouldn't ask you that."

"Another time. *Get to Know Your Rabbit* is bound to have begun." Betsy checked her watch. She drank some soup.

As he talked, for the most part she kept her head attentively lowered, as if she were reading. He talked to her temple, her chin, her neck or shoulder, or to his hands. Occasionally, she would look up at a word or phrase. Her smile flickered as if it were part of the rhythm of her face's life. "In nineteen-forty-eight," Alan began, "I went to a party at my cousin Marjorie's —the daughter of that same rich uncle. It must have been something my mother made sure my father wouldn't make an issue of, or we didn't mention it to him. I remember looking forward to it intensely. I went to school with girls, so I didn't know many girls outside of school, and I didn't have enough friends at that time anyway. I was supercilious and odd, a jerk—I mean, I had a few friends, but I think it took some doing to cut through all my opera-loving. My passion was embarrassing. I talked too much about the opera to the wrong people. I was not tactful in the way I tried to impress my classmates."

"Like me with my spiffy communications parents."

"Well, I wouldn't have minded you. I'm sorry I wasn't there. My cousin Marjorie was my exact contemporary and went to the Park School, which was all-girls at the time. It made me feel absolutely cosmopolitan to go to this party. A whole new country of people. I an eligible bachelor. I wore my blue suit. My suit. I'm sure it took me an hour and a half to dress. Standing there by herself at this party was Marjorie's classmate Rosamond Lewis. What I remember is this: Rosamond Lewis was very serious. She was also lovely, but an important part of her loveliness for me was this almost stern quality. I admired people who were beyond their years. People who acted their age seemed like fakers to me, as if they were merely pretending to enjoy being fifteen. I wondered what Rosamond was even doing at bouncy cousin Marjorie's."

"Is this the one you almost married?"

"Hear me out. She had disturbing hair, dark, thick, full of ripples, and this preoccupied face. It could easily have been taken as disapproving, or impatient. She was slender, and not particularly tall, but she gave the impression of being bigger, or older. Even her name was grown-up. The other girls were all smaller and more dressed-up, it seemed to me. Shinier. I asked Marjorie immediately, who was *that?* and peppy Marjorie introduced us. I felt like glue. And Rosamond and I talked. It's

73

accurate enough to say that Rosamond told me about a paper she was writing on the TVA or about her volunteer work for Wallace—this is Henry Wallace, not George.''

"I know about Henry Wallace. We voted for Truman. I made a joke about how the grass was Dewey, so Dewey belonged in the ground.''

"Which your parents quoted for months afterward. Rosamond establishes her intellectual credentials. I match her with a recent performance of *Lohengrin* or something, *Parsifal*, right? And then we danced. Clearly, I exempted dancing from being teen-age. It's what I had come to the party *for*. In those days, you may have seen in movies, there was slow, close dancing.''

"We did that, too.'' She made a shy smirk.

How close? "Okay. I wasn't sure I was supposed to be dancing with her, that even though she knew how to dance she was meant to be danced with. As I recall, in any case, we were keeping a gingerly distance. We were strangers, and she was so impressive that distance seemed right, just as well. Then someone turned off the lights, and Roz pushed against me and held herself there. I wasn't sure if she knew what she was doing, if I should back away a little, but I decided to take a chance. I was absolutely, you know, hard. Miserably excited. I worried about the lights coming on. I worried how long they were going to stay off. I didn't know what was going to happen to me, but for the time being I wanted to stay there forever. It was so draining, without drainage. I felt poisoned with my own stuff. We danced in this slumped way, as if one of us might end up hanging over the other's shoulder. Sexual poison. Like carbon monoxide or something. Do you have any idea of the impact? In the dark. No one to see. The feeling shared but not mentioned.''

"Sure,'' Betsy said, with a vigorous wistfulness.

"I had to go into another room when the lights went on, partly to conceal myself and also because there was just plain so much heat in me and so little air. I was suffocated with desire and also truly grim. I leaned way out the window to breathe. It was like being on a ship. It was a spring night, overlooking the park. The street lights and the moonlight were all the same. The trees were bright green in the dark. I leaned way out, waiting for her to come and find me, find out what was wrong, but she never did. I think other people came in, or looked in, and they saw my back, but I don't remember being paid any attention at all. I remember breathing that luminous green darkness, and being amazed and furious at the power of what had happened. But it was as if it had happened only to me. There was no one to run out with into the spring. I stayed in there so long waiting for her that when I went back into the living room, she had gone home. I was better off hanging out the window. The yearning out the window, on this nightship, was like thick gloom, but there was something absolutely satisfying about it. I was by myself on a wide deck. I couldn't fall off." He stared past Betsy's fine chin. "It's not the point of my telling you, obviously, but was it ever any kind of a problem for you, the dancing?"

"If I liked the boy, I liked what happened. It was safe. Safe excitement." She shrugged, as if to say that safe excitement might have been a silly law, but one not worth breaking.

He imagined Betsy as someone he had never liked. Women only pretended not to take sex for granted. Women didn't even understand the magic of their own underpants.

"So?" she encouraged him.

"I was scared to call her up. She was formidable, but I didn't want her to be evil. I didn't want to hate her. I would have chosen not hating her over her loving me. This is ridiculous, isn't it?"

Betsy looked disgusted. "You were fifteen years old, for God's sake! What's ridiculous?"

"It's not your dirty laundry, teenage dirty laundry."

"Everybody has dirty laundry. The writer's cardinal truth."

"It isn't the first thing one shows."

"Listen. You showed up on my doorstep. What did you expect to talk about?"

"You! Anything. Us. My fee-lings. I don't know. Apparently I wanted to talk about me, I *said*. It's just that I'm noticing I'm without safe passage."

"I said to you before, the only way I can know what I'm

75

doing here is to know whose house I'm in. I have no right to ask you to talk. But one should not show up on a doorstep without a reason. I'd rather you said too much. It makes you less suspect."

"Let us hope." It was possible she was asking him to do what she could never do. "As a kid, on the telephone, Roz usually sounded as if you'd interrupted her in the middle of thinking, which was no great help the first time I called. But she remembered me from the party the night before, and we got married. She remembered me from the night before. I sometimes stuttered at that age, by the way, and I'm sure I tore at my face while I was asking her for a date. She was somewhat more cordial than she sounded. That was her way. We went to the movies."

"What did you see? Don't leave out the important stuff."

"*Johnny Belinda.*"

Betsy nodded as if she had known, pleased.

"I did not suggest that we dance when we got home. We occupied a couch. We only kissed. My recollection of it is that she was intense and strained, that we were like a dried wishbone. And of course it was strange, to me, because we already knew each other better. But I liked her better. She was more recognizable."

"Did you ask her why she hadn't come to find you at the party?"

"I don't think I could have. Would you have come to find me at the party?"

"Oh, probably not. But I'm sure I wouldn't have left. I wouldn't have imagined what was wrong, but I would have been concerned, I think."

"More than anything, I wanted to take her to the opera, to the opera house. The season had closed by the time I met her. We wrote each other over the summer. She wrote these wholesome letters from work camp, folk-song sessions, hikes, her contempt for her schoolmates' interest in clothes. If she ever got hold of her parents' money, she was going to give it all away. I teased her about her folk songs, union songs. I *hate* folk songs. She accused me of being decadent. She was like a little Ninotchka. I never let her out of my head. I was idealistic only about personal love, but I took some kind of security out of her interest in the world. It made her good. She was so well *informed*. That was very impressive to me. She was your Miss Current Events. It was so respectable. I respected it. It was less drab to me than my parents' physics and chemistry, which I didn't understand at all, anyway. And beneath this good citizen, this well-informed good citizen of fifteen, sixteen, there was all that sexual mystery for me to solve. That fall, I took her to *La Traviata*. The most crucial date in modern history. Did you ever have one of those?''

"They were all crucial." She laughed quietly at herself. "I worried about being liked too much and not enough. I had the dread but not the excitement. I'm afraid it took me a long time to appreciate anticipation."

"I would have liked you too much."

"Not for long. Or more likely not paid any attention to me. I kept mostly to walls. I was comfortable only at home in those days."

But then, grief. She had known serious grief. After her mother died, had she cooked for her father? Or did they have a maid? What had it been like at dinner, just the two of them? Silent? "Did you still live at Five-forty-five when you were adolescent?"

"Always."

Had her room smelled of her, like his sister's? What had it been like to be her, alone in her room? "Were you writing then?" Ever a boy in her bedroom?

"Oh, sure, I'd been writing for years already. I wrote soap operas and news bulletins for station WBETSY."

"May I read them? That is hilarious."

"I threw them away years ago. Two years ago. What happened at the opera? Move on."

"Here was this serious, beautiful, mysterious girl. Someone who had rubbed longing into me, which I'd never gotten out, but who was also, now, a live person, who lived in daylight, whom I actually knew. I called her by her name, spoke to her on the phone, had received letters from her. I wanted to make her my opera companion for life. I wanted to consolidate my longings. Opera was like the desire for completeness, and she, Roz, would *be* completeness. If the opera house was the opera the first time I went, she was the opera this time. During the performance, I kept looking at her, hoping to see her with an enchanted look on her face, shining, mouth open, weeping, anything. But she simply watched. Looked. What I remember is that she *liked* it, *enjoyed* it, but she did not love it. I must have interrogated her during the intermissions. I think I decided that because this was her first opera, she simply couldn't take it all in. Or that maybe it wasn't the right opera for her. Too soft-headed, decadent. Maybe she needed more politics. I thought, *Aïda,* maybe. But in the last act that night, with Violetta dying of consumption, I collapsed, sobbing, as usual. And *this* must have impressed Roz. And now I need tasteful language."

Betsy flapped her hand. "I'm a grown woman. I should tell you, you're a good storyteller."

He held his own hand, interlocking his fingers, and he scrunched over the table. He thought, I am fifteen again. "We went back to her house. What hadn't happened at the opera, in a way happened. I didn't know what to expect. I didn't *expect.* My plan had been to take her to the opera. Everything else I allowed myself to imagine about the evening was impossible. What I wanted was to be *received* by her, but I don't know what that meant, even now. Anyway, we were back on the same couch, of the spring before—she had a sunken living room."

"Where were her parents?"

"I guess asleep. The point was, if she said nothing about them, I wasn't going to. Anyway, back on the same couch, but this time she stuck out her hand, sideways, she was bowed over, sitting forward on the couch, and I saw the hand was meant for me, she was waiting for something from me. If this isn't precisely what happened, what it feels like to remember is that I took a huge breath—by the way, I had to take a breath like that walking beside you last night in the lobby." He looked up, shallowly, only when she hadn't said anything. She dipped her head, giving Alan a tiny, courteous smile. "The breath was the same, but I should say that the reasons were somewhat different. With Roz, then, it was as if I would have begun to cry if I hadn't taken the breath. I put my arm across her shoulder, and we fell back together, lying down, and I was so moved and excited I didn't know what to do. There was no place to back off, anyway. I was on the inside of the couch. The room wasn't dark, but subdued, about like a concert hall. She put her hand on me, outside, and I rolled onto her. I was burning. She wanted me there, held me there, and then she began making struggling motions, and I thought she wanted me off, so I jumped off, you know, alarmed, but she wanted to get her skirt up, and she took my hand and put it there." He couldn't look at Betsy. He was embarrassed by his euphemisms.

"Uh-huh," he heard her say.

"I couldn't see anything, because my face was in her neck—all this was in a panic. Then she pulled me back on top of her. I wasn't unzipped, I had everything on, even my jacket"—once again now he looked at Betsy, who lifted her head, acknowledging the detail with a quick, sympathetic smile, and he talked directly to her, driving home his revived panic. His heart felt as if it were being singed. "She was like a horse, she could have been trying to throw me, I didn't fully understand that she wasn't angry. She was trying to hold me there, at the same time, hard across my back, with both her arms, and I whipped around on her, you know, like an electric eggbeater that's fallen on the floor, and I was crying. She eased me off her and sat up and straightened herself out. We held hands again, but I could feel my heart going out like a match flame. I couldn't look at her. I could feel the cold spreading in me as if my chest were becoming a dungeon. And I left. I didn't see her for a year and a half."

"Your choice?"

He shook his head. "I had no choice. I was terribly shocked by the violence, our convulsiveness. It seemed ugly. It seemed unfriendly. The sex, or whatever it was, had *separated* us. I felt as if my coldness had been terribly rude, but I couldn't possibly afford to apologize. I had to wait until my rudeness had lasted too long to allow apology. I wanted to lose her forever. I could not stand the idea of seeing her. I could have managed if we had slowly worked up to something. Or if I had gotten ahead of myself, and she had stopped me. I wanted more than the real thing—I mean real sex—or less.''

''There wouldn't have been the real thing, though, anyway. At least I would imagine she was just as scared of that as you were.''

''Of course. I didn't understand. What was there to understand with? The whole point was that I didn't want what I wanted. I didn't want *in*. And getting in, we called it, was the goal back then, you know. 'Going all the way.' Not that we really expected to. Ever!'' They both laughed. ''But we certainly thought we wanted to; or whatever we could get. 'Getting in,' getting bare this, bare that. Anyway, all my frustration turned out to be terror. In effect, I loved my fear. I *wanted* to be yearning, leaning out the window. It was as if going all the way meant I'd never come back. Even though really Roz hadn't asked me. It was enough. Too much. Even the suggestion.''

''But isn't it always a surprise, with anything, at any age, when what you want fits with what there is, fits a corresponding space? It's either too small or too big. People are usually the wrong age for what they want, or in the wrong place, or with the wrong person. Fate's a bad fit. If I just said, 'Fate's a bad fit,' forget it. You must swear you won't quote me.''

''But *that's* what opera is *about!* What we want not fitting with what there is, with what's available. The great operas with happy endings are even more overwhelming than the others, if possible. In any case, I humiliated both of us. She called me. She wrote to me asking me to call her. Once she appeared at my house. I avoided her. The most important thing in the world was to avoid her.''

''What did you do when she came to your house?''

''I was sick, in fact. And that's what I told my mother to say. But I could have seen her. I did answer her letter, finally, by saying I'd gotten involved with someone. I behaved as if she'd tried to murder me. A year later, I wanted more than anything to go to bed with her, but I couldn't get up the nerve to call. I wrote, I think, and got no answer. I wanted to *see* what I had done that night, and do it again, taking advantage of it, and all the rest, lead the way. My mind was incessantly swooning with it. Finally, I asked cousin Marjorie if Roz had a boyfriend. No. I called her. Her voice on the phone seemed much more grown-up, fuller, more cheerful—I thought it was her mother. I asked to see her. She suggested a walk after school. On the walk, I apologized, said I'd been a fool. I told her I hadn't stopped thinking about her, and how badly I wanted to see her. She very nicely said no. She was way above it, no bitterness. I pleaded. I think I was quite urgent."

"I find that hard to believe."

"Do you. She went to Swarthmore, to major in political science—where did you go?"

"To college? Cornell."

"I'll wrap this up. I went to Columbia, and I joined the newspaper there right away, *The Spectator*. My parents were tremendously relieved I got into Columbia. They are sticklers, no question, and my sister was an academic star, the perfect daughter for them. I became music critic on *The Spectator,* and I started doing some campus political reporting. I seemed to be fascinated by political maneuvering, by the differences between what was said and what was done. Secrets. I sent a few of my political pieces to Roz, stuff on Stevenson in 1952, and she wrote back, welcoming me to the world and bringing her intellectual history up to date for me. I still thought about her a lot. Sometimes I was angry because I had made such a fool of myself and she hadn't given me a chance to come back, and sometimes I mocked her, to myself, because of her extreme seriousness. Her letters were like term papers. She was so pure. Not original, like you, at all. But her mind had excellent *credentials.* And what was trustworthy was that she made her studies very much part of herself. She used her knowledge, her erudition, personally. I stuck to that. And I kept thinking about the couch, reviving the scene with us advanced by four years now, when I really thought I knew what I was doing. I had girl friends, sequential girl friends of absolute importance, but I seem to have used Roz as a way of saying to myself that there was something more important than any one of these girls, something waiting, *decisively* decisive. I kept her around in my head partly to protect myself. Not from falling in love, but from having to decide that any of them were *it*."

"You slept with them?"

"Yes, a few. You mean, did I get over my terror? There was hardly even any bleeding. I loved it. I couldn't have enough of it. You know—it actually worked. The point was that I didn't want to decide my life, and it was as if I couldn't prevent myself from making a final decision without artificial aid—or prevent myself from imagining I had to make a final decision. I talked about marriage all the time. I fell in love with people I was sure I wanted to marry. Some of them wanted to marry me. Marriage was it. Fidelity into eternity. By the time I was a senior, I felt as if I'd been divorced six times. Anyway, underneath, I used Roz to keep my future alive. But she would have been surprised to know it. Occasionally on vacations we saw each other. And if I was involved with someone at the time, I felt as if I were cheating on her to see Roz. Roz and I talked politics, contemporary politics. We hugged and kissed hello and goodbye. It was very nice. I didn't push for anything. Quite the contrary. I was more embarrassed now about the walk than the couch. I didn't want her to know I thought privately about her. I took pride in being able to disguise it. I was better off this way. I seemed to know it would pay off. We went through Joe McCarthy together. Basically, she was much more leftist than I. I wasn't leftist. I loved the villainy in politics. It's still what I love. Nixon is a great baritone role. I think of Watergate every day as an opera. All it needs is a last act and someone to write the music. Anyway, with McCarthy—also a dream role for a baritone—Roz and I were equal in knowledge and equally emotional. That was 'fifty-four. One night around then, we reviewed the couch night, and it was nostalgic, it was tender. We were both involved with others at the time, nothing happened, but we touched each other's wrists or something; whatever it was, it was acknowledged, or indicated, that the interest might be revivable. I think she must have been gratified at my political growth, I swear. And she probably did have something to do with it in the first place. And I suspect she also liked it that I was such a political amateur in comparison with her. In any case, there was a distinct tenderness that night. I was so pleased, it was almost enough. We wrote each other more frequently, we called each other. This was now nineteen fifty-five, you were fifteen, the age I was when my troubles began. I visited her once at Swarthmore, when she ran a mock convention. Then it happened that we both ended our respective involvements, and in the spring of our senior years we actually went to bed. I had an apartment near Columbia. What I am about to say is about two specific people together. This is not locker-room bragging, not that it's bragging. I am not tattling on womankind.''

"I have to leave in fifteen minutes. Stop bragging.''

"The worst is to happen, but it will take the least time. This was now seven years after the couch, right? Except that everything worked properly, she was very much the same as she'd been on the couch. In a panic. In fact, it was very exciting for me, but she was so wild it was almost as if she didn't like it, or as if she would have been the same way with anyone else. She thrashed.''

Betsy laughed through her nose.

"It looked to me like *suffering,* not something she put up with, but like a nightmare. I vowed that I was going to make her more loving, calmer, more mine. And I did, to a degree. We didn't do it that regularly, but sometimes it was better. Out of bed, she was an absolutely different person. I told her I wanted to marry her. I told her how I had kept her with me, how I had thought of her as final. She was pleased. Or moved. *Complimented.* She said we had plenty of time, we should wait. Fine. After graduation, I went to work at one of my uncle's trade magazines, a bottler's magazine. Roz graduated with High Honors, and went to India and Asia for a few months. I visualized her as a professor who advised governments; I wanted her to go

to graduate school, in the city. She wanted to roll up her
sleeves, as she said. She went to work in Mayor Wagner's office, in the Press Secretary's office. We stayed over at one another's places. She was very busy, very happy. She let me teach
her opera. There were things she really liked. That gave me the
greatest pleasure. She loved *Boris Godunov*. I felt that she liked
me better the better she liked opera, that I had proved something about myself. The sex would improve in unexpected ways
at unexpected times. I felt I was in charge of that. She used my
hands. I was happy being her friend. She asked my advice about
things. In 'fifty-six, she worked for Stevenson in his New York
office. She was a sort of second-rank hotshot. Her sleeves were
rolled up. Her hair was cut short. She was one of those people
who become made up of telephones, like a cartoon on a *Time*
cover? Each step she took up in the world I worried was a
comedown. I didn't say anything. She was too happy. But I had
it in my head that if she did something as serious as getting
married, that she would become her old, fully serious self, step
out of her movie part and slow down, use all her brains. I
wanted to be permanent with her, retrieve her. I had asked of
her that if she didn't want to get married yet, that at least we be
exclusive. And that was no problem for a year, as far as I know.
But in the Stevenson campaign there was some drawing away
that had to do with more than busyness. It was on both sides, in
fact, but I only admitted it about her. Something was going on
with her. I waited outside her building one night."

Betsy looked as if a toe had cramped. "You shouldn't have
done that."

"I know. And it was awful. She saw me, and her body
jumped, and neither of us said anything. She passed me by, with
a guy, into her house. She called me the next day. She'd gotten
involved with this fellow in the campaign. Much older. She
married him. Roz has been married three times. She's divorced
again now. She still has her sleeves rolled up. 'Roz Lewis here.'
She's been in every Democratic campaign from 'fifty-six
through now, mayoral, gubernatorial, presidential. In between,

84

she's the press officer of some municipal or state agency or other. She calls me at the magazine. We have a drink sometimes. I don't *like* her. I don't believe I ever wanted to marry her. It wouldn't have lasted. But I couldn't stand the idea of losing her, that groin in the dark, and all that seriousness, which did begin as great adolescent pomposity and ignorance, but I saw it grow. At her peak, age twenty-one, she was impressively knowledgeable. She threw it away. She became an imitation of something. She got lost in the ordinary world. She chose to. She boiled down." Alan watched his hands unclasp. "There was no prize there. And that's the story." He looked at Betsy worriedly, as if he had been reporting on a situation of immediate concern. He sensed his expression as grime on his face, and he fitted a small smile into it. But then it seemed to him as if he were appealing to her, so he swallowed the smile and made his forehead go smooth. He felt no less strained.

Betsy's eyes were not quite on him. She appeared to be adding up, in her head, everything he had said, or to be thinking about something else.

"What's my score?" he said. "Be candid." He smiled again, more naturally.

She looked at him as if he were distracting her, her lips parted and taut. "How can I be candid so fast? I have to think. And I have to leave." Then she lowered her head a little and placed a hand on one of his so lightly and quickly that if he had not seen her do it, he thought, he would not have known she had meant to. "You're generous," she said. She stood, and he with her, reaching, without success, for the hand she had withdrawn. "Only because I talked so much," he said. "You're being facetious."

"No, I was not being facetious. Now I'm the spoon that knows what's in the soup. So I'm thanking you for the soup."

"Are you going to tell me what you've learned?"

"Sure, when I know. There's no time now, anyway. I must get home." She swung toward the kitchen door. He followed her out. As they crossed the living room, she said, "One thing

85

does spring immediately to mind. And that is that everyone boils down. Don't you boil down? It's sounding like a mild perversion."

"I don't think I give myself a chance to boil down. But I don't believe you do boil down."

"That's just silly, on principle."

"I mean, I would love to know what you boil down *to*. Whatever was left, in your case, would be—it would make no difference."

"Thank you. I'm going to assume that's a compliment." She stepped toward the closet.

"Yes. I didn't mean to be at all ambiguous. Let me." He drew her pea coat from the hanger and held it open for her. She turned her back to him and put her arms into the sleeves. He refrained from pressing her shoulders.

She walked to the door, standing there sideways to him, slightly bent, as she had been last night in the lobby, in her listener's position. "So," she said. "Nice to see you again." She looked at him, then, her face amused and puzzled, as if surprised. "Anyway." She came to him with her hand out. He took it and she quickly kissed him on the cheek.

He held on to her hand. "And *will* you have any better idea of why you were here, do you suppose? I'll be back next Thursday, by the way."

Her look was straightforward and without gravity. "I think so. I hope so."

"So you can come back?"

She nodded once, slightly, smiling slightly. "I hope so. Will you give me a call? But not from London?"

PART TWO

4

Alan was not surprised, while away, to long for her. What he had not expected—he had no precedent for it—was that, having known her for a quarter of an evening and half an afternoon, his thoughts of her would be at all fearful or angry. At the start of his trip, he had imagined that he would be dying at every free moment to get back to her vicinity, to see what had happened, what was going to happen, to make it happen. There were no moments free of her. While he was in parliaments, offices, pubs, cafés; while he was in bed with Juliet Jeans in London; while at Covent Garden and the Cologne Opera, Betsy smudged his concentration. He had to look around her in order to see. A few times, during interviews, while asking questions or scribbling answers, he realized he hadn't heard the middle of his own question or the beginning of the answer, as if he'd nodded off, and he had to fish for the missing part. On streets and in lobbies, he imagined her coming toward him, not quite poker-faced, having flown to London, Paris, Bonn, Rome to surprise him. Most often, they were again in his kitchen, where they sometimes kissed at the table, or reached for each other, rose together, clasped, left for the bedroom. In the bedroom, sometimes in the kitchen, he lifted her sweater up her back, over her head. He smelled skin. Her look was grim with the moment, but not shy. Or she was in bed with Curtis, but thinking of him; or she was at the movies, thinking of him in Europe thinking of her at the movies; or they were together at the movies, or at *Traviata;* or she replaced Roz on Roz's girlhood couch, and the frenzy was a success. He was beside her at her mother's funeral, she weeping into his shoulder, he a cousin, a secret adolescent lover. She was at his funeral, stricken, lost. He was at her funeral, sobbing not quite discreetly enough against a pillar at the rear, the other mourners wondering who this grieving stranger could be. She appeared at Kennedy for his return, went with him to his apartment, her apartment, having left her marriage, Curtis having flown to London on a client's behalf, Curtis having died. He attended Curtis's funeral, impeccably dry-eyed.

But also, in fantasies that jumped like flames against the inside wall of his forehead, she declined to see him on his return, coldly, with no explanation; he couldn't reach her at all, her telephone number having been changed to unlisted; she had been involved for months in a blissful love affair, and he had misunderstood her interest in him; she was packing to move with Curtis to Texas, California, Chicago; she was packing to move alone to Quito; at lunch at the Palm Court, Carla List was entertaining her with anecdotes of his insensitiveness; she met with him to tell him she'd had second thoughts and decided it would be best if they didn't see each other again. She gave him different reasons at different meetings, the meetings held in the doorway of her apartment or by the fountain in the plaza of Lincoln Center: she was drawn to him, she didn't know why, as she'd never been to anyone, but must resist; she was drawn to him for reasons she disliked and must resist; she had discovered, from their talk in his kitchen, that she was available to love someone other than Curtis, but it couldn't be Alan because his record for reliability was so poor. Or his collection of ticket stubs was disturbing, suggesting murder, dismemberment, castration—face it; his concern with the perfect moment was irritating, childish; his passion for opera permitted him easy emotion and allowed him to forget how ungiving he was outside the opera house. She needed someone more safely human—not Curtis, but someone other than Alan.

On his flight back, jarred by Bloody Marys and the sunny sky, he wondered how he could have allowed someone he barely knew (and who had nearly every right not to want to know him better), to bully him with her rejections, to take him over for the purpose of exhibiting unfriendliness.

He decided he wouldn't call her—let the thing drop, or at least ride. She could call him. He would keep for himself or for someone else the cashmere scarf he had bought for her. Then the label wouldn't have to be removed. He didn't need this clangor. In his attaché case, along with three opera programs and the envelope containing the Covent Garden and Cologne ticket stubs, was a fat, nearly complete *Newsworthy* piece that smoothly incorporated the interviews by making a theme of their disagreements. At Kennedy, he looked for Betsy as if they had arranged to meet. He took a taxi straight to the office.

Among his messages, typed up for him by Mrs. Hawthorne, was one from Curtis Ring. Also one from Madeline Pursey—it took him a moment to figure out who this was—and one from Roz Lewis. "Did either Mr. Ring or Mrs. Pursey give any idea of what they wanted?" he asked Mrs. Hawthorne, sensing that his question wanted to be yelled. "If they had, I would have written it down, Mr. Hoffman." And she gave her peevish giggle. Mrs. Hawthorne's sourness could benefit Alan when turned on others. Not that she was protective of him; rather, literal and scrupulous in general. And when she took instructions from him, it was with a version of pleasure: she actually nodded, wrote them down. Alan was scared of her even though he had come to understand that the older she got—she was now sixty-three—the happier she was to be treated as a servant with a job to do in which she could prove herself mistake-free. He brought his piece into Bob Manners, reporting briefly on his trip and confirming their date the next night for *Les Troyens,* and returned to his office to await Bob's reading. He unpacked Mrs. Hawthorne's Liberty scarf and presented it to her, grinning. She was garrulous with appreciation. Alan kissed her on the cheek; his eyes teared. He went back into his office, closing the door, and lowered the blinds most of the way. He sat down. His heartbeat was harsh, his chest and forehead were damp. He blotted his forehead with a handkerchief. He looked up Curtis's office number and home number in the phone book. The office number was the one in the message. He wrote the home number, obscurely, on his memo pad. He dialed Betsy, vowing to say nothing to her about Curtis's message. The phone rang three times and he hung up. He phoned down to the Selfridge for a meatloaf on rye, Russian and lettuce, a cinnamon Danish, and a black coffee. He skipped Roz, in Lindsay's office. He had not told Betsy that once every eighteen or thirty months he went to bed with Roz, the first revival having taken place between Roz's first two marriages. He hadn't spoken to Madeline Meltzer Pursey in a year, since she'd invited him to her wedding. His parents wouldn't be home for a few hours yet. He would drop by tonight or tomorrow with their presents. His mother would say, "Oh, darling, this is too fancy for me." She would wear the handsome, conservative silk scarf out of loyalty. His father would wear the paisley necktie, with the wrong shirt or jacket, on a family occasion, reminded by his wife. And because of what he wore with it, it would look silly. Alan made two business calls. He tried Betsy again, letting the phone ring eight times. Out to the movies. With her lover. *Crudele.* So he called Curtis. Curtsy. Could Mr. Hoffman hold on a minute? Mr. Ring would be right with him. To ask what Act Three, Scene One of *Die Walküre,* with that tenderly coy message, was doing in his wife's desk drawer. To ask for a duel in Riverside Park. To ask for Carla List's phone number. "Hi!" Curtis Ring said.

"How are *you?* What can I do for you?"

"You can meet me for a drink. Did you just get back?"

"I was in Europe." Had he said meet him for a drink?

Curtis laughed. "I know. I'd like to talk something over with you."

"My pleasure." He knew about Europe from Betsy? Mrs. Hawthorne? "When did you have in mind? Today I don't see how I can. We close the magazine tonight. My boss is reading my story at the moment."

"Understood. I don't know that there's any desperate rush about it. You'd know that better than I."

"Something I can do to prepare? Look up for you?"

"No, nothing like that. I need a favor, if it's do-able."

"Would you like to discuss it right now? I have a moment."

"We could, but I'd prefer in person, if you don't mind. It feels like that kind of thing."

"No problem. Tomorrow? Tomorrow would be okay." The back of his neck felt as if deeply bruised. "I'm going to the opera, but I could meet you before."

"How about the Oak Bar at five, five-thirty."

"You tell me. Depends what's on your mind."

"Five-fifteen. Let's compromise. If you're early, try to grab a table, okay, old man?"

"You're on."

"*Ciao*. Thanks." Ring clicked off.

"I need a favor, if it's do-able," was not revealing. "I'd prefer in person, it feels like that kind of thing," on the other hand, was stimulating. Also, "You'd know that better than I." Likely, it wasn't about Betsy at all. Or perhaps: I have leukemia, old man. Take care of my wife for me. He went out to ask Mrs. Hawthorne if she had told all his callers that he had been in Europe. "I know it sounds like an odd question. I have a problem in there."

"Now, I know you wouldn't have wanted me to lie." Her face quivered as she smiled. She was still feeling happy from her present.

"Do you recall specifically telling Mr. Ring that I was in Europe? If it sounds as if I'm grilling you, I'm not. This is nothing about you." Alan felt ridiculous, frowning and apologizing at

93

the same time. It was imperative that Betsy should not have told Curtis that he was in Europe, imperative that she be loyal to their secrecy, and that she not be careless.

"I don't remember anything specifically at all, Mr. Hoffman. I'm sure I told him what I told everybody, or else I told his secretary, that you were abroad and would be back Thursday, the first of November." She asserted the last of her goodwill.

"Thanks. Pay me no mind. Jet lag." He circled his ear with his finger. He went to the men's room and washed his face. The delivery man from the Selfridge was waiting for him when he got back to his office. While he ate, he considered further: I need a favor—stay away from my wife. If it's do-able—don't stay away from my wife if you can't manage, but would you give it a try? Maybe Curtis was being entrappingly polite with him, in order to knife him at the Oak Bar. Jealous husband stabs rival in posh watering spot. No opera tomorrow night.

Mrs. Hawthorne buzzed him. "Betsy Ring."

Busy with the Ring family! He picked up, his blood tickling his temples like plush. He said, "I tried to get you. There was no answer." Why was she calling him?

"I was at my daily flick. *Ben-Gurion Remembers*. You mustn't miss it. How was your trip? Last week when I called, you answered your own phone."

"That's Mrs. Hawthorne, my masseuse. She does not listen in."

"I would like to see you."

It was as if the tip of her tongue had slid across his heart. "Me too. Is something wrong?"

"You lodged in my head." She drew out "lodged" a little.

"And you in mine. I've been back here about en hour. In fact, I called you right away. How did I lodge? A splinter?"

"No, not a splinter." She laughed. "About as well as could be expected."

"I'd like to do it right now, but the magazine closes tonight. I can see you tomorrow morning, before your movie."

"Tomorrow morning would be all right. Are you sure it's convenient? You don't have to go to work?"

"It's convenient, yes. I'm spending most of the day at home. I can call you when I wake up."

"May I call you instead? Somewhere between nine and ten?"

"Whatever's good for you. Let me give you my number."

"It's in the book. I tried you at home. I'm surprised you're listed. Did you have a good trip?"

"Why do you ask? You were there for most of it. What do you mean, you're surprised I'm listed?"

"I just think you'd get bothered from time to time."

"Because of the magazine?"

"In general. It was a minor facetiousness. Sorry."

"I'll hear from you in the morning?"

"That's the plan."

"I'm glad you called."

"I'm glad you're back. See you."

The telephone unzipped his sleep. He lifted the receiver to him with his eyes closed, holding it as if he were in love with it.

"Damn, I woke you," Betsy said. "Is that you?"

"I was just on the verge of saying hello."

"You're fast asleep. This is Betsy."

"I'm still on Italian time." He opened his eyes. Nine-forty.

"Do you want to sleep? Call me back? Never speak to me again?"

"I'm up. I'm awake. Here I am. Just one moment, please." He cleared his throat, away from the phone, but without covering the receiver; he did not want her to think he was speaking to someone lying beside him. Into the receiver, then, he vocalized an arpeggio. "There. Just tell me where you'd like to meet. I can be ready in an hour. Forty-five minutes. Do you want me to come up to your neck of the woods?"

"I love the idea of living in a neck of the woods, in the first place. Whenever an expression like that is applied to me, it makes me feel unique. No, if you don't mind, I'd prefer to come to yours."

"No, that's fine. I'm apartment forty."

"I'll take the bus. I'll be along. But you can't go back to sleep now. I don't want to wake you twice."

He took a shower and shaved, his skin conscious of his excitement at the idea of meeting her here before noon. He made his bed. He wished that he had honestly informal clothes to wear for her, a sweater that looked as if he had just picked burrs off it, blue jeans he had worn for a week. He put on the gray herringbone suit pants he would wear later and, over his T-shirt, a gray sweat shirt Bob Manners had given him in the early sixties that said on it RENATA CALLAS in pale-blue block letters. He got the newspaper at the door. He made instant coffee and toasted a piece of wholewheat bread, which he spread with peanut butter and honey. He rapidly read the coverage of the Saxbe and Jaworski nominations. He brushed his teeth. He took off the sweatshirt and considered a turtleneck. A turtleneck would be stagy—for receiving a Carla List; his green velour shirt the same. Had Carla found a new listener for the old play-by-play? He put on a black crew-neck sweater. He decided not to leave Betsy's present on the bedroom bureau. He brought it into the kitchen, then to the couch in the living room.

When he answered the door, she entered as if someone had given her a gentle shove, and she didn't quite look at him. She removed her pea coat immediately and handed him a paper bag, smiling quickly. "Lunch," she said. "Thank you," he said. "Nice to see you." He'd been smiling all the while. He took her coat and the paper bag. He put the bag on the mail table and turned away to hang up the coat. Were they going to have trouble talking now that they were here together again? Was there now no place for them to go? Stuck in the foyer. My God! he thought then, she was here again. Why was she here? He turned around. She was again in brown and green, brown corduroy pants, green sweater. Her face was clearing of strain. "Either you are wearing what you were wearing last week, or it is reversed," he said.

"Very sharp of you."

"It is reversed, correct?"

96

"Correct."

"Stay here a minute." He hurried to her present and brought it back with him to the foyer. "For you. Not a moment too soon." He handed her the green box.

"I get a present because you guessed right?"

"Yes. You have to open it. The box is not the present."

"Thank you." She seemed embarrassed but not displeased as she undid the ribbon, opened the lid, lifted the tissue. He looked in with her. Green, brown and white plaid. She lifted it out, put it to her cheek. "It is beautiful. Distinguished. I'll have to think if I can wear it in my neck of the woods, on my neck of the woods."

"It will be noticed? We can take the label off."

"I think it will be all right. I'll have to think. But I love it. Even if I can't wear it. If I can't, will you?"

"I'll see. Put it on."

She hung it around her neck. "So," she said.

It would be the perfect moment to enfold her. "So. So. So. Where do you want to go?"

"What are my choices? I would just like to look into your bedroom, which I never did see, and then we could sit in the kitchen again? I prefer it to your non–dining room."

"Do you have something to tell me?"

"Just talk."

"This way, please." He took the paper bag and led her across the sunny living room. "What's lunch?"

"In the bag? Tunafish sandwiches."

"I'll put them in the icebox."

"Refrigerator?"

"Yes."

She followed him into the kitchen and out, and into the bedroom. "There's really nothing to it," he said. "A bedroom." They stood between the high bureau and the double bed.

"That spread!" she said.

"Indian."

"If Chagall were Hindu. It looks like a nightmare about par-

97

adise. I didn't see in this closet the other day. There must be a lot of good stuff in here.''

''You're making me a character. You're researching a male clotheshorse.''

''It's simply that I'm closet-nosy. May I?''

''What's mine is yours.''

She passed around the bottom of the bed to the closet and looked in. He followed her to sit behind her, on the edge of the bed. His scarf seemed to love her neck. ''Two tuxedos? And white dinner jacket? Why aren't these outside and your outside blazers in here?''

''It's because more people see into the closet outside, and I don't like to show off my evening clothes.''

She laughed. ''I see.'' She nudged suits and jackets along the bar. ''Mod you're not.'' She turned her back to his clothes and sat down in the closet door, feet crossed. ''Do you know what it is? I'm interested in the difference between your personal boldness and how carefully you dress. You dress boldly, too, but it's so careful, and you are not careful. Maybe you are, but it's not apparent.''

Alan stood up; he sat down again.

''What was that for?'' She looked irritated.

He wanted to kiss the side of her neck, draw away the edge of green sweater, kiss her shoulder, see how she would accept his kiss, how she would refuse it; but he had known, just as he stood, spiced air surrounding his heart, that the kiss had no immediate motive but desire. On standing, and feeling as if he were hanging from nothing, he had sat again. ''What did you decide about our talk last week? Or, the subtitle is, How did I lodge in your head?''

''At different angles on different days.'' Her expression didn't lighten or add anything to her answer.

''Yeah?''

''Well, here I am. I don't know. I liked eliciting all that emotional history from you. I liked it better than I liked what you actually told me. I have mixed feelings about what you told me.

98

I thought, while you were away—at first I thought that the way your life has happened must be the way you've wanted it to happen. Then I thought, That's not true. He is troubled by it. Or maybe it's the way you want it but you're troubled that that's the way you want it. I think I can believe that you hate it that you're attracted to the kind of women you evidently end up with, your so-called histrionics, dead ends. You're much better than that, but still, you do it. So then the question is, Do you deserve better? You don't lack for histrionic flair yourself.''

''But you're not.''

''Histrionic? No, not much, anyway. I've got my own problems.''

''And where are they?''

''Where are they?'' She shrugged. ''Around. I do think you —the only way I can put it is generous. I think you wish you could be generous, wish you had the chance to be. That you wish you could give up the perfect moment and all that. Then I wondered, Why hasn't he gone to a shrink? He should be going to a shrink, should have been going long since. Have you ever?''

''Nope. Have you?''

''Yes, for a while. After my mother died. But just because you had told me a sad story didn't mean that you were a sad person. A visible child, in a way. I wonder why you didn't turn out to be a writer, of fiction, or an actor. I mean that I don't feel sorry for you. You're missing a lot, or maybe you don't miss it, but you lead a perfectly good inadequate life, like anyone else. Even without commitment, you're full of commitment. That's what comes through. What's the alternative? You said you'd reached the dead end, dead end of dead ends, but your way isn't the only way of doing that. You get excited by things. Maybe it's foolish, or reckless, what you do, the equivalent of not saving money. But other people regret not living like you.''

''They do? I think you're being kind. Don't you ever get excited?''

''Oh, sure. About my work sometimes, I'm excited. About

my publication coming up. But that's like being excited because you're going to watch cannibals. I was excited when *The New Yorker* bought my first story. And when it came out.''

''I felt very excited this morning, when I was getting ready for you.''

''Oh, I was excited yesterday, when I called you. Scared, but excited. Anyway. My conclusion about your life is that you're not so badly off.''

He smiled at her. ''Oh, but you're wrong. Please tell me, how are you?''

She blushed but kept her eyes on him, as if, although inconveniently naked, she were not sufficiently embarrassed to cover herself.

He recalled that he had kissed Carla on the floor last week. He would prefer not to repeat the position. With a dry, meaningless frown, he gazed at Betsy, who had remembered him, assessed him, so seriously. What was in it for her? ''Look,'' he said. ''Do you want to eat? I'm not hungry.''

''No.'' She looked at her black boots. She looked at him, then, as if she were calm with fear. From the bed, he reached out a hand to her. Even if she had reciprocated his motion, they would have been inches too far from each other to touch. He was about to stand, to walk to her, to help her to rise, cause her to rise, when suddenly she stood—unsat—and he stood with her. He glimpsed wretchedness. ''What's wrong?'' he asked. Before he could think what to do next, her head was beneath his chin, his eyes were closed, he was carefully but completely holding her. She was pressing his shoulderblades as if she were shaking, as if she were smothering her shaking. He said, ''What can I do for you?'' He now registered the impact of their collision. Keeping one hand hard against his back, she moved the other to his chest, beside her head; he imagined her for an instant as a baby asleep against him. He took his deep breath. What would have been, with another woman, the moment for maneuver or declaration, the moment in which lust pauses beneath the archway of solemnity before staggering through it, now flustered Alan. He lowered his cheek and tucked it against hers, as though he were listening to her skin.

She cleared her throat. "Can we talk?" Grains of distress stuck to her voice. She cleared her throat again.

The question, coming from her, sounded to him like a pledge of love. "*Please.*"

They drew apart, briefly grasping hands. Her eyes were wet. "I'm sorry."

"Sit. Let's sit." He pulled her easily, or she went, in the direction of the bed, where they settled, side by side, at the edge he had just left. Not looking at her, he laid the back of his wrist on the back of hers, which rested between them. His ears waited.

"It is a goddamn big step. I know I'm going to tell you. It is your fault. You reminded me last week of the possibility of talking, by talking so fully about yourself. And I'm not being facetious. It touched me."

"How wonderful. And I was worried about throwing myself on your mercy." He looked toward her as if they were in the midst of reminiscing about old times.

She returned his look. Her expression was lightly anxious. "That's part of what troubles me. I don't feel you were. But I think I am. So I don't want you to misunderstand me. Not yet." She laughed.

"What do you mean?" His wrist still lay on hers.

"I'm not sure. I'm not asking for your advice. I want relief. Temporary relief. But I have no idea if telling you will relieve me. It may make it worse. It's you I seem to want to tell. And I don't quite know what that means, either. There's some luxury in it for me. And it may be unfair. Misleading."

"Oh, take a chance. Unfair to me?"

"Or to me, possibly. Or to both of us. Or to Curtis. I think I'd better just say it all."

"Yes, but just—" He let his head fall toward hers, a slow plunge toward the alarm of reception in her face; feeling her hand, on the bed, shifting to receive his hand's clasp, he closed his eyes. He kissed her cheek, and then, as though he were a diplomat taking liberties, her neck. He felt her other hand arrive on his shoulder. His shoulder seemed to sink. Now, almost frightened, short of breath, blind, he moved his face across her cheek, wondering if he were ruining everything, and kissed her mouth. Her lips curled open. Their mouths hung open together. Their tongues met at the tip, the formality of the touch unable to prevent a jolt. They pulled away together, and embraced. His breath had slashes in it. He opened his eyes. He was looking over her shoulder at his bedspread. He was hiding out on a promontory above a valley; her hair, to the right of his ear, was the edge of a woods. Her arms were firm around his back, bands of warmth. He talked past her. "I feel as if I'll break, spill."

"Where do I send the pieces?"

"I mean it. I have never felt this way. It is the first time."

They released and examined each other. Betsy smiled in a crumpled, embarrassed way, and gave a tiny, soft snort, the breath of a thought. "You probably don't remember feeling this way before because you feel this way all the time."

"Not true." He was certain of himself. "I promise I won't break on you if you'll promise to believe me. My nerves are coming out of my skin, my lungs are coming out. I'm coming out of my skin. I feel as if I have no clothes on. I'm double-naked. I've never felt that way."

"I'll believe you. Shh." She touched his hanging curls with her fingertips.

"If you don't talk now, I will rape you."

"Part of your interviewing technique, that must be. Excuse me." She flipped her legs onto the bed, her knees pointing at him. Stretched roughly parallel to his pillows, she leaned on her right arm, looking down at the red, turquoise, and yellow flower in the center of the spread. Alan shifted to face her, drawing his left knee onto the bed, the other foot remaining on the floor, his position that of a courtly listener. Betsy said, "Curtis is like a stage-door mother with me. He's turned into some kind of en-couraging tyrant."

"Backstage mother. *Stage* mother."

"Backseat driver, actually. He has all these suggestions for me, for my fame. He thinks I'm going to be famous now, or he badly wants me to be famous now, or he wants to be famous for me, in addition to being the exceptional lawyer he already is. He's writing stories now, in the evenings. He drinks port and writes."

"What do you do while he writes?"

"Read. Sometimes go to a movie with a friend, so that Curtis will not catch on that I'm movie-going in the daytime."

"Just a second. Where does he write?"

"Why where? Because of your message?" She smiled.

Alan nodded.

"Don't worry. It's folded way in the back of that file drawer. It's irrelevant. Mostly, he writes at the dining table, anyway. In longhand. Maybe the port goes better in there. A British memoirist. Maybe he's writing his memoirs."

"You haven't read anything?"

"One of them, the first thing, a long story. It was all imitation of about five different writers. Not so bad, really, but fake. About a judge. An eminent old WASP judge dying on the Riviera. This judge has not seized life, he feels, appearances to the contrary, but merely judged others. Do you know it? I picked out everything good to say that I could. He seemed satisfied."

"What's he done with it?"

"I don't know. Do you mean is he trying to sell it? We haven't discussed it. He hasn't shown me anything since, either. But he writes a couple of times a week. He asked me about ten days ago why I wasn't more prolific."

"Uh-oh."

"I said I wondered, too. But since then my bones haven't stopped grinding. My bones grind. This powder is piling up, and I breathe it all day."

"How does he like *your* book?"

"He said things like 'fascinating,' 'challenging,' 'beautifully written.' Blurby things. But I don't blame him for that. To others, he says it's 'fabulous.' I blame him for that. But there's no question that he's proud of it, or me, in his fucking proprietary way. To me, he also says he hopes it will have the audience it deserves, which means he wishes it were less inaccessible. So do I, sometimes. So he shoves all these ideas at me for making *me* accessible instead, these promotional ideas—a travel article on Ecuador, Ecuadorian artifacts, get a travel magazine to pay my way. Or an article on contemporary brownstone life, on literary brownstones, brownstones in novels. The latest conception is a piece for *Esquire* or *New York* on a group of contemporary New York women's literary careers, the five-hottest-women-writers-in-New-York kind of thing. So that I'll be the sixth. He wants me to be in the red-hot center. His imagination is tireless in my behalf, and he's forgotten who I am. Do I sound as if I'm complaining?''

"Go right ahead." Curtis would be ideal for Carla List.

"Is it unbecoming?" Betsy swung her legs like a mermaid to the other side of the bed and laid herself out, again more or less across the bed, leaning now on her left elbow. Alan noticed that she kept her boots clear of the spread. "I feel as if he's squatting on my face. It's my fault, too. I know it. I'm so mad at him that I'm unable to be angry. I keep avoiding his suggestions, deflecting them politely, and I'm avoiding him in the process. He tells me to push the people at Wynn, Marcovici to get me on the telly, as he calls it, and radio shows when the book comes out, and I keep reminding him, without losing my temper, that they've already told me that it's almost impossible for books like this. But he brings it up again, as if he were senile, or malicious. It's as if he were telling me that he thinks I've written the wrong kind of book. He wants me to be Jacqueline Susann who writes like Doris Lessing.''

Alan arranged himself now so that he was lying across from Betsy, his chest opposite her legs. He felt careful on his own bed. It seemed to him that Curtis must want an interview for Betsy.

"He called Woody Allen a Renaissance man the other night.

He's a follower in this way, a fast follower. I've always been able to forget that part of him, or ignore it, because I could always remind myself how good he was at what he does, and how smart he is. It's always been the reassurance. If I remembered how intelligent he was, then the bottom could never fall out. That's why I told myself I could marry him. His tolerance of me and his intelligence. Curtis remembers everything he's ever learned, which includes a lot of history and a lot of science. And he uses it. He puts things together well, synthesizes. He sees situations without bias, and people, usually. When he's involved in an issue, he stays cool-headed. He's not innocent and he's not cynical. He's the least stupid person I know, except for the faddish stuff, which I decided was a form of relaxation for him. Lots of people have that problem. But it's as if his brains were infected now, as if they actually smelled. I can't get that out of my head. I've stopped admiring him. I can't stand to look at him smile. I think of him as a fool. I want him to understand how he's behaving without my telling him. He makes me feel stupid, too.'' Her lower lip pushed out, she brooded in the direction of Alan's gray-socked ankles, her cheek squashed in her supporting hand.

Alan blinked hard. ''You have to tell him you're angry.'' He looked along the low-lying diagonal connecting his face with hers. ''You have to. How can he not know that you're angry? I mean, what happens at night?''

''Sex, you mean?'' She glanced at him and returned her eyes to his ankles. She did her head-bouncing, side to side, in a slow, sad version. ''It's not the problem, not yet, anyway. Either he doesn't feel like it or I don't. Or we just do it. I pretend he's the young Peter Ustinov. Or a bearded Peter Sellers. I don't know what's going to happen. I'm not prepared for it to end. The idea seems fatal to me.''

''What idea? Fatal to what?''

''We were both ready to marry each other when we did. The timing seemed like good luck. We had good understandings. We were peaceful. We smiled a lot at each other. We left each other alone. We were sweet to one another. We liked each other, admired each other. Admiration is essential. I felt like a grown-up, finally. One of our good understandings, I thought, was that we were not going to have a child. For the last few months, however, he's been wanting us to have a child. And he knows I don't. He says he thinks it would be good for me. Evidently he wants me to be famous and have a baby as well. A pioneer writing woman who can type while breast-feeding. With additional photos, next page, of our floor-through.''

"What would be wrong with having one?"

"If I say it aloud . . . it's the kind of thing it doesn't help to try to justify. He's had one. I don't want one. He knew that from the beginning. He's suggesting adopting now, a minority child. It's all since I sold my book, this inventive behavior of his. It's as if I had done something wrong, and he's trying to make it all right between me and the world. He's changed into a monster parent. I feel far less disloyal to him than I expected to before I began talking, but I'm sadder." She dropped flat and laid her cheek in her elbow. "Why did I tell you all this?" Her hand dangled over her head, a flag of lassitude.

He had nearly been about to move over to her, to comfort her. "Don't take it back, for God's sake! That's rude."

"Don't you remember how embarrassed you were when you talked about yourself?" She lowered her dangling hand to a pillow behind her.

"You're right, I'm sorry. Ah! But you told me not to be."

"But I didn't call you rude. I feel foolish. I've told you what I should be telling him, I guess. Your advice is correct. I told you I didn't want advice."

"Maybe you're not telling him you're angry because you feel there's nothing left to save."

"That's what scares me. The point is that our getting married made such sense. Suddenly it makes no sense. The suddenness is what's scary. I decided a long time ago that the best thing about being alive was that there were things to find out, always things one didn't know. But this isn't what I meant."

"But so it goes. Things are very sudden." In opera as in life, he almost said. "If I know anything, I know that."

She raised her eyebrows at him and instantly lowered them. "I used to have dreams after my mother died that I was hanging on to the wing of a plane by one hand or finger, or one toe—not through any wish of my own, you understand—way out in the universe, at night. There were plenty of stars, but their light was as far-off as it is from here. I was flapping around in a black wind, very cold, and I never fell, but I was always about to. It wasn't a secure position, if you know what I mean."

Alan laughed and shook his head. "Terrible. Who was flying the plane?"

"The doctor said I was, but I could never see myself. The plane was dark. He also told me what a mature dream it was to be having, but all I ever felt about it was panic. It was like being already dead but terrified I was going to die. I had the dream again a week ago, the first time in seventeen years, the day after I was here, the day after you left."

"Oh, hell." Alan sat up to sit beside her, laying a hand on her shoulder, gazing at her shoulder. "I'm sorry I wasn't there, seventeen years ago and a week ago."

"What could you have done?" From her elbow pillow she looked worried.

"I don't know. This." He slid a little away from her, so his face could reach hers, taking his hand from her shoulder so he wouldn't press on her. As he closed his eyes he felt her right hand against his chest. Bent in his swoop, he opened his eyes. She sat up, facing him, making a love seat of the bed. She removed her hand from his chest. "Is this because things happen so suddenly? So it goes?"

"Didn't we kiss once in a previous life?"

"Yes. You were a precious goblet."

"Would you lay out your objections to doing it once again?"

"I have no objections, but it adds to the complexity."

"A kiss!"

"There is no such thing."

"There is for me."

"Then the last one will have been enough. Why are you turning us into a saucy lad and a modest lass at the front gate? Is this your routine?"

"Absolutely to the contrary. You're missing the whole point. Would you prefer me to be more direct?"

"I would most prefer to avoid the issue. At least to postpone the issue."

"Why did we kiss? Why did we embrace in the first place?"

"I am not being helpful in the situation, I admit." And she started off the bed.

"No, don't get up." He had hold of her arm. "I feel cautious. That's not a routine, for God's sake. I don't want to spoil anything. I am being very careful, you see. Not bold at all."

"No apology necessary." She looked airily at him, as if there were nothing left to say. "We could have our sandwiches."

"We could. Are you finished with your problem?"

"For the time being. Until I get home. Until Curtis gets home."

"Look. I am not hoping to extract a quid pro quo. I am *drawn* to you. I want to be close. I am not trying to cajole you, deceive you, into screwing."

"I don't think you need to explain that."

"I simply want to be close."

"You'll have to explain what you mean by close."

"Just next to you, on the bed. Try to restrain yourself."

"You're crazy. But all right. I'm crazy." She did not move.

"No. You are not." He stood briefly, to turn, and he lay down facing her, his eyes inches below her arm. He looked up at her with quizzical tenderness. Her expression was also quizzical, but unsettled. Her eyelids seemed unusually busy. He watched her lift the scarf from her neck and put it high up on the pillow, to her right. "Cheers," she said, and slid onto her stomach and down, her face tipped in his direction but toward her shoulder. Her eyes were closed. Solemnly, he laid his left hand between her shoulder blades, as if the space between her shoulder blades were decisively intimate. His heartbeat boomed. Betsy suddenly squirmed closer, tucking fully under his arm. His mouth was at the top of her forehead. She seemed to smell essentially of skin. They might have been married, snoozing. It could have been a day ago that he had kissed her. He felt again as though they were out of doors, now under sun, on a meadow, or that they were the meadow, their cells secretly, minutely breathing. Her hand came down on the bottom of his back.

"Why me?" she mumbled, opening and closing her eyes. "Why should I feel at all safe with you? What do you want with me? Is it because I'm married?"

Why was she asking him questions like these just when she had moved her hand to the bottom of his back? "No. If you were unmarried, I would have asked you to marry me by now. I don't know all of the why yet. It's because of the way we have talked, *that* I know. Because you are so unobvious, hard to grasp. Because you are so serious; mostly that. I think you must make me feel unridiculous."

"Meaning I'm ridiculous."

"Exactly. No! Because you take me so seriously and because it's impossible not to take you seriously. You are your uniqueness all the time. Not eccentric—unique. You're original."

"Is that so uncommon?"

"Why don't you *know* that? Almost everybody is ordinary or nuts. Both."

"I've never been serious with anyone who wasn't uncommon in at least one attractive way. One important way."

"How many?"

"How many men I've been serious with?"

"Yes. Do you mind?"

"Five."

"Including me?"

"Well, no, not just yet."

"How many men altogether?"

"Thirty-five or forty."

"You're kidding."

"About eight, I guess. And you? Eighty? Ninety?"

"I don't count. I know I've been to approximately twenty-two hundred and seventy-one opera performances. Women may be something like ninety or so. Maybe it's a hundred. Maybe you're the hundredth and you win a trip to Hawaii. But you're not screaming and jumping up and down, so I can't be sure. Ninety is only about four a year since I began."

"But how do you meet them?"

"At the office—new researchers. At other offices, at interviews, parties, receptions. An occasional standee at the opera. At concerts sometimes, especially balcony lobbies. And through friends. I have some solidly married friends who dote on me, believe it or not. Husbands, wives, children. Children adore their Uncle Alan."

"Do your friends warn the women they're going to introduce to you that they may be the fifth or sixth performance of the season?"

"I don't request it. They'll warn *me* if someone's vulnerable, or if someone's predatory, for that matter. You have to understand, some women are bachelors, too, or simply still single, whatever. They know what they're doing, more or less. Or a woman may act self-destructive, in any number of ways, without being at all destructible."

"Don't you ever go to the ballet? Wouldn't that be an additional source? Those little long-haired balletomanes? Little Gelseys?"

"I've never gotten hooked. Dance looks to me like people explaining something to the deaf. I keep wishing they'd say something."

She giggled gently. "Did you just make that up?"

"No, in truth. And none of this conversation has anything, *any*thing, to do with you, needless to say, or I wouldn't be talking this way."

"I know. My uniqueness."

"Do you go to the ballet?"

"Maybe four a year. Curtis is fond of it. It relaxes him. I could go more. I like it for exactly the reason you don't."

"Has your hair ever been long?"

"Always, mostly, until this year. Don't you like it this way?"

"Not as a rule. But I love your face. It opens up your face."

"Have you ever had a beard?"

"No. What happened to Curtis's other marriage?"

"Evidently she was dissatisfied. She wanted him to join a large, fancy firm. He was always getting offers. He still is. She seems to have disapproved of him more and more comprehensively. So he got out, to his credit, after five years of it. Actually, he should have married me first and her second. I've wondered if he's been doing to me what she was doing to him. He's so much more chic now."

"What did he see in her?"

"She's attractive, in her way. It's called 'Junoesque'? And competent. Forceful. She dazzled him, he says. Maybe he liked me because I was small and quiet."

"Did she get married again?"

"To a big broker, Roberts. Apparently a bastard. Antoinette owns the Velvetree."

"What's her name?"

"Antoinette Loesser."

I'm sure I went out with an Antoinette Loesser ten or twelve years ago."

Betsy looked deadpan at him.

"The most awful woman I've ever known. I asked her what kind of restaurant she wanted to go to for dinner and she said, 'Let's go to Lutèce,' as in 'Let's go to the movies.' "

"And was it fine?"

He smiled. "I took her. I learned about yachts. She told me all about a yacht she'd been on. She was twenty-four, twenty-five. The guy who owned the yacht was sixty."

"Sounds like the right Antoinette. Well. We have an awkward transition here." She shut her eyes again.

"Please." He jiggled his hand on her back. "I could have

kept it to myself. In any event, I'm not bragging. And I had no way of knowing she'd be marrying your husband."

"They were still married when you interviewed him." She talked to her shoulder.

"Interviewing the husband of a woman you once went out with before she was married to him is a mere misdemeanor."

"How was the sex?"

"None! She wouldn't have me!"

"Tough break, all that dinner down the drain. If it will help, Curtis says she was not nearly as good as she looked as though she should be."

"Thanks, but I'm sure I've been turned down by better since."

"There must be a whole flock of married women in your ninety."

"Not true."

"None?"

"A few."

"What's a few?"

"Five, six. They weren't you."

"What happend to them?"

"They poisoned themselves with arsenic. What about you?"

"Poisoning myself, or married men?"

"Yes. Aside from your husband."

"One."

"Really? This is before you were married."

"Of course."

"Did it last long?"

"No. It was unpleasant. Perhaps you went out with him."

"I'd have to know his name."

"Mr. Tony Bennett."

"Was there really someone?"

"Yes, why not? Women do it, too. I don't like this kind of questionnairing. It's like scouring pots. I wonder if we could be quiet for a minute. A minute of silence."

"Excellent idea. That's our transition. Transition is everything, you know, Wagner said."

"Did he. Except that there must be something to make a transition to."

Was she telling him to make it, or was she telling him he'd be wasting his time? *"Silenzio! Silenzio! Silenzio! Si-len-zio! Olá! Olá! Olá!"*

"You don't hear a peep out of me."

"That's the chorus in *Pagliacci* singing at full blast, telling itself to be quiet."

"I'm learning quite a lot. What made you think of that?"

"Awkwardness and anxiety. Nothing." In the silence, after a moment during which he wondered if she would stop him, he moved his hand down her back, over her brassiere strap. Did she wear a bra regularly, or was today an exception so she wouldn't seem too prepared if her sweater came off? Or was that the kind of question considered only by men born in the Great Depression? He thought it probably was. His hand, having reached the well of her back, moved up a little. He slid it again toward the bottom of her sweater, thinking about dipping his fingers under and nudging the sweater up just enough to take the step onto skin. But he feared she might jump, as if awakened by a stranger, even by a friend. As his hand moved up again, he pressed her sweater up with the base of his palm. Betsy gave a tiny sigh. At her noise, Alan felt as if his lungs had slipped. He reached for the bottom of her sweater, inserting his hand, laying it on the indented smoothness of the bottom of her back. He splayed his fingers. A precious nausea fluttered coolly in his chest. Her fingers fiddled for entrance. With his right hand, he pulled his T-shirt from his pants. She moved her sweatered arm under the T-shirt straight up to his right shoulder. Her hand felt like sunlight, a bath. She looked asleep. He did not move his hand. She was one gesture ahead of him now, one gesture bolder. Beginning always whispered to him that the end was only a few days or weeks away. His lust traveled directly downhill. He and women rolled down hard earth, rumbling out of sight like loose wagon wheels. Then he was at the top of the hill again, by himself. He didn't know what to do. He kissed her forehead. She tilted her head up to him, still as if asleep. He

113

moved down the bed a few inches; she curled away, onto her back. He leaned over her. He had his hand under her hair. He gazed at the naked face concentrating on expecting him under closed eyes. He had asked for another kiss. Closing his eyes, he lowered his face carefully, as if he were blind in the dark. When he kissed her, he did not press his mouth on hers. He feared burying her lips. Each time their tongues wrestled, he stopped, as if she had won, as if he were exhausted. He lifted his face and looked down the length of her body. If his hand reached down, anywhere, she was there, stretched, to touch. "My boots," she said. He looked at her. She had opened her eyes. Her expression appeared to be slightly cross, as if there were a glare in the room. A wrinkle of embarrassment or self-consciousness lay like a shadow beneath her lower lip, such as he had seen on her after their earlier kiss. Then, as she blinked, the complexity dissolved. She studied him.

"What are we going to do?" he said, sounding to himself as if someone had just died.

"Take off my boots?"

"Yes."

She sat, the green arch of her back before him as she leaned forward. He put his hand on the center of her spine. He heard zipping. The mattress lurched a bit. She dropped her boot over the bottom of the bed. Another zip, another tug, another dead boot. Her hands appeared at her waist; she was about to pull off her sweater. No, he said to himself, his hand jumping at hers. He withdrew his arm with a snap, but not before he had touched her. She turned to him sharply, on her knees, sitting on her heels. Was she going to take it off from the front? "I owe you a warning," she said. He patted the space beside him. She stayed where she was.

"What warning?"

"If we stay here, I can't stay here like this. Without going ahead. Or we can get up and eat. Or I can go."

"*Leave?*"

"Not necessarily forever. And I'd rather stay than get up. It's just this. If we do go ahead, I want you to know, if you care, that there's a chance it may not happen again. Not because that's the way I am, or even the way you are. It's because I've never been in this situation. I just don't know. If I weren't with you, I wouldn't be somewhere else. But I have nothing to promise. I don't know what you want or expect. I want you to decide." She dropped back down beside him, on her stomach, her arms crossed under her chin. She eyed him without expression.

He kissed her hand and watched her eyes, his face as close to hers as it could be without touching it. "I care *only* that if it happens, it happens again. I won't be able to stop with once. I can't. It's got to be the beginning only."

"You don't know. I don't know. We don't know how we'll feel. We don't know what's around the corner. Especially I don't. Don't you see that?"

"We must stop talking again. It's ridiculous. Between us, we're seventy-three years old." He would have to take his chances. "It scares me because I feel so strongly."

"Then let's arise."

"Betsy." He clasped her shoulder. "I can't not. I can't not." He felt grief-stricken. He had more to say. He wanted to talk for his body. He wanted to tell her in different ways that, if they began, there would be no ending, that this was it for him, that he wanted to protect her forever. He wanted to tell her that he wanted to stay here but didn't want to hurry. He could wait until tomorrow or the next day if he knew she would come back tomorrow or the next day. He didn't want to start using her up, the cloth of her skin—he wouldn't say that; he could never use her up. She was all original. Then he thought, But if I give up this moment, I will probably lose her. She has put herself on the line. He wanted to say that he loved her. He felt the bump of a sob in him, but no sob. "Betsy."

She gave him a gray smile. "It's not as if it weren't a big event for me. Whatever happens after."

He put his hand on her shoulder. "Shh. No after. After is only us." He rocked her shoulder to suggest she turn over again. She didn't move. He took his arm from her shoulder and reached his hand as far down the back of her leg as it would go, to the bottom of her corduroy thigh. He drew his hand up the thigh and sloped it off her, fitting it beneath her hip. He rocked the hip, discreetly. She turned. He raised himself, watching his hand, not her face, and moved his hand across her belly, under her sweater. If he looked at her face, he feared, he would say that he loved her; he had the sense from her that the less solemn he could be, the better off they would be, they including him.

"Can anyone see us?" She lifted her head off the bed. "Across the street?"

"It would be hard, but I'll lower the blinds." He left the bed and tugged the blind cord, darkening the light by three hours. He shucked his sweater and T-shirt, dropping them on his loyal silent valet. Would she say, What on earth are you doing? He sat down on the side of the bed and looked at her with neutral sadness. She sat up abruptly and pulled off her sweater. Skimpy, low white brassiere, half containing slight breasts. Watching him watch her, her expression austere, she unhooked the brassiere. He helped it off, uncovering aureolae almost as wide as the breasts, raspberry nipples. He lowered himself, their arms pouring over each other's shoulders. Together they let go a whisper of exclamation. She felt like powder against him. It was true he had never felt like this. With his chin he loosened the hold of her right arm, and he kissed her breast, slid his cheek across it, his tongue, inhaling the private skin. Her hand stepped down his chest, wheeled like a breeze on his stomach. They both floated in the same lemony dimness, he thought, a private afternoon light of light after death. One day they would be alone in space together, like Tristan and Isolde in the new Met staging. The Met, where they had met. They would be alone forever in an eternal conversation of their bodies and low voices, space a bed. She would be saved forever from the solo blackness she had described to him. No one he knew had ever told him such a thing as that dream. Her griefs were substantial. She was so reliably substantial altogether. A slight woman of

116

such substance. She could never evaporate. As she lowered her hand on him, his heart slammed and the blood dropped like a wall from his head. What's my name? he thought. He retrieved his name but the name was strange to him. With a moan of a gesture, he grasped the top of the inside of her thigh, which was angled vertically, his wrist at the verge, against the corduroy, of the crinkling bulge of secrecy. When he was young, a vagina had been so secret that nobody had ever seen one. The world knew of it, every once in a while mentioned it. It was both dangerous and delicate, an illness, vagina, above all contagious, or a blowsy black plant, a vagina; you might touch it by mistake and become poisoned. Or you might step on it in the woods in August, a deep softening disguised by grass, and break an ankle. A shocking danger, a magnetic wound, gash and hair, and beyond question the most important of all things. His adolescent performances of *Parsifal* glimmered with the secret—Amfortas ill with his wound, "Amfortas," in the softness of its syllables, vaginalike; also "Gurnemanz," "Monsalvat." "Grail" became girl, holy girl, hole-y girl, hairy grail; "Parsifal," a fall into a hole covered by parsley tufts. "Kundry" contained "cunt." "Titurel" was a silly bonus, which, even though not part of the scheme, helped to confirm it. He had never told anyone these associations. They were punishable. He would masturbate imagining girls at school, naked, in the roles of Zerlina, Susanna, Sophie, Mélisande, Mimi, Kundry. Kundry, sexual slave, age fifteen, sixteen, seventeen. Ellen Kundry, Sally Kundry, Wendy Kundry, Heather Kundry. Roz Kundry from out of school.

Betsy's palm left him. From the side of her breast, he looked down. She undid the button of her pants, lowered the zipper. He saw a wedge of black tights, the skin of underpants showing through. He moved his hand down to lay it on hers. He drew his mouth across her warm nipple, went to the other breast. "Are you going to take off your pants?" she asked. "Yes. I'll help you with yours." He pushed with her, not looking, his thumb sliding down her naked buttock. He stood again, not looking at her, shoving off the rest of his clothes, hearing behind him the final flurry of her undressing. They met on the bed. He glimpsed her but did not look. Their rolling together, two billows of warm air, was so light and rapid that he ended nearly on her. His penis lay on her hip, about to crack like ice in the sun. She covered it with her hand. Vengefully, he clutched her, pressing wetness out of deep hair. He looked down, then, at the surprisingly wide, high fan of hair, a large badge of adultness on her almost girlish body. Her eyes closed, her face lolling at him, she was smiling tautly in suspense. "Please look at me," he said. She did. Her eyes were unguarded. "You don't have to wait," she said. She stroked him, just once. "I want to take our time," he said.

"Next time."

"You said no next time."

"I might never go home. Don't talk."

He revolved the heel of his palm, collecting and smearing her slickness. She began to lap her body at his circling hand, her absorbed expression making her look oddly shrewd. He felt as if her hairs were tingling curls of electricity. Even naked, he felt more naked than he ever had, precariously excited, but what was happening and about to happen would be only the ultimate of the usual unless it were to be the first and not the last time, unless it were to be the first of numberless times in which they belonged to each other with increasing permanence. She was turning the event into an electrocuting lay. "Betsy."

She kissed him with her tongue, heavily coating his lips. Her tongue had gained weight. Her glue was on her breath, smelling about like everyone's, thus making her more special—her touch of the universal a form of tact toward womankind, noblesse oblige. It would be embarrassing or rude to stop here, to deliver a speech of love, to hope that before he gave himself, as if he were a girl in a joke, she would say she loved him. She wanted *this*. He would rather have wept in her than come. He would have to take his chances. He would have to count on what she had said—that if she weren't with him, no one else would do—

118

and pray that his value, whatever it was to her, would carry over to become indispensable. It was as if he wanted to be pregnant with them; they would come out of him as a couple, unified for life. He moved onto her, her legs rising like gates, and thickly into her, his heart draining.

When it was done, he lay for a moment with his eyes closed, his hand on her arm, imagining himself alone. He felt as if he had landed, boneless, in a grove reserved for those slain at the moment of the attainment of love. He was in a conscious coma. He was worried that she would want to get up. Once she was up, leaving would come next. He opened his eyes uneasily, as if he were waking on the first day of his life and feared to learn what he would find before him. Her face was tilted away from him; he wondered if she was crying. Her forearm covered her forehead. She sprawled. She looked larger, longer, than she did with her clothes on. He laid his hand on her hip. He kissed her on the neck. "I'd like to get under the covers," he said. She looked at him sleepily. "Alone?" she asked. "Not alone. Will you get up for just a second?" "For just a second." They left the bed on their respective sides. Alan swung the bedding down. They got into bed. Alan pulled the sheets up. Nonchalant in his relief, he lay on his stomach, his head in his arm, the arm next to her body, Betsy half over him, her bush like damp wool against him. Her arm crossed his waist and her hand covered his. "Why don't we just stay like this for a couple of years," he said.

"The phone hasn't rung at all," she said. "Did you turn it off?"

"No, I am innocent. You won't stay here like this for a couple of years?"

"It's one-fifteen. I can stay for an hour. Don't you have things to do? Don't you have to go back to the office?"

"I have a few things to do, but not 'til later, and I'm going to *The Trojans, Les Troyens*"—he carved "*Troyens*" with exuberant nasal vigor—"with my friend and boss, Bob Manners. Before that, I have to drop in on my parents and see a guy on

119

business. I would like to cancel everything, tell the opera to cancel the performance, and stay right here with you forever. What do you have to do?''

''Go home. Be home. Try to work. Think. One or the other. I don't feel I'm with someone who's been with ninety women at all.''

His eyes wettened. ''Well, you're not, now that you're here. They've all disappeared from history. But then what? You are now going to disappear from history, too, taking me with you, leaving me neither you nor me? I can't believe we'll just stop with this. It makes no sense. It's impossible. We're lying here like two soft-boiled eggs who've been friends for years.''

''It seems impossible. If you're asking me would I choose not to see you, of course the answer is no. If you're asking me will I have to decide not to see you, the answer is I hope not. I'm only saying I don't know. I don't want to make any promises I'm going to have to break. I'm not even sure yet why I would have to break them.''

''I'm going to starve for you as soon as you leave.''

''I'll have to see what it's like when I get home, and later. What waking up tomorrow is going to be like. But I'm happy lying here. I feel lucky. I'm sure I'll be unhappy not lying here.''

''Please.'' His eyes filled again.

''A big part of the Curtis problem is that I have enough money of my own to live on independently for about six months. If I ever left, I would have to go back to teaching, if I could get a job. But I have got to write. I'm a writer. But I can't write. All this is part of it. I'm not going to continue to live off someone I can't stand, if it stays this way. And I'm never going to live off anyone I like again.''

''Your father left you nothing?''

''It's a long story. The upshot is that everything got used up by his illness. What I have is my advance from Wynn, Marcovici in the savings bank, and a few dollars. I don't expect to be rich, ever.''

''Maybe once your book is out you'll be able to write again.''

"I tell myself that, but it's begun to sound like a lie. It puts cold air in my blood. But it can't be. My life depends on it. Remember? If I've run out of ideas, I'm dead. I've had only a half-dozen ideas in my life. Would you like to do it again?"

For an instant, he didn't comprehend. "Sure. Now, you mean?"

"While we're here and all."

"In just a moment, by all means. My heart only finished applauding a little while ago. Why don't you move in with me?"

"Closet space? Curtis doesn't know he doesn't love me. Or maybe he loves me and I don't know it. Maybe I love him and don't know it. Maybe the air will clear and things will be better than they ever were at their best. I doubt it, but no one knows anything yet. Not even you."

"I do. I know everything, I promise you, but it doesn't help yet."

"And what is everything?"

How could he, of all people, say to someone like her, on their first day, that they were destined to last? He was going to stick with her all the way, no matter how difficult or dangerous, wherever it led. The longer it took, the more likely they'd be to make it, not the less likely. "It's very good. Everything is very good. The whole point is, our future is worth pursuing. That means absolutely everything, don't you see?"

5

"I saw Hoffman this afternoon."

"Hoffman." Betsy refrained from making it a question. She cut a bite of calve's liver.

"At the Oak Bar."

"Splendid. Who's Hoffman?" Her breath could have been extracted from her in lung-shaped blocks. "You mean Alan Hoffman. From the opera?" Two sips of wine.

"That Alan Hoffman."

"Why did you see him? You ran into him, you mean?" Another bite of liver. On the gulp, she extended her neck toward her husband, to her left at the head of the living-room dining table. She was wearing that afternoon's clothes; she hadn't taken a shower.

Curtis smiled, keeping his own counsel while he sliced his broccoli. And she knew. He said, "Since I've come to understand that you regard your novel as a private document, I decided to take it on myself to start something up on its behalf." He ate, chewing at her until free to talk again. "So I queried him, Hoffman, on whether they might interview you at *News-*

worthy, when the book comes out, assuming you're going to allow it to be published."

"Yes." She could not lift her face to him. Her neck seemed too weak for what it had to support. "And what did Alan Hoffman say?" Then she thought to add, "Between the two of you, you'd find a way?"

"No. He said he'd like to help, but it would depend on the reviews, his bosses, on you, on the book. He didn't mind my asking. We had a good time. He was full of his trip. He saw lots of government people. I got a full-scale briefing. My mistake is that I told you."

"That is not your mistake! For God's sake!" Her head was up, feeling flushed. "Why didn't you ask my permission before speaking to someone on my behalf? And why did you tell me? Did you think I'd be grateful?" Was she screaming at him?

"I don't know, Betsy. I guess I thought you'd be amused that I saw him, since we had that funny drink with him the other night. I didn't ask your permission because I knew I wouldn't get it."

"How was it arranged?" She didn't know whether she sounded panicky or merely querulous.

"I called him last week, and he was in Europe. He called me back yesterday. We had a drink. It seemed to me a good chance to accomplish something for you that you might tolerate. I'm sorry I told you. I'm sorry I did it. I apologize."

She lowered her head. She had no difficulty subduing her voice. "I have tried to get it through to you that I want to be left alone about my book. I have an editor. Wynn, Marcovici has a publicity department. There are salesmen. There are bookstores. There are critics. I am thirty-three years old. I have tried to tell you I do not want to do these promoting things you want me to do. It's just a bunch of careery shit. No magazine would buy those ideas, anyway, from me, and what's more they wouldn't even help in the way you hope they'd help." Curtis was eating. Alan at *The Trojans. The Trojans?* In a row, in the

123

dark, with his friend Manners. Wasn't he thinking of this afternoon, just the same?

"I think this subject has had it. It sounds to me, frankly, as if you're so scared the book is going to die on you that you want to keep aloof from it. Part of your maternal instinct."

The dullness in her was like indigestion that had spread to her arms and legs, gaseous fatigue. If she went up to the clinic at St. Luke's, would they give her intravenous Alka-Seltzer? "I guess that's a possibility. But it's not the reason I'm not killing myself trying to get on the Merv Griffin show with Nabokov and Zsa Zsa Gabor. I agree the subject has had it. Do you think maybe you're trying to provoke me out of the marriage? Because you've discovered you're married to the wrong woman and you're unable to say you don't love me?" Her bluntness embarrassed her. Her face felt stiff; her eyes stuck to his beard.

Curtis paused in his eating. "Oh, but I do love you," he reproved. "If I didn't love you, I wouldn't be so concerned that you've been so unhappy recently."

"I see. Well, I can't write. The best thing you could do altogether is to leave me alone about all this. Maybe you should quit. Maybe I'm impossible."

"You have not been a joy to live with." He took a swallow of wine.

"I wasn't a joy to live with when you married me. If you could ignore my book, it would be much better." She felt hopeless saying it. "It could be. Pretend it's a cold-sore you're overlooking, or something. You used to be so good at not noticing me in a friendly way and letting me come around. And we were friends just the same." She smiled involuntarily for just an instant with one side of her mouth. It was more that they had never been enemies. She knew they had never been enemies.

He pulled away from the table a bit and crossed his legs, leaning back, in his white shirt, the pants of his gray pinstripe. His hands held his knee. He looked past her. She looked nowhere, blankly. The conversation had hurt him. Or he was getting set to tell her he wanted to leave her. Or he was thinking about a case. His mouth was closed like a scar in a hank of hair. Had she married him because he had left her alone? Because he was doting but distant? Brilliant and doting but distant? Why had she not asked him to shave his beard before they got married? His face needed translation. What had she done? She couldn't remember anything at the moment beyond how easy it had been to do it. He'd had the apartment, his postmarital brownstone. He made money, adult money. He had established himself. On his own. So why didn't he see what she wanted? Curtis, in general, had been her first adult. Others had been delightful or sexy or odd, but they were young birds compared with Curtis. He was established and he did not parade. He did not wear his medals. Admiration and demand barely kept up with him. He was the definition of the man who knew what he was doing. The way to put the problem, it suddenly struck her, was that he coveted less than he had achieved. That was his weakness, his secret. He ogled clichés of success. She was his current cliché, failing to develop. "Are you counting on me to be a star? The big time?" The words had escaped, tangled in heartbeat. Her mouth hung open.

"I'll get some coffee." Curtis picked up his plate, leaving behind his unused salad plate, and went into the kitchen. "Will you be having coffee?" he asked. She heard him scraping and rinsing the dish.

Tears prepared to raise the bones of her nose. "No." She must have been inaudible to him. "No, thanks," she said. She swallowed pain. She did not want to cry. Curtis came in. She turned her head from his view. "Are you done?" he asked. She didn't know what he meant, so she didn't reply. He took up her plate. "I'll do that," she said. But he carried it away. "I'm going to the office after my coffee," he said from the kitchen. She stayed where she was. He'd be going to the bedroom and the bathroom before he left and if she went into the study and closed the door, he might come in to say good night. She didn't want to talk, didn't want to look at him. She heard him fixing his coffee. This must be what people called an impasse. She was participating in an impasse. Would it be on the late news?

When he crossed the living room, behind her, she asked, "Why do you have to go to the office?"

"I'm glad I have an office. Aren't you?"

Meaning that he made their money there? Jeff, the last man before Curtis, had been so sweet that he smelled of sweetness. Sweet, tall, lean. Prentiss's most popular teacher. Gung-ho. In his own home, his own bed, he behaved toward her as if he feared offending her. Cumulatively grateful, apologetic, removed. She would not have been surprised to catch him sucking his thumb. Forty-two years old. The secret of all the serious men before Curtis was their childishness. It was that which had become exposed, pink skin under their attractive feathers. Timid. Or reckless. Whiney, dependent, possessive. Curtis's secret had been subtler and had taken longer to show. Or else to see. Betsy cleared the rest of the table and washed the dishes Curtis had rinsed. When he left the house, he didn't say goodbye. On the kitchen phone, she got the Met box office number from Information and called to find out when *The Trojans* ended. The phone rang on and on, deserted. Was there a *Trojans?* A chorus of contraceptives standing guard over Helen, having their way with Helen? She thought of calling Andrea, in Toronto, to tell her what was happening; but Andrea would be too interested.

She took a shower and got dressed again, green tights over green underpants with yellow roses, brown suede wraparound skirt, black turtleneck. Nine-thirty by the bed-table clock. Sitting on the bed, she looked up Alan's number and called his house, senselessly, her eyes trespassing through his apartment while the phone rang. No one home but us tickets. What should she do? What did one do in this particular circumstance? Wait for him outside the opera? She thought of calling Curtis to find out what was on his mind; the thought receded. She recalled for the third time since she had come home that in a brand new way she was once again no longer a virgin. It had not sunk in. It did

126

not feel strange or monumental. She did not feel that the wrong man had been in her, or that she had "cheated." Did such thoughts not come out until the next day, like a bruise, or stiffness? She wanted to be back with him, doing the same, only more so, the works, guzzling. He was not the type who didn't. They hadn't known each other well enough this afternoon. And then she would go to sleep with him. They had arranged that she would call him tomorrow, at home, if she possibly could, if only to say hello. (If only to say goodbye, he had said.) Curtis usually worked on Saturdays (but never before on a Friday night), so actually, though she hadn't told him, she might be able to see him tomorrow afternoon. She smiled, like someone in love. His childishness was so mature. It was as if his singularity, his peculiar gaudiness, had become his profession, or his companion. It was just this, she thought, that she probably liked best about him. His flamboyance was convincing. Despite his premature intensity, she could almost believe he wanted to be hers. She imagined tomorrow, the center of the day, under his covers with him, surrounded by him and his covers. She thought of making him a ticket. She thought of colored paper, purple, black, red, green. Crayons. "Crayolas." A scene of colored paper, Crayolas, scissors, glue, concentration, she and Maude Lofting, when they were ten or eleven, drawing and cutting— valentines? Christmas cards? Gowns?—in her bedroom at Five-forty-five West End on a dark-gray afternoon, the kind of afternoon she had regarded, around that age, as medieval, exciting because it was grim. While she and Maude had played, Thelma, the maid ("housekeeper"), was in the kitchen, humming and cooking pot roast, both.

In the study, putting her sick notebook aside, Betsy took a piece of typing paper and her scissors and cut a full-length strip off the top, then cut the strip in half, crosswise. "ADMIT ONE," she printed, in heavy pencil. "BETSOPOLITAN OPERA HOUSE. FRI. AFT. NOV. 2, 1973, ONE P.M. APPROX." Vul-gar! To allude in this way to the afternoon just spent seemed coarsely nostalgic, arch, highbrow locker-roomy.

127

(She was giving a review to her ticket.) She dropped the strip in the wastebasket and attacked the other half. Revision was everything, superseding even transition. "TICKET. ADMIT ONE. TIME: OPTIONAL. DRESS: OPTIONAL. ORCHESTRA AND BALCONY." Box? Tch. "PRICE: UNKNOWN." *Dramatique!* She cut another strip and redid the ticket, on the typewriter. She put the ticket in an envelope, sealed the envelope, leaving it blank, and placed the envelope in her notebook. She removed the first-draft ticket from the wastebasket and took it to the bathroom, where she flushed it.

"How come you didn't call me last night?"

"How could I call you? You think I didn't want to call you? All I wanted to do was call you."

"I expected you to know, to sense with your quiveringly sensitive antennae, that Curtis went to his office after dinner. You could have called him to discuss the possibility of my *Newsworthy* interview further. And as he wasn't home, I would have answered the phone."

"Why didn't you call me at the opera? I'm going to get a beeper so you can call me whenever you're alone. He told you about meeting with me."

"He did. Oak Bar and all. I was sorry not to be able to make it."

"Don't you see why I couldn't tell you?"

"I hope it is that he didn't tell you what he wanted until you met and you didn't want both of us worrying."

"That's exactly right."

"In that case, you come off smelling adequate."

"Better! Heroic! How could I know what he wanted?"

"How was the opera?"

"It was wonderful. But it did not take your place. I could hear it, but I barely stopped thinking of you."

"Good. What did you do after?"

"Manners and I had a drink, two drinks. No, three. And some food."

128

"Same place?"

"No, at The Magic Flute, up the street. What are you doing?"

"On my bed."

"What are you wearing?"

"My nightgown. And you?"

"Nothing. You have stripped me. What color is your nightgown?"

"Let me see. It's yellow with teensy brown bears and giraffes."

"I'll buy you a nightgown. And when do I see you? Do I see you? I have got to see you. Where is Curtis?"

"At work. Somewhere. I can see you."

"You can? Today?"

"Today."

"You were very unsure of anything yesterday."

"It couldn't be helped."

"Did something happen?"

"If I'm going to see you, I'll tell you then. I'm available any time today until midafternoon."

"All I have to do is read up on the War Powers bill."

"That shouldn't take long."

"All I want to do is see you. All I wanted to talk to Bob about was you."

"You didn't, did you?"

"No, I didn't. But he asked me what was wrong."

"Why? What was wrong?"

"I gaped at you a lot."

She smiled at 'gaped.' "And then how did you explain the gaping?"

"Fatigue, preoccupation, you know."

"Did you visit your parents?"

"Yes. They were flooded with pride. My sister, Fran, just won some big science award in Washington. I have to call her."

"Is she married?"

"She has two kids. Her husband's also a biochemist. I want to see your book. Do you have extra galleys of your book? Or a

129

carbon? This is for me, not the magazine. I'm not kidding around.''

"I'll see. Maybe I can get them on Monday. I should be getting the real live thing any day. But I'll stop by Wynn, Marcovici on Monday and see about galleys.''

"Please. Does Curtis usually go to his office on Friday night?''

"He doesn't.'' Her answer, meant to sound matter-of-fact, sounded clipped in her throat.

"Will you come here? Or do you want to eat out? Or your house.''

"My house! No. Shall I make new sandwiches?''

"Where does Curtis eat on Saturdays?''

"Around his office, I guess.''

"Where's his office?''

"Fifth and Forty-third.''

"I'd like to eat out somewhere with you and spend the rest of the time at my house. Is that too greedy of me?''

"I'm going to have to settle for your house. Eating out would make me nervous.''

"Why don't I buy the sandwiches? What do you like?''

"Tuna fish.''

He laughed. "Oh. What did you do about the scarf?''

"Nothing. It's in the closet.''

"Okay. When will you be here?''

"An hour.''

When he opened the green door, he was in a white terrycloth robe, supporting on his left arm a body of roses in green paper.

"My! Sexy greeting. To say nothing of expensive. Did you go out like that?''

Kissing her lightly, he handed the roses to her.

"Either they or I must go in a vase. Are these instead of sandwiches?''

"No, I got rose sandwiches, too.''

130

In the bedroom, where he brought the roses in a vase, she undid the belt of his robe and opened her jeans while in his embrace. Guilt was no nearer than the thought that she didn't feel guilty. Curtis could have been in Hawaii instead of downtown. It felt to her as if the more direct she and Alan were, the more intimate their intimacy, the further they were from danger. He eased down her pants. They touched each other, receiving voltage, before she removed her clothes and he dropped his robe and they entered the bed, at first lying together as if on a beach, stunned, after a marathon swim, then beginning to swim, to swim under, to disappear, circling and nosing, meeting and falling away, eventually clasping to lift and bump bottom.

Their arms like straps across each other's backs, they lay with their cheekbones touching. "You have me all," Alan said. "You cannot take yourself away or I am helpless."

"Shh. You said that yesterday, and here we are again."

"What happened last night, with Curtis?"

She described the dinner conversation. "I feel better today, but at the moment I felt like a little girl being punished for talking fresh at the table. I came off as both mean and ineffective, or clumsy. He couldn't have been calmer, or smugger. I didn't make a dent."

"But you told him. That's the important thing. Now you're clean. Now you're not responsible for withheld resentment. What happened when he got home?"

"I seemed to be asleep."

"Do you know when he got home?"

"Somewhere around midnight."

"And how was it this morning?"

"Cool. No discussion. No frank but useful exchanges."

"What happens tonight?"

"He abducts little Curtis and hijacks a plane to Cuba."

"What are you doing tonight, I mean."

"Having dinner with our friends the Simonsons, Marilyn and Steve."

"Who are they?"

131

"She's my agent. Not mine alone, you understand. He's a lawyer."

"Dinner in or out?"

"Supposed to go to the Russian Tea Room. Buffalo-grass martinis. Maybe a little grass at their house to warm up. What about you?"

"I'm going to a very, very early Verdi opera in Queens."

"With anyone?"

"Not as of now. I haven't asked anyone. Probably not. But you're more than welcome to come. What do you do tomorrow?"

"Nothing planned. *Tales That Witness Madness* and *The Possession of Joel Delaney* are at the Symphony."

"They are?"

"What about you? Tomorrow."

"I'll be working, here. Come here if you can."

"I'm sure not."

"What's going to happen to us?"

"When I find out, I'll inform you within ninety days. I might point out that what happens to us is not entirely up to me or to what Curtis is going to do or not going to do. You may decide in a week or two that you don't want anything to do with me. How do you know I won't 'boil down,' like Carla or eighty or ninety others?"

"You're being silly. It is truly inconceivable to me. I'm not blind. I have at times in my life known what I am doing."

"Maybe you just like the thrill, the secret."

"*La Forza del Clandestino.* Nonsense. You're the thrill. What about you? How do you feel?"

"When might I give you up?"

"I mean how do you feel?"

"Well, I'm lying here in your bed, covered with mutual goo. That must say something. I'm not looking forward to going home. To my husband."

"But would you rather stay with *me* than go home?"

"I'd even go to the airly Vurdi opera with you in Queens. The

132

difficulties are not of my choosing. It's too early for difficulties. I hope this isn't a fully serious conversation."

"The problem is, I didn't know the night we met that you were unhappy. You're available."

"Not exactly. I'm more available than I seemed to be the night we met and less available than I would appear to be at this moment to a disinterested passer-by. Please be cheerful. Are you feeling guilty? Don't imagine that you've stolen me."

"No. In fact, when Curtis and I met yesterday, he seemed like your agent, not your husband. In any case, I'm not having any fantasies about being tied up, castrated, and thrown into the river. All I've been thinking about is you, your value. And the uncertainty. Naturally, I'd like you free."

"Well, we know you're not used to uncertainty in love, don't we?"

He lifted his head and laughed loudly at his pillow. "That's extremely funny. You might *say* I'm not used to uncertainty in love. What a dig!" He turned to her. His eyes were wet. "You are ineffably adorable." He hugged her. "You see, what comes out of your mouth—you don't say anything that isn't luxurious to listen to. It's like magic."

"I thought last night that the sudden freedom seems like magic, that eleven days ago I'd never heard of you, and now you know everything important about me." She couldn't decide whether to give him the ticket or not. It might seem too definite, promising, to him. But it spelled out her interest. It spelled out her hope for something. (That he would be reliable?) It spelled out her gratitude. But Curtis might be subsiding into his wry reasonableness this very afternoon. In a week or a month it was possible she would no longer be angry. You could swallow huge changes and forget what you had swallowed. Then the ticket would be obsolete or rude. But she had made it in friendliness. If the friendship were to stop, she owed him the friendliness. "I made a present for you last night. A tiny present."

"I want it."

She sat and she stood (her prizewinning ass to him; it had

always gotten the compliments), thinking her bureau was in the wrong place. But then this was not her bedroom. She reached for her bag, on top of the bureau, beside the vase of roses, and brought it back to the bed. Alan had raised himself to his elbow, his face happily curious. She settled beside him and handed him the envelope, on which she had written that morning, "For Ah!" "This is the way I would like it to be," she said. "So you'll know. Don't forget."

He fingered open the envelope, now looking courteously puzzled. He read the strip, shaking his head, turning it vertical and again horizontal, again shaking his head.

"You're allowed to laugh once."

"The laugh is included. It's overwhelmed." Tears swelled on his lids. He looked at her and clutched her. He said into her neck, "I simply will never forget this. No one has ever thought of this. And I don't care what the cost turns out to be. I am not going to let you pass me by."

She lifted him away to look at him. His tears were breeding and running. "What about you? Don't you cost anything at all?"

He wiped his eyes and rested his head on the pillow, holding the ticket, smiling at her. "I was just about to add that. I plan to be nothing but a boon to you."

She put her hand on his cheek. "You don't have to say things like that. I would like a rose sandwich. Rose, ham and Swiss."

On Monday morning, when she got to Larry Turnbull's office to pick up a set of galleys, he handed her as well, from behind his back, her book. As if it were bread, she sniffed it, and looked at him, giggling. Turnbull said, "Don't worry, all our authors smell their books." She examined it everywhere at once, taking off its jacket—a topographical map of Ecuador in pale-yellow, blue, and red, beneath "*Ecuador*   A Novel   By Betsy Harris" in black, all spelled right, no bones broken. It was, she thought, as if she had written the country: Ecuador, by Betsy Harris. She touched the grain of the blue cloth binding, decided to love the mustard-yellow type on the binding's spine. The back of the jacket carried the paragraph from the third chapter in which Condamine was introduced. Larry had wanted a Meg Derry photograph there, Betsy's face fully covering the back. She had refused twice; the second time she had refused Dan Wynn. From the outset, she had imagined no photograph of any size anywhere on the jacket. The absence of a photograph would extend the mysteriousness of the book. She skimmed the jacket flaps, unable to help smiling in her revulsion at the junky highbrow prose. Her book was in the world. Her revulsion was part pride. "Ginger Wolf is a fugitive in a nightmare Andes, escaping both herself and a real enemy or two. . . . All is not grimness, however, as Ginger discovers she is being aided from afar by the benign and powerful Charles Marie de la Condamine, who soon magnificently materializes—master and measurer of the Equator; mathematician; peacock; aviator; gymnast; lover. . . . A novel shuttling across centuries and continents, and between levels of myth, romance, parody, and acute physical and psychological terror and joy . . . without sacrificing suspense and narrative flow. In the words of noted critic Frederick Garland, 'Ginger Wolf is a richly multifaceted creation, one of the most coruscatingly original heroines of modern fiction. . . . Betsy Harris is a talent in a thousand.' " By her wish, her biographical note contained the titles of her stories and their places of publication and nothing about her. It was, she saw, almost as if her name were a pseudonym, she was so without identity on the jacket. Her real name was Betsy Garbo. She confronted the dedication. A gravestone. "To Beatrice and Theodore Harris, and to Curtis Ring—three blessings." She looked at the book's last page, 224, and kissed Larry Turnbull on the cheek.

"I've had a cancellation," he said. "Like to lunch?"

For an instant, she forgot where she was going now, so she stumbled over her regrets.

"Soon, then. You're entitled to a bit of celebration, after all. It looks beautiful, don't you think?"

She laughed, a breath. "I do. I wonder how it reads. Is there any news, by the way? On bookstore orders?" She felt as if she were poking herself in the eye.

"Everything's moving along nicely."

"No figures?" She cleared her throat.

"They're not handy at the moment. My recollection is that they're improving all the time."

"It's like talking to a doctor."

"The doctor is telling you not to worry. Nothing is sick. Call me later and make a lunch date."

"Thanks. Thanks for the book."

"Go home and write us another one immediately." His hand dusted her out.

Walking, she could easily make it to Alan's by twelve-thirty. So, on this high blue-and-yellow November morning, a city-movie morning, a *World of Henry Orient, Breakfast at Tiffany's, Barefoot in the Park, Touch of Class* kind of morning, her parents sailing overhead and able to see, like gulls, her book and galleys in the large Wynn, Marcovici envelope she carried, she strolled up Sixth Avenue, unsquelched by the buildings, smiling at her fellow pedestrians, an American novelist and a woman of secrets. She wished she could enjoy her secret, since it was so novelistic. She wished she had no secret. She wished, although she was eager to get into bed with Alan, and possibly too eager to tell him what she had figured out about him, that she were having a bit of celebration, after all, with Larry Turnbull-Bore, amid the odors of perfume, rolls, table linen, wine, at the Italian Pavilion; that she could be solely, for two hours, the new novelist, as sleek as book-jacket paper (what Curtis wanted her to be), without any life at all outside her existence as the new novelist. During their first lunch, nearly a year ago, Laurence Turnbull had said she must call him Larry; she could be sure he wasn't going to call her Mrs. Ring or, God forbid, Ms. Ring. Why on earth, he wondered, had she gotten married at all? Such a nuisance for a writer. He and Edna had been divorced the year before, after thirty years together, both of them incomparably better off, Edna with some decorating jobs and selling her crewel work; their son, Hardy, doing splendidly as assistant manager of McLaine's.

Betsy's enjoyment of the lunches with Turnbull—that is, of the restaurants, the food—had made her a little slow to realize how tedious they were. Out of his initial well-being crawled Larry's anxieties and complaints. About Hardy—did the lad really want to spend his life working in a restaurant, no less a pseudo-pub, for all the success of McLaine's? About Edna, whose dessication seemed to cause him so much regret that Betsy wondered why Larry hadn't stayed married to her; about Larry's former career at philistine Brown, where he'd been teaching *Humphrey Clinker* when she was a student at Cornell; about his former, sole, and unappreciated novel, *Recessional* (he had inscribed a copy to her), which had seemed to her like ten novels she hadn't read concerning academic corruption, ambition, betrayal, and sex. She ate and listened, a few times, happy to eat and look. He never suggested an unnerving kind of interest in her. Actually, she seemed to have little to do with him, except when he mentioned his hope that she was, or would soon be, starting a new novel, or when he reported on *Ecuador*'s progress through production, or when he quoted a phrase or passage from it so easily and precisely that she could have been Jane Austen. His knowledge of her book was such that he appeared to have memorized the text, and he understood it as well as she wanted anyone to understand it.

He was tiresome, foolish around the edges, advantage-taking. She had come to deflect as many of his lunch invitations as she felt she could afford to. His tweediness was devout. His weak chin looked dented, reminding her, for a reason she couldn't decipher, of a football coach. Sometimes a silly swatch of orange-gray chest hair showed at his button-down collar. But he was a figure in her life, occasionally a dream figure, a benign orange bear with unsexual Cordovan cock and balls. More privately, he was someone to call in an emergency. She figured that he owed her time if she should ever need it. What he could do for her, she didn't know, never specifically imagined, but he was a generation older than she, and potentially considerate, concernable. She would not want him to be, as her friend Andrea had been from their sophomore year at Cornell, the trustee of intimate information. He was an all-purpose fantasy of emergency aid, a stretcher-bearer.

Alan was as vivid as a model at his door—brown-and-blue glen-plaid suit pants, wing-tip shoes the tan of a foreign currency, cream-colored shirt unbuttoned at the neck, maroon silk tie pulled down. "Did you just finish dressing?" she asked after their quick kiss. "You're a dapper menace."

"I just beat you here. Why were you in such a rush on the phone this morning?"

"I don't like talking to you on your office phone. I wanted to get to Wynn, Marcovici and up here."

"Those are the galleys?"

With a smile, she raised the envelope.

"I may read them?"

"They're for you."

"I'm going to get a separate line for you to call me on at the office. You have two nights and a day to tell me about. Rereading your ticket twelve times isn't the same as talking to you, somehow." He kissed her again, as if to show her, it seemed, that he wasn't complaining. "You're wearing the coat of the night we met."

"I'd like to take it off."

"Please." They removed it together, and he hung it up. "I think you look gorgeous, extremely polished, a symphony, a serenade, in beige. But if you want to equalize the situation by our both taking everything right off, I'll go along with it, to be polite. But first I want to hear about yesterday and Saturday night, if you don't mind."

"Let's sit in the living room for a while. We haven't sat there. I like the couch. When are you due back at work?"

"I'll stay however long you can."

"Is that all right?"

138

"The only thing wrong with it is how long you can stay."

"Do I get to see your European interviews?"

"I just brought the issue home. It's out tomorrow. What you get to see is my by-line. You have to understand that seventeen people with sterling-silver cleavers chop up everybody's work down there. I'll show you later. Let's talk."

She sat on the couch, and he sat in one of his Victorian chairs. "But I have to show you," she said. "Come here." She undid the manila envelope and slid her book out, not looking at Alan as he stood and came over to her. She was showing her parents something very important she had made in school. He took it from her, sitting beside her. "My God," he said. "Look at that." He kissed it, and then kissed her on the cheek. He flipped the book to the back. "No picture of you?"

"You don't need a picture. I'm here."

"Is this for me? Is this a surprise?"

"This is my only copy so far. I need to hold it for a few days. But at some point soon I get ten copies. I have a few sisters of my father to send copies to, a few friends, a few old teachers. You may have all the rest."

"What about Curtis?"

"And Curtis gets one."

"Ah! He gets his own copy. That means he's moving out?" He smiled, holding her shiny book on his glen-plaid lap.

She laid the envelope on the floor. "Why don't you have a coffee table?"

"I think about that twice a year or so and then I forget it. It's the kind of thing it's easy to forget you don't have."

She held her hand out to him. Instead of taking it, he put his hand calmly on her arm; it seemed to her that the calmness padded a gesture of suspense. "I don't have anything significant to report to you about the weekend," she said. "I hope I'm not going to disappoint you."

"Let me hear."

"Well, Curtis has resigned from my book. He defended his motives, but he conceded he'd been mishandling me, was how he put it. He said I wouldn't hear another word from him about it. He chuckled some. It was awkward. We've never been through anything like this. You must understand—Curtis hates mistakes so much that he never makes any.''

Alan took her hand. ''When did this take place?''

''When I came home from you Saturday. Before we went out.''

''How did you respond?''

''I thanked him for seeing it.''

''That was all? And what did he say then?''

''He said, 'Peace.' ''

''And then?''

''There wasn't a clinch and a fade-out. He touched my shoulder, I think, and we went about our business.''

''Did you get home before him on Saturday?''

She nodded.

''And how was the evening with the Simonsons, Marilyn and Steve?''

''I got stoned. We all did. How was your opera?''

''Not so bad. *Un Giorno di Regno.* 'King for a Day.' His second opera. Lucky to see it. I was concerned that you were trying to reach me or that you were waiting in the lobby—I mean my lobby here—that something had happened, or that you were free and I was missing a chance to be with you. Anyway, how does it all leave you? Where are we?''

''Did you take someone to the opera?''

''In fact, my parents came along. We picked up an extra ticket. We had fun. And once again, where are we?'' He let go of her hand and stroked her arm just above the elbow.

''My feelings toward you haven't been touched, as far as I can tell. I think of that as part of the problem.''

''What *are* your feelings toward me? What are you feeling toward Curtis? Gut feeling.''

''Well, a little better.'' She laughed slightly. ''Nothing great. It's like a shirt that's come back from the laundry.''

''Explain.'' He again held her hand.

"Maybe it's wrong. I'm improvising. What I mean is that the stain's not gone but it's faded some. It's the same shirt, but it's cleaner. Does that make sense?"

"Was there sex? Any sex?"

She saw him gulp. "It barely registered. That was helpful to me. It wasn't one percent of what it is with us, with you and me. And it was never twenty-five percent of what it is with you and me. So? Where are we? You tell me."

"I have no choice about us."

"Don't be ridiculous. Of course you do."

"You want *me* to make the decision? My only question is, do you want to continue with me?"

"Yes, I would, if I can. I would like to try."

"I would keep the seismograph registering. Do you think we're all sex?"

She scraped from her tongue, against her teeth, the words, "Don't be a prick," and swallowed them. She kept her eyes on him and her hand in his.

"I'm sorry. Why would you like to try continuing?"

"Because you make me feel wholehearted, I suppose. So far, it's worth the risk to me, and the probable confusion."

"Why wouldn't you consider leaving him?"

"I consider that I've virtually left him. I just live with him."

"Move in with me."

Her teeth clamped so that her jaw ached. She breathed until her anger had passed. "I hope you don't really mean that. I will have known you two weeks tomorrow. For one of which you were not in this country. To move in with you would not be a serious thing to do. Yet. Tell me you understand that."

"I mean that I know I could make it work. I wasn't being frivolous."

"How can I leave him? With what reason?"

"That you no longer love him."

"I can't quite say yet that I don't love him."

"You can't say it to *him,* you mean, or you still love him?"

141

"This is stupid. Whatever happens is going to take time to sort out. Maybe he'll leave me, instead."

"How would you feel about that?"

"I don't know. I don't think I'd try to stop him. Everything depends on time. That should be obvious." She kissed him and kept her face available. "I was not away from you Saturday night or yesterday or last night. I thought about you hard, all the time. You were pasted to the inside of my eyes. One of the things I thought was this. Your saving of tickets is charming and odd, and it may even be touching, but I figured something out, or it finally came to me. The way you go to the opera and the concerts and your ticket-saving and the way you go through women—you look as though you've just discovered a horrible new smell. Shall I go on?"

"Yes. Hurry."

"Forgive me for this. I have to say it. The more operas you go to and the more women you collect, the more you're avoiding the future, the more you're pretending there's no ending, no such thing as ending, no death. Everything gets repeated so rapidly, ecstasy and loss, over and over. So there's no time for ecstasy and no time for loss. No time to settle in. And saving the tickets, used tickets, is a way of saving against time. Of hoarding. It's like a form of thrift. The tickets will get you into heaven, or eternity. A long retirement."

"I must say, I've never thought of it so succinctly. If you go to the opera, it's certainly true you get to see a whole lot of ecstasy and loss. We call it E and L. Maybe I'm a rubbernecker at heart. Your immediate predecessor, Carla, said the tickets were a picket fence, by the way, or just a fence, I'm not sure."

"This has been said to you before?"

"Let me assure you that without question yours is the deepest and most elegant interpretation of me I've heard."

"Should I leave?"

"Why don't you just finish, instead?"

"Okay. I'm finishing right now. I think it's like this. I think you and I have to give ourselves plenty of time. If you want me the way you say you do, you're going to have to find out if you're right. You're getting the very best of me as it is. I can tell because I know how you're making me feel. I want to be with you all the time, excluding about four minutes ago, when you asked me to move in with you. If I were living with you, and my work weren't going well, or not going at all, just what's happening these days, you would probably regret having insisted on how much you adored me. And if my work were going well, you might find me absent while present. Not everyone might, but you might. And you might be right. There's a good chance you're better off this way. That we're both better off. I come to visit you and I go home. It lacks something in coziness, I admit. I don't like going home. But at least you're here. And I come to you."

"But you wouldn't stay absent though present. You talk as though you'd be frozen in one mood. In any case, I'd be gone all day. You'd have plenty of time to be absent."

"I'd miss our twelve-thirty meetings. The thing is, you've never had to practice patience. It may be that I'm not meant for the long term, either. It may be that I'm no more a wife than you are a husband, or whatever the secular equivalents are."

"No. I cannot let you tell me I would not make a good and lasting husband to someone I loved and admired. Admiration is essential, as you said on Friday. I could be absolutely trustworthy. And you don't know how you might change under the right conditions."

If there were such a thing, she thought. "All I've been saying is there are no decisions to be made yet. We can't talk about my moving in with you. I'm trying to keep on top of things. I want to let things get figured out." She put her face in his neck, kissing it, and her hand on his chest. His hands circled over her back, the circles rising and widening. She thought of her book dying. She thought of herself drowning in the winter ocean she had dug in her brain, the ocean of the month of January, white, below an encircling cliff. She thought of never having another idea for a book or a story. She reminded herself that this fear

143

could turn into an actuality. She thought of living with Curtis for forty years in silence. She thought of living alone, knowing no one. She thought of herself as a hooker in white boots in the blue shadows of Seventh Avenue. She imagined responding to an ad in *The New York Review of Books,* placed by professorial man seeking civilized relationship with woman 25–40, to share love of books, Bach, walks in the autumn woods, and unprofessorial sex, and discovering that the man was Larry Turnbull. She imagined Alan on his knees, telling her that his love for her, to his agonized regret, had vanished. "You are turning me into a stove," she said.

"Is that good?"

"Very."

"Then why won't you trust me?"

"Maybe I will. Why do you trust me?"

His left hand clasped the back of her neck, his fingers sprung in the underside of her hair. "Because I'm in love with you." His voice cracked. "You don't know what it's like."

Startled out of her body's leisurely welling, she looked at his sudden creases of pain.

He shook her look away with closed eyes. "You don't understand that you're a prize. Nothing you say can change that."

"Then I'll say nothing." She kissed him between his closed eyes. She lifted her book from his lap and lowered it to the scarlet rug.

He read her galleys in one night. He said her book made him think of Nabokov, explaining that he meant it made nature glamorous, exotic, as Nabokov did. When Alan was very young, he told her, six or seven, he had awakened one morning in the bungalow his parents rented on a lake upstate, and, from his bed, had heard a parade passing on the dirt road about fifty yards behind the cottage, had heard the band music, imagined the instruments in the sun, the costumes. He hadn't gotten up to watch, for fear the parade didn't exist; if he went to look, the road would be empty, not because the parade had passed but because he had dreamed it or supposed it. Nor had he mentioned it to his parents, nor had they spoken of it. He had let it go in order to hold on to it. Nabokov's butterflies and flowers, the details of the mountains and tropics in Betsy's Ecuador, were like the horns and flutes and the brilliant uniforms on the country road, as magical, except that what Nabokov and she described had the miraculous extra power of being in front of your eyes.

If he could say something like that to her, Betsy figured—her judgment of his reaction to her book was at least as important to her as his reaction itself—she shouldn't sniff him like a Chinese Communist puritan looking for evidence of bourgeois deviationism. Still, as she had done with other men, and earlier with boys, she examined Alan for conversational road-hogging, soloistic sexuality, burdensome humility, idolatry, insincere rhetoric, voracious dependency, friendlessness, errors of grammar—the conventional crimes of intimacy. But whenever she found something, or thought she found something, it was so trivial she felt petty to have noticed it, or it was too big and theoretical to worry about, and easily replaced by the liveliness of his pleasure in her, the brand-new quality of his nerves; by the unusual and reassuring mixture of his documentary knowledge—petrodollars, congressional subcommittees, lobbying, Golan Heights, names of mayors countrywide, two-hundred-mile limits, separatist movements, Vietnam historically, militarily, diplomatically—with his loyalty to the anticipation, appreciation, and tenderness that seemed to govern him. His excitement over her had revived her original sense of her own full lust, ten to fifteen years behind her, which she had not expected, or thought she would ever want, to wake up to again.

If a great singer, or a new singer being praised along Alan's grapevine, were to appear in an opera he had been to fifty times, or just recently been to two or three times, he was as eager to attend as if he had never been to that particular opera before. He could go to the same opera three times in eight or ten days. (If he wasn't going alone, he always had someone to go with—

Bob Manners, a retired girl friend, his mother or father, a college newspaper friend, a British businessman, a Congressman from Indiana, a wife or husband whose husband or wife couldn't tolerate opera. His habit cost him over six thousand dollars a year, more than a quarter of his net income, though some of the expense was deductible. Ninety or a hundred women, thirteen winter suits, ten pairs of slacks, eleven jackets, twelve pairs of shoes in good condition, ninety neckties, forty shirts, twenty sweaters and turtlenecks, two thousand records, catalogued, including over four hundred recordings of operas. More than forty-six hundred ticket stubs from all the auditoriums of his life. No coffee table.

She enjoyed and she envied his statistics and the freedom from obligation they implied. During their bed talks, he said over and over that all he wanted was to belong to her. She wondered if he wasn't going to get fired, returning to work so late after lunch. He never failed to stay with her for as long as she could stay. He promised her his time was his own. He could work at night if he had to. He would give up all the opera he needed to, for her, with no regret. She observed, intending to amuse, that her world's record of afternoon movies—her only notable statistic—was in danger of being overtaken. One couldn't brag about missing *The Valachi Papers* or *Shamus* as one could brag about having seen them. Alan smiled and patted her, applauding her irony. Then she saw the point she herself had exposed. "I now have a good reason not to waste my time at the movies, although the reason has even less value as an excuse to anyone but me and you than being unable to write. But if I've stopped wasting my time, when am I going to start writing again? There's a way in which I would like to stop being free, too."

"But you will. It will come. *And* I do not believe I will lose you in the process. I'm convinced."

"Assuming you're too good to give up entirely, we won't even be an issue if my brain turns to dust out of disuse."

In the meantime, as she noticed that Curtis was spending

146

more time than usual downtown at night, she began going to the movies after dinner, or, if he wasn't coming home to eat, before dinner. Sometimes he came with her: polite of her to ask him, polite of him to join her, an unspoken mutual bargain. Twice she went with Susan Paul, who taught first grade at Prentiss and had so many personal problems that she could fill up an after-movie coffee hour without requiring any help: divorce, analysis, a sexist, anti-Semitic boyfriend who had punched her in the eye, aging parents in Brooklyn, roaches, a leching super, hostile colleagues. A useful companion, since Betsy had nothing to tell. Betsy asked Alan if he would like her to fix him up with Susan Paul, a perfect case of Hoffman histrionic.

Even though, when "resigning" from her book, Curtis had conceded some mishandling, in his closing of the matter he seemed to have replaced his concern for her career with an air of supercilious leniency, still parental. If she wasn't going to listen to him, then her life was her lookout. She and Curtis talked about his practice. A pornographer named Jack Mansfield, who had become Curtis's most offensive client, provided anecdotes. They talked about news events. (Through Alan, she knew more than she was used to knowing.) She and Curtis agreed a lot, she noticed. She nodded at him a good deal. When he would agree with her—"True," "Hadn't thought of that," "That's right"—as often as not her eyes teared. He no longer wrote short stories at home, and she didn't ask if that's what he was doing downtown. They still had sex, but no more than once a week. She chose to take some pride in her avoidance of revulsion, her "toughness," and in being able to initiate the sex on one occasion, when she had been fearing he was holding back because he knew something and was trying to find her out by testing her willingness to abstain. She had to work on concentrating, so she decided that she must seem to him to be involved. It was harder to have sex with Curtis on the days she couldn't see Alan. On those days, she had to talk herself out of being sulky. It was as if she had converted to Alan's emotional time. The substance of their days varied insignificantly—talk, sex,

147

food, sometimes a nap, and sometimes sex again—but each day had the importance of a day attainable once a week, once a month, sometimes once a year.

Early in their bed-ridden November, a few days after she had attacked him with her ecstasy-and-loss theory, he confessed to her that nothing truly terrible had ever happened to him—the knifing last summer came the closest; his experience was absurdly tame for someone forty years old. It was undeniable, he said, that his ecstasy, when not musical, had generally been tense, whipped up, hurried along by some degree of drunkenness for which liquor was not necessarily responsible. The ecstasy he experienced outside music, he experienced before it was time to be ecstatic. He would pump his idea of her importance into a new woman like a publicity man. Sometimes women told him off right away, but usually they fell for it, just as he did. They praised his enthusiasm. He wasn't "jaded," like so many men. He was "refreshing." He had never lost anyone to speak of but Roz Lewis, and the painful pain with Roz had been not when he'd lost her but at the beginning, the night he'd met her, after they'd danced, and again the night on the couch, when he'd panicked. "Provoked to enter; forbidden, unable, and unwilling to get in," he had said to Betsy. "Unrecapturable bliss," she had teased. He had responded: "Only now, with you, is it worth doing right. I'm home with you."

He had never been in the hospital as a patient, and never been seriously ill, unless—he had then delightfully shifted moods, as if apologizing for the solemnity of his complaining—you wanted to count his madness and attempted suicide at four, syphilis at five, and TB at eight, the common crop of childhod ailments. All of his serious suffering had been spent on music, his tears shed for dying sopranos, composed pain, beautiful sounds, perfect notes, the heartbreaking slow movements of certain quartets, quintets, and concertos, which, when they were not tragic, were so beautiful they felt tragic. He was by no means alone, she should understand. People flocked to musical pain, throngs collecting in concert halls and opera houses for the sake of suffering, safe suffering, paying to suffer, to weep. Three thousand people would gather to hear Schubert's *Die Winterreise,* a song cycle about a rejected lover wandering across a winter landscape, pining to death, death by rejection, loneliness, *not* frostbite. But those people bring suffering with them, she had said. "Yes, and I take it home with me, or as far as it will go. I take it out for a few drinks, anyway." Was it a pose? she asked him. Pretending he had never suffered in order to get her sympathy?

Fatigue, strain, had not roughened his skin. There was no gray in his hair. The sketch lines at his eyes and on his forehead seemed to have been established by forty years of nothing more than squinting, smiling, and frowning. His nose was just long enough and his eyes small enough to save him from the prettiness his mouth and his curls nearly achieved. He was neither short nor tall, neither slender nor stocky. He came out on the small side, a youthful shape and size. Though he didn't look like anyone she had ever known, he was not unusual looking. But he was unusual. When she looked for his age on him, she reminded herself that he was unusual. He told her she deserved all the credit for the carefreeness of his face. If she didn't believe him, she should see his memories of the ten days with Carla, or of the Janet Lawrence episode, the Elaine Ratazzi episode, the Jill One, Jill Two, or Jill Three episodes.

She lay in his bed as if it were her bed. But the possibility that his remarkably unscuffed life contained some kind of irresponsible future was what she had to put aside as too big and distant to worry about; the possibility that, barely having been hurt, he was innocently concealing—she perhaps now helping him to conceal—harm. Harm to her, to himself, to someone else. She took it no further. She would be reminded of the possibility not when he referred to the women of his past (his affairs hadn't lasted long enough for him to do lasting damage, she supposed. People survived rejection. Men had survived hers, she theirs), but when he presented a new plan for their doing something together. He had not recently asked her to move in with him.

He was asking her instead to be out with him, all over the place —a movie, lunch, or dinner safely off the beaten track, Staten Island, they could take separate ferries; meeting by accident next summer in Finland, or anywhere she'd like. What about going to the Meri Mini Players, an auction of English pottery, a rock concert? Wherever he was without her, which was everywhere but his apartment, her absence distracted him. He was dying to be in the world with her. He understood the problem but insisted she was being too cautious. That's because she had to be cautious for two, she said. Above all, of course, he wanted to get them to the opera. They had already missed the season's good *Traviata*s. Would she, seriously, think about *Rigoletto* on December fifth, a Wednesday? *L'Italiana in Algeri,* a Saturday matinee, December eighth? *Tales of Hoffmann,* believe it or not, on December eleventh, a Tuesday, or the nineteenth? *Tristan* in January? In January, she told him, she would be published and unable to leave her house. (Death by publication had already begun. Two advance reviews lacking enthusiasm were tinted with a useless respect.) It wasn't that she didn't want to do things with him, she wanted to, but how could it be worth taking the chance? It was ridiculous, he said, that he had been out with her husband but not with her. He compromised: they would sit way the hell up in the Family Circle; maybe she'd feel better about going with him if she couldn't see the stage well. The Family Circle was no help, she said. Curtis had plenty of poor clients, any one of whom might recognize her. Then they could sit separately, he proposed. He just wanted to be there with her.

On the first day of her period, they went to see *Le Sex Shop,* the noon show, at the 23rd Street Cinema, on Eighth Avenue, entering separately, meeting in the next-to-last row. They had a sandwich afterward at a luncheonette near the theater.

"See? Not a soul. You're not nervous."

"Yes. I am. There are no strangers anywhere. I've seen no one unfamiliar."

He laughed. "Come on."

"This is not to be taken as a precedent."

"I love you too much to let you irritate me."

"Shh."

Otherwise, he couldn't have been more thoughtful and steady unless she'd let him be. He always got to his house before her, or within two minutes, so that she didn't have to stand in his hallway feeling like the one person at a party no one is talking to. His lovingness seemed an extension of his punctuality. His first and last interest was in being with her. He was untemperamental, as trustworthy as he had told her he would turn out to be. No melodramas. No untimely phone calls. In bed, he touched her with a concentration she had never felt on anyone's hands or lips or tongue. What he did to her he did as if she were at the moment doing it to him. When he drew out of her, he winced. So did she. He held her with as much interest as he stroked or kissed her anywhere.

The subjects of *Ecuador* and its nonsuccessor were less irritable to his touch than they were to her own; she had exempted him from intrusiveness. One day, he handed her a typed list of all the South and Central American countries, as a source of ideas for further work. "You can do country by country," he said. "Everybody needs a specialty." Instead of smiling in the miffed way she hated more than her mouth muscles did, she was pleased by his joke, giddily played with it. But the puns—on Uruguay, Montevideo, Peru, Lima, Chile—came out thin and silly.

On December first, a Saturday (Curtis off with little Curtis), during a post-sex doze, Alan said to her, "Your nightmare about hanging on to the wing of the airplane—what about that for a novel?"

"Are you leaving me?"

"What a strange question. Why do you ask me that? Open your eyes. Look at me."

She did. "Isn't that funny? I can't imagine why I said that. Because I was half asleep."

"Are you leaving *me?* Why should such a question have crossed your mind?"

"It doesn't have anything to do with you, with leaving you."

"It must have been my mentioning the airplane."

"What made you think of the airplane in the first place?"

"I think about it all the time. It gives me pangs. It makes me want to guard you."

"You're guarding me at the moment to my complete satisfaction. I don't feel like writing another novel."

"I want to guard you all the time and forever. I would like to make everything you want possible, and to make you want everything I want."

"What could the novel be? Just a girl hanging on to an airplane? From sixteen through senility?"

"I don't know. Maybe it's just a poem. That's *your* job."

"In a way, it's odd I've never thought of it myself. Maybe because it sounds like science fiction. Betsarella zips from planet to planet on the wing of a plane, seeking her missing parents, Gurk and Za."

"Not bad."

"I hate science fiction. Detest! 'Sci-fi.' I hate hardware, Mission Control, Apollo, all that."

"That's not quite science fiction."

"I think you've given me an idea. A science-fiction novel without any science. It would take place among planets, but as if on earth. Or under earth. Like Orpheus or someone."

"*Orfeo* was one of the very first operas, if not *the* first. Seriously."

"We'll collaborate. A novel with music. You sing the novel on accompanying records."

"To collaborate, we would have to live together. Otherwise, there's not time."

"We'll get an office. Then I won't have to sneak seeing you. We'll have a queen-sized couch in our office."

"I have not brought it up for a long time. I have been extremely patient."

"I'm not giving you an award for patience just yet."

"Do you see that I love you with my head screwed on straight?"

"Yes to the first part, maybe to the second."

"Do you love me?"

"Yes, still. After all these weeks. I'm afraid I do. Every day, when you ask me the question, I am reminded that I love you."

"Allrightallrightallright. If Curtis left you, or if Curtis flew off to the big courtroom in the sky, would you move in with me?"

"If the apartment next door were vacant, I'd move in there."

"Not economical. What do you think would happen if you told him you wanted to be on your own?"

"That's what I'd like to know. I keep my ears open for clues all the time."

"In a way, after all, he's left *you*."

"Maybe."

"Nothing new has happened or been said?"

"Nope."

"Why don't you talk to him?"

"Because I have you to talk to. Because you and I have such voluptuous conversations most of the time. I feel that everything about you and me is voluptuous most of the time."

"That is a wonderfully nice thing to say. Why don't you talk to him about separating, is what I mean."

"I would prefer if you did it for me."

"Okay. At the Oak Bar."

"I'm kidding."

"It doesn't seem exactly my place. But I would, if that's what it took."

"Listen. Won't I keep for a while? Take the long view. I'm still a little drowsy, aren't you?"

Betsy got home at three-fifteen to wait to hear from Curtis. Curtis called at five, saying he had tried her earlier. He was extending the day with his son to go to an early dinner at the Cattleman and another movie, and then he was going to see Jack Mansfield at the Hilton for less than an hour. He should be home by eleven at the latest. She said fine, she would stay home and go to bed early.

She delayed calling Alan. She didn't want him to skip his concert to be with her, and she didn't want him to ask her to go with him. She wanted to be alone in her house. She would stick her nose in the TV. There was chicken in the refrigerator, wine. She would make salad. She called Alan to tell him the evening's layout and said she wanted to stay home and do nothing. Not think about anything but him. Lounge, slouch, TV. She would see him Monday, possibly tomorrow. Did he mind? Was he hurt? Because he shouldn't be. No, he said.

He called her back an instant after they had hung up. "Change your mind?"

"Once it starts, I'm going to want to change my mind. Once you're no longer available to call. As of now, I am adamant. Adamantine."

"Okay. Do you love me?"

She laughed, but her eyes were suddenly wet, and she filled with exhilaration. "I do. And what's more, I'm glad you love me."

"Are you crying? Shall I come up and give you a kiss?"

"It's thirty blocks out of your way. Sixty, round trip."

"I'll be there a little after six for one minute. All right?"

"I'll want you to stay."

"In that case, I'll be able to leave. What are you doing for food?"

She told him. She was elated at the idea of his coming to give her a kiss, coming solely to give her a kiss. She meant to do something while she was waiting for him, but she couldn't figure out what it was supposed to be. She flounced through the newspaper, reviewed the unpromising TV page. Maybe she should go to the concert with Alan, or go home with him, cook dinner with him. Or should she compose a farewell letter to Curtis? It occurred to her that since Alan had said he was coming to give her a kiss, she had not imagined Curtis coming home and surprising them. The buzzer sounded at ten to six. "It is Alonzo, a penniless student," said the voice in the intercom.

"Alan?"

"*C'est moi.*"

She buzzed open the downstairs door. She watched him springing up the stairs, dark overcoat, smiling at her. She let him in and shut the door. As they looked at each other over their kiss, pleased, she wanted to leave with him or to have him stay if he could stay permanently. She didn't want to live with him but wanted him to live with her?

"I brought you dessert." He held out a paper bag to her. "Vanilla, hot fudge, whipped cream, walnuts."

She took the bag. "You are sweeter than it. Come in the kitchen. I'll put it away. Would you like some? Or some chicken?"

"I have a cab waiting. My mother invited me for a quick dinner. Want to come? Come with me. I'll bring you home to them."

"You haven't said anything to them, I hope. About me."

"No. They never ask anything any more, anyway. I cannot tell you how I would love to surprise them with you, if you were free."

"Tonight I'm free." She smiled, annoyed with herself.

"I mean free." He gave a wistful grimace.

"Maybe I will be. Your cabdriver is going to be joining us up here." At that moment, a horn squawked twice. "Go." She kissed him again. "Thank you for my dessert. I will think of you with each mouthful."

"Shall I call you during intermission?"

"Probably better not. Maybe I'll be able to see you tomorrow. I don't know. Curtis's pornographer is in town."

"Then you must come."

"Do you love me?"

He laughed, looking like a surprised winner. Then he hugged her. "I will give you the answer tomorrow. In the meantime, take the long view."

After dinner on her bed, with the sundae in the freezer for her to look forward to, Betsy was luxuriating in an hour-long TV drama about an elderly, sadistic, crippled multimillionaire

155

whose young blonde wife was trying to have him murdered. Late in the drama, the multimillionaire's private plane came in to land at his private airport, in Arizona, where sycophants awaited him, along with the blonde young wife and her hot-eyed boyfriend, the rich man's nephew. At the instant the plane touched down, Betsy's brain swelled in a violent rush (she was scared to move), filling with black sky, the black wind, her plane, the stars, then, close-up, populated planets, blue people, black people, bright yellow people on the moon, chasms on the moon, buckling bridges over the chasms, bright yellow people sliding off the bridges, as if involuntarily skating. The planet China, the planet Africa, the planet North America, everything would be the same but different, the earth tossed into the universe, the Chinese filling the U.S., Canada, Central and South America; South and Central Americans packing Scandinavia; Africans running Europe. Someone inside a plane. Not hanging from a wing, or not until later. Inside a plane, alone, being flown by someone invisible, hidden, unknown. Maybe the plane was leaking fuel. Or a spaceship, if necessary. She could love science if she had to, hardware, Mission Control. While she was writing *Ecuador,* studying maps, history, climate, natural resources, annual this and that, the lackluster country, way high up on her list of lackluster countries before her dream, had stayed climactically glamorous and significant, throbbing and blinking with messages. Predestined. Like Alan's opera house. Like fiction itself when what you recognized was something you'd never seen before. Nothing more unlikely than the magnetic appearance of Ecuador in her life could occur, she sometimes thought, unless it were to be the actual reappearance of her parents, which she had often imagined so vividly that she would wonder if they were actually dead. "Quito" and "Ecuador" had bred in a box on her desk, a dream growing in daytime, in real life, visible and touchable. The kind of experience that made the heart feel important, famous.

Walking so as not to jiggle anything in her head, Betsy went into the study and, with the same caution, sat. She scribbled almost a page in her notebook before she recognized that she was lifting the pattern of *Ecuador* to outer space. Embarrassed, but sidestepping dismay with a sharp shake of her head, she remembered what she had improvised to Alan that afternoon. *Ecuador* had been escape. This would have to be pursuit. Endangered pursuit of parents, kidnapped parents, a kidnapped family, maybe, a husband, someone beloved. But no Gurk and Za. Real names. No science fiction, but not no science. Science and fiction. There would be other passengers on the plane, or spaceship; maybe they were the missing family, behind sealed doors, dead, or conversing, laughing, screaming. Whispering. Captive. On each planet-country she visited, she would have an adventure that threatened her mission or her life. The plane would be a brain in the dark, always in danger of permanent darkness, not crashing, but extinction, disappearance. Other planes might eventually be discovered following hers, shark-planes or guardian-planes. One planet could be overrun by starving wolves, raping wolves. Or cows, predatory cows that moved as rapidly as panthers. One planet could be overrun by Joan Crawford. The book would have to be funny from time to time. If there were five adventures, two of them, or the middle one, would be comical, in the manner of a sinister comic book. The adventurer didn't need to be female. Have it a boy, sixteen, a young man, twenty-one. Neil Armstrong. Jack Armstrong. Jeff Jackson. Tom. Ted. Ron. Ron? Ronald? Ron Malone. Ron Malone exposed to various traps and seductions, seduction by hermits, seduction by murder. Lust. Incest. Guilt. Watch out for allegory. This could be one repulsive allegory. Avoid Seven Deadly Sins, Four Humors. The crucial thing would be to make it dangerous, perilous, floorless. It would have to be real, as real as daytime life, as real as daytime life carefully mixed with nightmares. As ifs coming true. Ron Malone fighting for his life. As real as someone forcing you off the edge of the earth, off a planet. She would prefer a Boeing 747 to a spaceship. She would land a 747 on the moon. She would read all the astronaut stuff. She would adjust the fiction to the science after research.

Everything on the planets would be the same as on the earth, but different, remade. When Ron Malone got back to earth, the earth would be stripped, like an emptied house. He would live on the plane, alone, or not alone, humming through space. The plane would be his planet, a mobile home. She sketched out, more or less skimpily, five adventures. She wrote, "Happy ending?" She returned to the bedroom, the TV talking to itself. She kept it on as she got ready for bed, and avoided thinking about what she had written down, fearing it would fail her. She watched the television set more than she watched the television, until Curtis got home. She went to meet him at the hall closet. He hung up his sheepskin coat. She followed him into the kitchen, now remembering the sundae in the freezer. "How is little Curtis?"

"Not so little and not so good. I think from now on you might call him just plain Curtis. I'll know who you mean."

"Okay. There's a sundae in the freezer. I bought it earlier, but I don't feel like it now. You're welcome to it." She stood by the sink, watching Curtis from behind studying the refrigerator shelves. In boots and jeans and a sweater, in this case an unbecoming honey-colored turtleneck that feminized him, he always looked as if he were wearing borrowed clothes. She preferred him dressed up. She had never told him.

He brought out the sundae. "My God. A mountain of sinfulness. Don't you want some? Why did you bring this into the house?"

"You start. I doubt it." Standing, he began to eat it. She hoped Alan would be amused. Curtis eating the sundae made a ménage à trois with two people missing.

"How was your day?" he asked. His feet were crossed. He looked into the sundae as if it were impertinent, and dug up another spoonful of it.

"It was all right. What's wrong with your son?"

"He's not getting on with his stepfather. I'm going to have to do something."

"Like?"

158

"He says Roberts teases him about his reading. He's having reading problems. I'd like to strangle Roberts."

"What's wrong with Roberts?"

"Nothing new. He's a son-of-a-bitch." Curtis laughed. "How's that? Making fun of a nine-year-old boy with a reading problem. I've got to talk to Antoinette. I've got to get the visitation agreement revised and spend more time with Curtis."

"Antoinette doesn't help?"

"Evidently she tells Curtis not to be so thin-skinned."

She would have liked to show more interest, but any further questions or comments from her about Antoinette would draw Curtis quickly past criticism of his first wife to criticism of Betsy's unwillingness to be a mother. Or so it had been. "How was Mansfield?"

"Mansfield. I have to spend part of the afternoon with him tomorrow. He's taking an evening flight. He says he wants to meet you, by the way." Curtis looked at her briefly, and went back to eating the sundae.

Her cheeks were heavy with heat. "Me? Why?"

"He needs writers. Wants you to write for him. The authors' names are pseudonymous, so you wouldn't have to worry about that, and you could make a pile."

"What did you tell him?" Her heart was bouncing across her chest.

"I'm just kidding, for God's sake. Don't you want to finish this?"

"No, thank you."

He sealed the container, returned it to the freezer. She moved out of his way as he came toward the sink to rinse the spoon. He ran the water. "Okay. I'm beat," he said.

"I have to clear the dishes off the bed."

"Don't overdo. What dishes?"

"From dinner."

He was behind her as they walked down the hall. "How many for dinner?"

"We were just eight." She was relieved to see that she had

159

turned off the study light. It was as if her new idea were as important to protect as the secret of her and Alan. She did not want her husband's approval.

On Sunday, when Betsy phoned Alan, she told him how his suggestion had spilled all over her brain. Cauliflower au gratin. She felt semi-resistant, inhabited by strangeness. The situations and scenes she had sketched were uncomfortably unfamiliar. She was going to have to do a lot of reading to get comfortable. Back issues of Curtis's *Scientific American*. She would go to the Public Library tomorrow morning. She wouldn't be sure she knew what she was doing until she could use space travel and planetary information to feed the events of her novel and, at the same time, the information began to cause and control the events on its own. "It may not work. It may not work. But it feels as if it's supposed to happen. So thank you. I'm going to call my seven-forty-seven the Alan Hoffman."

Alan laughed. "No you're not." He said he would bring home clips from *Newsworthy*'s morgue and books from the *Newsworthy* library, if she needed them. She could do her research at his house if she liked. Also, she should visit the Planetarium. Also the Space Museum in Washington. He'd meet her there for the day. "I am thrilled, needless to say. When do I lose you?"

"I don't want it to be you or it. I need both. Each should benefit from the other."

He laughed again. "You sound absolutely unlike yourself."

"It's just love, love, love. Let's talk about it later. I can be down in an hour. We don't even need to talk about it. I don't plan to get lost. Except possibly in the Planetarium, where I haven't set foot for twenty-five years. A novel is not a substitute. You are not a substitute. I'll see you in a little while." When she hung up, she tightened her skin against a giddiness in her cells. She sensed a shifting in the cells of the future, a movement of curtains against her eyes. Curtis about to announce a change. She imagined herself answering in freedom, whatever he said. A huge gate swung open, she passing through it, with all her belongings following on a truck—her desk and her typewriter, bureau, clothes on hangers. Alan, in a white suit, waited on the other side, arms out to her, a long view, a lawn succeeded by fields, a horizon of tranquil hills, green and sunny.

Before she left for the library on Monday morning, she had to phone Turnbull to tell him her idea. Offhand, it sounded grand to him. He asked her to give him fifty or sixty pages and something of an outline. She had been making herself scarce. What, he wondered, had happened to their celebratory lunch? Now he had the satisfaction, at least, of knowing she had been up to something useful. He had rung her several times at home, but no answer. She accepted his offer of lunch a week from tomorrow, Tuesday the eleventh. She would cancel it, press of work, if she couldn't see Alan earlier or later that day. She would not give up a moment of him that she wasn't spending on work.

The next day, Alan brought home tear sheets from *Time, Newsweek,* and *Newsworthy* on the space flights, as well as an astronomy textbook and some astronautical books she had found unavailable at the library. Also, a gift, *Events in Space,* by Willy Ley, for grades nine and up.

On Wednesday, they both arrived in his lobby at the same moment. They pretended not to know each other. In the elevator, he grabbed her. She let out a minuscule scream, and they kissed most of the way up. As he unlocked his door, she asked, "Don't you think people have done it in elevators?"

"Going up, absolutely. On the way down, you have to assume that any pesky voyeur could get on at any floor." They came into the foyer. "Are you asking this for your novel?"

"Who can tell? I got three hours of reading done this morning. I keep interrupting myself with ideas."

He kissed her on the forehead. "Congratulations."

"Not yet."

He got rid of their coats. Turning back to her, he said, "I have a lee-tle surprise. A small discussion will be required." He snapped a heavy-looking white envelope from the breast pocket of his gray tweed jacket. (The jacket supervised a cobalt-blue shirt and a canary-yellow woolen tie.) "Now, I have here"—he flapped the envelope—"fourteen opera tickies, seven sets of seats for performances starting this coming Saturday afternoon and going over the following ten days or so. All the seats are separate. The closest we are, in one case, is across an aisle from each other. In most cases, you're a row or two ahead of me, or behind me, depending on how we arrange it. All the seats are in the Dress Circle or Balcony or Family Circle. One set has us in Family Circle boxes on opposite sides of the house, facing each other across the whole fucking *theater,* at the very top, a mile high."

"You sound as if you're not making this up. May I see them?"

"If you won't abuse them." He unsealed the envelope and handed it to her. Inside were seven sealed ticket envelopes, each marked in Alan's hand with the abbreviated name of an opera and the date and seat numbers of the tickets within.

She gave him back the envelope, frowning as sweetly as she could. "So expensive."

"But they're each inexpensive. Which in fact makes them harder to get. I'll have no trouble unloading what I want to. You're not to worry about that. You can let me know as soon as you know Curtis's plans. There's no reason I know why this Saturday afternoon shouldn't be as free for you as most recent Saturday afternoons have been. I'm assuming that would be a little easier for you than evening. If we go this Saturday, *L'Italiana in Algeri,* we hear Horne. The opera's light and brilliant. It's never been done at the Met before this season, and it's not long. I recommend this Saturday." He returned the envelope to his pocket as if it were a sword. "Okay?"

She could see his tight smile withholding hope for her agreement. "I can hardly say no to such imaginative stubbornness, can I? You only mean for me to come to one, not seven."

"I mean one, of course, for the time being."

"Would you just explain to me the advantage of our going when we are not sitting next to one another?" She feared her expression might be too benevolent to conceal her irritation.

"What do you *mean?* When can we sit next to each other? You won't. I'm ready to sit next to you tonight, all the time, with your arm next to mine on the armrest. I think about it all the time, imagining you loving being there as much as the movies. There's no advantage to this at all. It's ridiculous. I know it's ridiculous. I just thought you would find it easier. And funny, maybe."

"It's a little as if we'd be slipping into the theater on the lookout for some assassin, like agents."

"I'm not going to force it. I want you to come into the dining room and write down the dates for yourself. If you decide you can't do it, you have my guarantee I'll forgive you. But I hope you'll do it. You have a choice of one *L'Italiana,* two *Tales of Hoffmann,* one *Rigoletto,* one *Magic Flute,* and two *Simon Boccanegra*s."

"The point isn't what. It's how. When. I'm going to try." Could she possibly ask him not to come with her? Or let her take someone? And she'd report to him? "What do we do at intermission? Strike up a conversation?"

"That's what we did the first time, after all. The fact remains, you know, that we spend almost all of our time very far apart. I just want to break you in." He put his hand on her shoulder, smiling as if the issue were amusing him.

"Here I am." She embraced his waist. "So near and yet so near."

He unbelted her embrace and held her hands at her hips. "I just want you to write down the dates. It is truly disgusting that you and I don't do anything at all together outside the house. And you are the one being stubborn. The world is being deprived of the affection we would show it together." He escorted her from the foyer, his left hand high on her back. She felt as if he were showing her into a roomful of people she didn't know.

She learned from Curtis that evening that he was going to see Antoinette, and probably Roberts too, on Saturday afternoon. A client had given Curtis house seats for Saturday night's preview of the *Pajama Game* revival. Did she want to join him?

"Of course. Did you have someone else in mind you wanted to take?"

"Just because I have the tickets doesn't mean you want to see it."

"I'd like to. Thanks." If there was such a thing as a day tense with entertainment, Saturday would be it. Still, she had better get the opera over with. It would probably be easier for her than she was imagining it would be.

On Friday, Alan gave her her ticket, the one for the Family Circle box.

"Do you realize that today is Pearl Harbor Day?" she asked him. "I just realized."

"Today, not tomorrow. Look. The worst that will happen is that someone sees you at the opera, alone. It's such a remote seat, I don't think anyone will see you at all, except me."

"What do I wear? If I get home before Curtis, I can't be all dressed up if I've been to *Bang the Drum Slowly* at Loew's 83rd. And forgive me, but what about intermission? Do we ignore each other?"

"Wear what you would wear to the movies. I'm glad to give up my fantasy of you in your wine suit. At intermission, we'll meet at the bar up there, behind the Family Circle, and we'll play it by ear. Everything will be fine. I promise."

On Saturday, she waited out Curtis's departure, shredding the minutes as if they were Kleenex. She rushed into the wine suit and ruffled blouse she'd worn the night they'd first met. She would tell Curtis, if it became necessary, that she had dressed early for their evening, since she assumed he would be wanting to go out to dinner. She got to her seat with twenty minutes to spare. She saw no Alan across the theater in a Family Circle box, unless he had disguised himself with a wavy blond wig and glasses. Her oblique view of the stage was so steep, and the ceiling of the theater lay so weirdly near her head, she could imagine she was on a planet, or nesting under one. The ceiling was an inverted lake of golden pancakes, the roof of God's very own pancake franchise. Chandeliers hung below her, clouds.

Her boxmates were assembling, cordially minding their own business. Still no Alan across the filling chasm. Like a good girl, she studied the synopsis of the opera in her program, but the plot was either too simpleminded or too complicated to comprehend. Zulma, Mustafa, Ali, Elvira, Lindoro, Isabella, Taddeo. Kaimakan. Pappadummies. A chorus of eunuchs. She would like to ask him, her tutor, how was this opera like life? A touch on her shoulder. She jumped, looked around and up. Black blazer, scarlet tie. "Welcome. Have a good time," he whispered. He sprang away, an acquaintance in a jungle. He emerged a moment later on the opposite bank, bowing his head to her before sitting down, and then flourishing a pair of opera glasses, with which he dipped around the theater, stunt-flying, slowing, stopping to include her—a kiss of a pause. She held her program over her face.

The set was surprisingly simple and charming, the chorus of eunuchs intentionally funny. She was not used to drollery on the opera stage, nor to this lack of fuss in a production. When Marilyn Horne appeared, she astonished Betsy with the informality of her power. Standing there, she shot off notes like a markswoman firing a rifle at a cascade of targets and hitting them all. The ovation confirmed for Betsy that she was witnessing an event. She remembered the great ones her parents would recall at the dinner table—Caruso, Josef Hofmann, Babe Ruth, Toscanini, Joe DiMaggio. She herself had seen only DiMaggio, once, from a seat as high as this one was, with her father, in Yankee Stadium. It occurred to her that she could protect her enjoyment by leaving at intermission, beating Curtis home, she hoped, getting out of her suit and into movie clothes, home clothes.

She took her coat with her when the houselights came up. In the lobby, she approached Alan, who was smilingly approaching her through the people closing in on the bar. "Pardon me, Mr. Opera," she said. "You don't know me, but I just want to say I'm having a great time. It's impressive how elegant such silliness can be."

"Elegant, yes, but by no means silly, if you think about it, my dear. Act One—a woman on a search for her shipwrecked lover. Fidelity? Perseverance for the sake of love? She finds lover. Act Two—lovers will escape from their captor, from under his very nose, because they are *meant* to be happy, and they sail home to Italy and freedom. It's not such a far move from *Fidelio,* where a wife saves her husband from death. He's in prison. Maybe love is an escape from death. It's brilliant, in fact. I didn't catch your name. May I take your coat?"

"Ginger's the name. Discretion's my game. Will you forgive me if I go home? We will continue this interesting talk soon? I really hate to go, but if Curtis comes back perturbed from his meeting with Antoinette and Roberts, it would be just as well for me to be there."

"Leave now?"

"I think it's a good idea." She had never seen him glower.

"Did you *plan* this, to leave now?"

"I did not. I'm enjoying myself. But it seems smarter to be there. I'll be too nervous staying. I'll probably be able to see you tomorrow, anyway. And Monday. And Tuesday. And so forth. Will you forgive me?"

"What can I say?"

"Say you understand. Don't be mad."

"It seems awful to let you go when I can't kiss you goodbye."

"Shh. Tomorrow. Monday. Tuesday. I told Turnbull-Bore I would 'lunch' with him Tuesday, but I'm planning to cancel it or see you after or before, or both. Whatever is best for you."

"You have to work on your book in the morning. Better for me is I see you every day and every night. Better for me is I see you tomorrow."

"If I can, I will, as always."

"You *didn't* plan this?"

"Not until ten minutes ago. Are you listening to me? If you'll invite me, I'd love to see the rest of this sometime. Sitting next to you. I loved it. It's like a musical in Italian."

166

"There are a few more this season. Three more." He shrugged at her.

"Please don't look disappointed. This was a risk for me."

"I want to stop *risking*, Betsy."

Did they look as if they were having a fight? "I know. Me too. I am trying harder than you think. Getting home now is part of it." She was whispering now, and feeling silly.

"What does that mean?"

"Because I think he's in the process of rearranging his life in a way that may help us. I'll speak to you tomorrow as soon as I can, or Monday. We're just at the beginning. Don't spoil it."

"Why didn't you tell me any of this?"

"Because he hasn't told me anything. Just a hint about the custody agreement. I don't know what it means yet, but it has possibilities. We can't talk about this now."

"I didn't bring it up. Should I go home now, too, and wait for you to call?"

"No! I won't be able to. Stay here."

"You have got to come tomorrow." His head moved forward in emphasis.

"You mustn't forget that you are where I want to be." She kissed her fingers and touched his cheek, giving him a quick, hopeful smile. "Goodbye." She felt his fingers touch her back as she took off, trying to keep her or pat her. She looked around and waved. She could be home by four-fifteen or four-twenty. Had he said this was not a long opera? She wished she'd worn jeans.

She imagined in the taxi that she was racing home because she had been told her house was afire: Miz Ring! Oh, Miz Ring! The day was turning the color of stone but remained sunny on top. No snow, naturally. December nowadays was merely the prolonged nude end of fall. Snow was old, and Alan loved old things. If she lived with Alan, would it start snowing by Christmas again? Actually, she had never cared much for snow. But if there was no snow, why should anyone have to bother with the

167

cold? Snow made the cold less cold. If she lived with Alan, might she change her mind about having a child? Little Ticket? Tyke-et. Tykette, if a girl. She had the cab let her off at Ninety-fifth and Columbus. If Curtis should see her, she wanted to be walking—some errand or other. She mustn't walk too fast, though, or he'd wonder why the hurry. But she was in a hurry. She walked fast, noticing the heaviness of her coat, along Ninety-fifth. Garbage like stiff clothes in the street. A nap was what she wanted. If Curtis found her in bed, frittering the day away, she'd be safe. She hoped Alan was not sulking in his box. She would sneak him a call later, if she had a chance, to make sure he'd calmed down, cheered up. If he was not sulking, she wanted to be next to him, being knocked dead by Marilyn Horne, pleasing him. She did not want to go out tonight. There were so few places it was good to be. Bed with Alan, bed alone, her desk again these days, movie theaters. Where she most wanted to be at this moment, she supposed, was in Alan's bed; by herself in Alan's bed. Even more than that, she wanted to be out of her suit.

At her building, she looked up to see if Curtis was looking down from the living room (parlor, he liked to say). Unless he was peeking, he wasn't there. Would he jump out at her from the closet, the bathroom, with a "Yah!"? Nothing to do now but do it. She entered the dusky vestibule, remembered that she had already gotten the mail that day, eaten an English muffin, seen half an opera. She took the stairs alertly, peering up, over her right shoulder. She unlocked her door, listened, called a weak "Hello?" Closing the door gently, she listened again. Bedroom door open, sad late light in there, like a deaf relative. Study door open. She threw her coat on a hanger as if she were concealing a person in the closet, and took off her jacket and unbuttoned her blouse as she made for the bedroom. Maybe Curtis wasn't coming home, had run away with Antoinette and their son, leaving an enraged Roberts, a baffled Roberts, a repentant Roberts, who would call her, Betsy, wondering if she knew where they were.

168

The bathroom door was open, the bathroom empty. She dropped her blouse and jacket on the bed and sat down on the dark-blue spread to remove her half-boots. Her right foot was in her hands when she heard the jingling of keys in the outside hall. She turned on the bed-table lamp and stood up, her eye on the Cornell sweat shirt hanging over the back of her chair in the study. She was in there when the hall door opened, and pulling down the sweat shirt when the hall door slammed as if it had keeled over. She next found herself, with a pounding heart, standing in the doorway of the bedroom watching Curtis at the hall closet. "Hi," she said. "How did it go?" Did her coat smell of outdoors? Had he seen her on the street? Followed her to the opera and back? He clumped toward her. His face was surly with concentration on something fixed before his eyes. He didn't seem to be looking at her, though he looked straight at her as he walked straight toward her. She stepped back to let him pass, so he wouldn't shove her. He had come home like this last year, when an impressive client, from Curtis's class at Princeton, had accused Curtis of padding his bill and refused to pay it. Curtis had taken Courtenay Rostand's necktie and pulled it over his shoulder and driven him out of the office, using knees and elbows. He had wanted to kill him, he said.

Curtis removed his suit jacket and threw it on the bed beside Betsy's jacket and blouse. He tapped the back of his left fist against his bureau and walked by her, out of the room, down the hall, twitching his knuckles against the walls. She felt both impatient and foolish watching him pace. If his anger had nothing to do with her, she wanted the chance to be sympathetic. She had to wait for him. He walked at her again, in his white shirt, brown-and-white-checked tie, with the same sullen display of preoccupation, raising his knuckles to the walls with each step. He walked by her again. She realized then that she was choosing to stay in the doorway. She noticed the wide rear of his hair, his wide waist. He sat down on the bed, leaning back on his hands, squinting into the study.

"What is wrong, Curtis? For God's sake!"

"We have to move. Or I do. I need an apartment with a bedroom for Curtis. Alias little Curtis, your stepson."

"All right. Let's discuss it. You don't have to act crazy." Why had he not asked about her discordant outfit or her blouse and jacket on the bed?

Still without looking at her, and sounding cheerful, even satisfied, he said, "Roberts readily admitted that he had teased Curtis about his reading. He hoped it would shake the 'lad' out of his 'slump,' were the terms he used. He said I should remember that it was not his, Roberts's, responsibility in the first place, but primarily mine, as I was the absent father. He observed that while he could not of course help but be grateful that I had run out"—Curtis, evidently amused, shifted his gaze to Betsy—"on Antoinette—'run out' is what he said—he did not in principle believe in divorce, for just this reason, just this sort of situation. No apology whatever for his behavior. Roberts looked to me as though he were practicing on me how to be insufferable, not that he needs practice. Exercising his insufferability on me. I wanted to punch him, knock him off his Guccis. You know, a charming, impetuous Cary Grant sort of knockout. I thought perhaps a touch of impetuosity might land me back in your good graces, but then I couldn't remember what they felt like, your good graces. So I didn't bother." The facetiousness in his smile was sprightly.

She found herself so startled by what he had said that she didn't know what to do at first, after her mouth opened. He had snuck up on her. Her lips felt strained. Was she smiling, too? "I think your instinct in wanting to punch him was fine. But I like your restraint more. I'm not particularly impetuous. I'm not an admirer of impetuosity. I don't know why you say that." One needed training for a conversation like this.

Now his smile appeared to be provocative. If there was a tinge of humility to it, she knew before he spoke that even the humility was hostile. "I only meant that a charming, impetuous, boyish act might atone for my vulgar ambition, my misplaced and unwelcome desire for your success."

His ornate talk was embarrassing her. She continued to feel an ache in her lips, but she assumed her smile no longer showed, if she had been smiling. "I don't know why you're looking so entertained. Your heavy sarcasm is unbecoming. Your desire for my success was not unwelcome. Is not unwelcome. You weren't being realistic about my book. You were bullying me." She had never said all of it before. She felt tardy.

He presented her once again with a pensive profile, his self-consciousness a target. Was this how Alan's histrionics behaved during their exit scenes? "How can someone like me be having a life that's suddenly such a mess?" he asked the study doorway.

"Why do you think your life is such a mess? Everybody's life is a mess somewhere. Who are you?"

He gave her his face again. He would not quit smiling, or smirking. "I realize that when I tell you I'm going to have to move, there's a possibility you're going to say you want to move with me."

She didn't know what she should say, what he was after.

"And there's a possibility you don't want to."

It was, she felt, as if she were trying to keep a closet door shut, and he were trying to pull it open, and he had just gained an inch in the tugging. If she said she wanted to move with him, she would be unhappy and a coward, and Alan would make her unhappier. If she told him she didn't want to move with him, or even if she temporized, she was out in the open, nowhere to hide. "Did you speak to your son, by the way? Before you left the Robertses'?" It was not an answer to his treacherously vague conjectures, but it was a question pertinent enough to require an answer—to divert him. When had she ever played 'for keeps' before? She'd never even used the expression until this moment.

Curtis had finally stopped smiling and looked friendlier. "I did." He sat forward on the bed and crossed his legs. "I spoke to him before speaking to Roberts. He said he didn't want to live there any more. I said I hoped to be spending more time with him. He said he wanted to move in with me, meaning us. I said I would do my best, but that that would be hard.''

''Of course, part of the problem is that Antoinette herself has more than a full-time job.''

''But you don't.'' The smile again.

He had just made an error, she was certain. She pocketed it for later use, if needed. It was probably illogical of her, but she felt safer now that he had made little Curtis's problem her fault. Keeping her voice levelly polite, she reached for another question. ''Why can't he continue sleeping here on the couch when he comes? You must have anticipated it when you moved here, that things might not stay the same with him, where he was. Or that things might not stay the same with you.''

''Before you moved in, when he stayed over he slept in this bed with me. And no, I didn't anticipate. I didn't anticipate remarrying, and I didn't anticipate marrying you. I thought maybe when we got married that at some point we'd move out of here and that I might rearrange the custody situation. But you were clearly not interested in him, so I backed off that, right? The way I've backed off having a child of our own. Early on, I wanted out of Antoinette so badly it may be I didn't think enough about him, where he would be sleeping at what age. I wanted a place that I wanted, it's quite true.''

''Seems fair.''

''I can't take care of him alone. If you and I move to an apartment with a bedroom for him, I still can't take care of him alone. He doesn't need that much care. He's nine years old.''

''I know his age.''

''He needs someone to be there when he comes home from school.''

''He doesn't have that now.''

''There's the housekeeper.''

They looked at one another steadily. She felt as if each pair of eyes were exerting opposition, that by the force of their eyes they kept what remained unsaid raised between them at the center of their gaze.

"I guess I could get a housekeeper if we move," he said. "You'd be home, with a housekeeper for him. Very cozy. It's not the money. It just seems silly. It would make you look silly. You'd better tell me, Betsy. What do you have in mind? We would need a study for you, I assume, if you wanted. Or perhaps you'd prefer to rent an office somewhere?"

"Why do you think I wouldn't move with you? What puts you in doubt?"

"The last six weeks, what else? We seem to have put a lot of distance between us." He stood up. Her heart lurched. The floor beneath her seemed to sink a few inches. With his hands in his pockets, he took two steps to the window, between the bed and the study door, keeping his back to her. The light outside was a clear black, ice-black.

"I would need time to decide." She pushed her jaw toward him and laid her hand on her bureau top.

He turned around. His hands stayed in his pockets. His dim smile made him look frail. "There we are, there we are. Why?"

"The last three or four months." She laughed a compressed, pointless laugh. "You know. The same problem as yours." She made herself keep her eyes on him.

"You believe we can't work any of this out?"

"Do you want to work anything out?"

"Does it make any difference if I want to?"

"I don't know." She shook her head. "It doesn't feel—"

"Do you have a boyfriend? Lover?"

"No."

"Is that the truth?"

"Yes. Do you have a girl friend?"

"No. But if I did, I wouldn't feel victorious anyway. I'm what's called a loser. I'm the kind of loser you wouldn't know it to look at. You know that kind?"

"I don't know why you say 'loser.' That's ridiculous."

"I appreciate the reassurance. Were you at the movies this afternoon?"

"Yes." She nodded.

173

"I saw you running up the stoop just before, when my cab turned the corner. Think about tonight. I don't know what the hell to do. Excuse me." As he walked toward the bathroom he jerked his head at her as if he were dismissing her. He closed the door.

Betsy didn't move, except to take her hand off the bureau. She listened to his noise. Was he saying, "Piss on it?" How many times had she heard Curtis pee? A thousand? Fifteen hundred? And would this be the last? What would he say next? She could think of nothing to say.

The toilet flushed indecisively; as he came out, she decided not to say, "It's not flushed." Should she tell him what movie she'd been to, or would she sound as if she were trying to cover herself? He sat down on the bed again, near the bottom, his hands pressed to his knees, his head bent. She saw that he was hurrying to breathe. He was about to cry? She had never seen his eyes so much as moist. He laid his chest on the bed, his cheek on her jacket. "Unbelievable pain," he said, in a whisper that sobbed.

"What?" she said, and hurried to him, kneeling. His face was white, melting, dripping its own color. His eyes were squeezed shut and his mouth was in a stiff grimace, as if he had been seized by the most unbearable possible memory. She put her hand on his shoulder. His shirt was damp.

"Lift my legs on."

She stood and took hold of his knees, raising his legs fully onto the bed, watching to see that his torso didn't collapse off the edge. His fly was not zipped up. She heard a soft belch, and the gurgle of vomit. Vomit the color of mushroom soup covered the side of her jacket and hung in his beard like shreds of cloth in a bush. His eyes were still closed, much more relaxed, and his mouth loosely closed. He looked serious, but no longer as if he were being broken. He looked as if he were dead. "Curtis? Can you say what's wrong?" She put her hand on his shoulder again and the other on his hip and gently pushed him onto his back. His head nodded away from her. She pulled down his

174

smeared necktie and twisted his collar open, wiping her hands on the sides of her sweat shirt. Her face filled with heat. His chest, his belly, were not rising and falling. Flat. Still. How did he manage that, unless he were faking, or actually dead? She blew out a long, shaky breath and began to sweat. The smell of the vomit had settled in. She breathed with her mouth open, trying not to smell. The top of her soiled jacket lay under the top of his back. She looked at the bed-table clock. Ten past five. He would start breathing again within five seconds. If she opened the window, it might kill him. She put her hand on his belly. Still nothing. She climbed onto the bed from the bottom and held her hand in front of his nostrils. Holding her breath, she lowered her cheek to his nostrils. No breath reached her. She turned his wrist over, feeling for his pulse; undid the leather wristwatch band, felt again. If it was after five, the opera must be over. Not a long opera. His wrist was empty to her touch at all points. Too definite, this was. You can't close it off like this because of me. Because of anything. I am not your life. You are letting down your son. She yanked his shirt from his waist, thinking the sudden movement could wake him, and placed her palm on the hairiness of his belly. His belly remained as still as her hand.

PART
THREE

6

Alan had felt jarred into gloom by Betsy's departure during the intermission—by its abruptness, by its self-protectiveness, by her insensitivity. He would not have done it to her, been so deeply rude. In his seat again, he couldn't concentrate on the opera; the stage was a TV set playing in another room. More disheartening than her leaving was that, in leaving, she had given him something so distinct to criticize in her. It was as if *this* were the rudeness. Then he began to think about what she had said while leaving, and suspicion attacked his gloom, giving it an uncomfortable vitality. She'd been placating him, coddling, conning, condescending, by hinting at a serious future ("I am trying harder than you think. Getting home now is part of it"), babying him to soothe his resentment over her flight, being sweet to him so she would feel less guilty.

And then the knot unsnarled, so easily it was as if there had been no knot, as if he had imagined it. It was not in Betsy's character to coddle. He thought back over the times she hadn't coddled, over the moments at which she had taken pains to be blunt. It was partly her toughness that made her trustworthy. In any case, she would not have hinted at a serious future in exchange for his not being angry at her for leaving after one act of the opera. It didn't make sense on the face of it. It hadn't made sense for him to be angry, either. He had nearly forced her to go to the opera in the first place. She had been uncomfortable at going with him, and at going with him separately. He was left, now, apologetic and foolish, lacking Betsy to apologize to, but with her hint to hold on to. Behind it, Curtis's hint. Words that meant business. Rearranged custody agreement. Rearrangement of Curtis's life in a way that might help them. He'd missed the value, in his peevishness, of what she'd been saying. His undeserved relief embarrassed him.

Belatedly, he breathed Betsy's message as if it had blossomed into achievement, news. What to do when the opera was over? Go home for an hour, hoping to hear news from her, even though she had said she wouldn't be able to call? Try to get rid of his ticket for tonight? How to sneak a message to her letting her know he could be available? His heart felt like a tulip. He wanted to see her immediately, surprise her, reassure her with his most cherishing smile, present her with the head of his beheaded sulk. He left his seat before the curtain calls began, as he almost never did. Standing on the steps outdoors, overlooking the illuminated plaza, he felt awkward and conspicuous among the departing audience. He felt as if he were setting out but didn't know where to go. The enormous opera house behind him, emptying of fellow strangers, was his house. It struck him at the moment that the opera house was so nearly his house in fact that he normally took his sense of it as such for granted. His apartment was two blocks away but seemed as distant as Paris. In a few hours, he would be back here, for *Tales of Hoffmann*, ha ha. It would be his fifteenth *Hoffmann*. He might eat at The Ginger Man, O'Neals', *Poulailler*. He might take a trip up to Betsy's house in a cab, blow a kiss through the cab window at her living-room windows, then say to the cabdriver, I've changed my mind, not getting out here, take me back downtown. It made no sense, was of no use, but it would at least be safer than phoning her. He walked down the plaza, toward the streaking yellow gleam of taxis. But she would think it silly when he told her he had done it. He had no way of letting her know everything was all right. He could phone, whisper a message, and hang up, saying wrong number. But that wouldn't help him find out what was going on up there. Curtis might answer, or might be standing by the phone when Betsy answered. Betsy might not understand what he'd whispered. If he called, worry would ruin his evening. So with a thrust of his arm, he blew a kiss over rooftops to Ninety-fifth street and veered toward O'Neals', impatient, and embarrassed to be alone.

He deserted *Tales of Hoffmann* after the first act, having spent much of the hour reviewing Betsy's assemblage of uniquely high-class virtues, and choosing among domiciles and other circumstances of their future. Toward the end of the act, he became preoccupied with the sense that the opera house he was sitting in—his house—had sneaked loose from the city surrounding it and, like a six-decked ocean liner, was gliding down the Hudson toward the Atlantic. No one but he knew. On his way out, he stopped at a youthful, round, and radiant female standee and told her that seat O-4 was hers if she wanted it. "Oh, neat," she said, "do you have the stub?" He made as if he were seeking it in his pockets and couldn't find it. He had always included in his collection the stubs for performances he hadn't completed. There were very few such cases, for one thing, and it wasn't as if he had cheated the easy way, by ever including the stubs of those who attended performances with him. "Sorry," he said, "it's lost. I'm sure you won't be bothered." She thanked him. "Have fun," he said. He put on his overcoat in the lobby and left the opera house. Walking toward his apartment, he was thinking that within the year, months, a week, he would dump the whole ticket collection. A grand gesture, to show Betsy he had outgrown it. Maybe tonight, right now. Maybe that's why he was going home. To dump his stubs. But where? In the garbage, just like that? What would he do with the tank? Get fish? One huge fish? What *would* he do when he got home? What was the point of being restless at home when he could be restless at *Tales of Hoffmann?* He thought of going back to the opera, the audience party; he swallowed the idea when he pictured disinheriting the adorable standee he had just gratified. Of course, he could let her keep his seat, and stand in her place. (However, if she saw him, wouldn't she wonder how he had gotten back into the house if he didn't have his stub?) But, he decided, he was going home for a reason. His restlessness was a condition meant to yield an event. He wasn't any more superstitious or astrological or E.S.P.-oriented than his parents or sister (great believers in proof) were. Yet it was true of his life, he felt, that almost always when he had wanted or needed something to happen—even if for no other reason than that something was, at the moment, better than nothing—it had happened. When he was bored, something leaped; when he leaped, something awaited. Not that his luck had been remarkably good; rather, that in his life a lot of luck had occurred. His family lived on proof, he lived on luck, good and bad luck, on suspense, on expectation, satisfaction, disappointment, on daily playlets, scenes: he would or would not get the assignment taking him to Austria during the Salzburg Festival, such and such an article would or would not be approved, the performance would or would not be what it was cracked up to be. There were unexpected tickets to hot-ticket events, and expected tickets that he spurned. There was sexual drama more or less on demand: a pickup, a turn-down, a thrilling beginning, an intimate and painful ending. His mother had identified very early his need for what she called "noise." He had not been happy as a child when a party was over unless there was another party in the near future to look forward to. It had been, in his long bachelorhood, as if he were married to drama, and the father of little dramas. Until Betsy, he supposed, he had been able to imagine that his life had a reason for being, a significance, just because, when he had hoped for a new stranger to fall in love with, when he had wondered who was around the corner, he had usually found the ready stranger, the ready stranger had been provided, without delay. Fate had left it to him to get rid of the stranger, to lose the stranger, but had soon come up with another. Now that he had found a woman who was a friend, a woman he revered, a woman he needed, who had learned and remembered him, who knew him—known and remembered by Betsy he felt loved, beloved, safe, saved—fate was leaving it to him to keep her. No *addios*, no matter how tender. He would still be loving her in the spring. He would be loving her a year from now—ten, twenty, and forty years from now. He would always nourish her novels for her. He would be the constant "without whom" in her dedications, the man behind her scenes. He would never fail to give her reason to keep on loving him. He would do anything to make her happy, nothing to disappoint her. He wanted to know her when all her hairs were white. He wanted years and years to look back on with her, he wanted to collect reminiscences, establish a history. Their anniversaries, their restaurants, their illnesses, trips, apartments, their closets, their child. No child. No roller skates, no bats and balls. But in their closets, coats that knew each other. Their friends: their friends treating them as a couple, familiar with their shared and unshared habits, their quirks, their famous lovingness. ("How they dote on one another, those two.") She would love him so much straight through their remaining forty years that whenever he came home she wouldn't want to write any more, and he would make her keep on writing until dinner. He would cook their dinner, or order it in, or take her out, or eat alone if she decided to work through. She would love him so much that, when they were in bed for the night, she would often tell him she couldn't believe she was the same person she had been before she'd met him, the night of October 23, 1973, in the lobby at *Il Trovatore* ("The Troubador," he must point out to her, a pining serenader, just as he had been, yearning for her, until that night). And then they had gone to O'Neals', after Carla had run off, and when she and Curtis had left the restaurant, she had come back to apologize, they would recall, in case she'd been rude, and the next day, showing up at her house, he had alarmed and beguiled her at the same time, and she had taken the risk he had offered, and they had transformed one another into doting, infinitely intimate friends, praising their luck over the years. A faithful, encouraging, admiring couple. His face was between her legs, her hands on his head. (Hard to believe he had already been there, many times.) She was weeping with tenderness. They were curled up together, after her fifth, seventh, novel, ten, fifteen, twenty-five years from now, and she was saying to him, "If you died, I would die. When you die, at ninety-eight, I will die instantly, in your arms, Betsy Harris, novelist, age ninety-one." By the time Alan unlocked his apartment door, he had wiped his eyes twice, and he wanted her to be in his house at this instant, he wanted to embrace his salvation, his Betsy, his matchlessly original, sexy prize. His undeserved prize that made him worthy of her. He could not believe his luck.

He flicked on the foyer light and bolted the door. Now that he had arrived, it was, as usual, as if he expected her to be there, as if she lived there and should have been home, calling hello, coming out to him. His apartment was empty of someone other than himself. He hung up his coat, feeling tired, sad, already giving up to the desolation waiting to greet him in the dark rooms to his left, desolation lining both sides of his route, living room, kitchen, study, bedroom. He was turning from his foyer closet door, wondering what music to put on the turntable, to make himself feel either worse or better, when the phone rang, way off in the darkness. Alan broke for the study phone, the study nearer than the bedroom, deciding as he lunged through the living room that it was Bob Manners, or his mother. Or it was Roz, or Madeline Meltzer Pursey, neither of whose calls of over a month ago he had returned. Shoving on the dining-room light, seeing that the phone was on the table instead of the floor, he swooped to it, grabbing off the receiver before the fourth ring began. His "Hello" spilled out, half voice, half breath.

"Hi," Betsy said.

"Is something wrong?"

"What are you doing there?" She sounded exhausted, or deeply peeved, as if he had lied to her for the hundredth time about his plans.

"What do you mean? I just got home, on a hunch, praying you'd call. Where are you? You sound angry."

"I'm home. Curtis is dead."

Alan dropped his voice. "Asleep?"

"Dead. D-e-a-d."

He looked around the dining room to make sure he was home. He thought of sitting down; he remained standing. "Betsy?" He felt as if he were in the middle of a sentence, the point of which had disappeared on him.

"What?" she said.

Her tone made him feel as if he were failing her in some way.

"What happened? Are you kidding?" He sat down. "Are you all right?"

"He came home not more than a minute after I did this afternoon. We were talking, he went into the bathroom, came out sick, sat down on the bed, and died."

Alan gave his forehead three gentle punches with his fist. "Heart—heart attack?"

"Yes."

"Where is he now?"

"In the morgue at the Riverside. Waiting to be cremated. They're doing that tomorrow, in New Jersey."

Alan shook his head as if he were disagreeing with someone in the room. "Do people know? Are you calling people?" Was anyone with her?

"Antoinette, I called. Curtis's parents, in Woodmere. Curtis's doctor broke the news to them from here. I spoke to them after. The Monroes, the Simonsons. They're calling people. Cathy, Curtis's secretary, is calling people. Dwight Monroe has called *The Times*. Everything's being handled. I think Cathy is going to stay overnight with the Rings. She knows them better than I do."

185

He wanted to ask her again if this was all a joke, but it had gotten too far along in the conversation for that. His breath seemed to be sinking to his belly. Would there be a funeral? Would he attend? "How do you feel? Are you alone now?"

"I feel as if I'm going to be so exhausted I'll be sick. But I don't feel in the least bit tired yet. As soon as I remember what happened, I try to think of something else."

"Like what?"

"Nothing seems to be good for long. I remember I have a book coming out. I remember I have an idea for a new book. I remember you. All my thoughts are like chips."

"Is anyone with you?"

"No! I had to fight to be alone to call you. It's amazing you came home so early."

That sounded friendlier. "Is anyone with you in the apartment?"

"Not now. Not yet."

"You should have someone with you. You should have me with you. Can you tell me what happened when he died? Would you rather not talk?"

"No, I called Dr. Kay, and he came right away. And Dwight Monroe. Riverside sent a station wagon, a service car, and took Curtis away. I went over there, to the Riverside, with Dwight and Dr. Kay, in Dr. Kay's car. Between us, we've taken care of everything for now. The mechanics of it were unpleasantly easy. It's as if everyone had been rehearsing for years, and they carried me along."

No autopsy. "Is there a funeral?"

"A memorial service. Probably Tuesday."

"Were you talking seriously when he died? Was he upset? Look, do you want me to come up?"

"I don't see how you can come here. I will tell you everything else when I see you. Maybe later. Maybe I can sneak down for an hour. Tomorrow, Curtis's parents may come in and stay over with friends. I'll probably never see them again after next Tuesday. I'm trying to figure out, at the same time hoping to avoid

186

having to figure out, what to say to them. Dwight and Sheila have invited me to move in with them for the indefinite future. Dwight just called me from his office, where he took it on himself to go to get Curtis's file, and told me there would be enough money so that I shouldn't worry about it for now. He will review my financial future with me whenever I'm ready. What I think is, I can never be ready. I have no idea how to behave toward Dwight. He's Curtis's closest friend, and executor, and suddenly he's my advisor. I've always liked him. He's the only person I know whose lack of humor helps make him charming. But now I don't know how to talk to him, or what will show. Marilyn Simonson is insisting on sleeping here if I don't sleep at their house. Everyone is being intensely generous and thoughtful, and my reaction is to want to be alone. It's as if they think I may jump out a window. I just realized I haven't called Andrea in Toronto yet. Maybe I'm worried she'll fly right down. Or maybe I want her to. Am I talking a blue streak, or 'blue street,' as I said as a child?''

"It's not a time to refuse friendship. It seems a shame I can't be helpful to you.''

"I'm sure you can. I just don't know how yet. I'm not actually sure it's smart for me to come see you tonight. Maybe I'll just go to a hotel. The Limbo Hilton. Where does one stay? I'm not standing on line to sleep here, with or without Marilyn, but at least if I stayed here alone my friends would have to understand it. The one thing against the rules is disappearing.''

"I agree with them. I think you should decide whether you want to sleep tonight at the Monroes' or the Simonsons'. Maybe you could stop here for a little while on the way there. I'd like to be filled in. Or I'll come up and get you and bring you here, or wherever you want to go, whatever you decide.''

"I'll see. Now that I know you're home, I'll see what I come up with and call you back. Dr. Kay gave me sleeping pills. They put you out for forty-eight hours and you wake up a year from now.''

"Well, don't take one until you call me back. Don't take any, or else I'm coming right up. I love you, Betsy.'' Tears, but they stayed out of his voice.

"I'll call you before ten. Stay calm."

"You'll be all right?"

"Yes." She hung up.

He hung up the receiver as if it were a suffering body. He put his forehead in his hands. Should he have consoled her? He had imagined Curtis dead less often, and much less vividly, than he had imagined Betsy dead, or himself. Curtis was to have been thirty-nine next week. Curtis and Betsy, with the Monroes and the Simonsons, were to have gone out next Thursday for Curtis's birthday to Perigord Park or Seafare of the Aegean. Betsy had been a little uneasy about the idea, because the Monroes and Simonsons were not made for each other, the Monroes finding the Simonsons "a shade loud," the Simonsons finding the Monroes "a bit uptight," but when Betsy had called them (after Curtis had said, "It's my birthday. I want them both. They can get along for one evening. Maybe this will be their breakthrough"), each couple had responded easily: "Fine, fine, love the Simonsons!" "Fine, fine, love the Monroes!" Alan was the secret vault of all Betsy's anxiety and information.

Had Curtis wanted to die? Had Betsy shocked him? Had he found her out just before he'd died? Was he really dead? Had they argued? Had he had a heart condition only Dr. Kay and he knew about? Curtis mortally threatened but selfless, not wanting Betsy to know? Curtis was not an evil man, not a bad man. Foolishly insensitive, overbearing toward his wife. Too wide a faddish streak. But these were not crimes, or not punishable by death. Alan pictured Curtis as electrocuted, and he flinched. Curtis had been an unsympathetic type. Now he was a sympathetic type. Perhaps he had pushed Betsy to be ambitious because he knew he might die any time. Alan rested his head on his hand on the table. He blinked, as if he had just come out of a faint. In his immediate view was the polished wood of the tabletop and his beige phone. It had been Betsy on the phone, at that. He felt as if he had fallen, or shrunk. Everything was enormous. He felt helpless. It was not pertinent, not becoming, for him to feel helpless. He felt a piercing of sympathy in his chest and then the blood of sympathy springing from the wound. He lifted his chest and dialed Betsy. She could not be left alone. If she needed some money for the next few days, he wanted to get to her before Dwight Monroe or Marilyn Simonson did, people he hadn't even met. The line was busy. What had she done with Curtis's wedding band? Had she taken it, or left it on him? If he was to be cremated, she must have taken it. Ring's ring. Alan recalled noticing it at the Oak Bar, a golden band.

He tried her number again. The busy signal stuffed the phone. He tried her again, right away. Unavailability in his ears. Closed teeth. *Nn—nn—nn*. He wondered if he was dialing because he didn't want to get up, move around, because the news would stay stiller if he stayed where he was, would be less evident.

As he was about to dial her again, the phone rang, causing his hand to jump. "Okay," she said. "I'm staying at the Monroes'. They have more room, easier room. I said I'd be there in an hour or so. How would it be if I came down for half an hour, forty-five minutes?"

"Do you want to come? I mean, I don't want you to do it if you find it too awkward."

"I don't. I'll be there in twenty-five minutes. I'm just going to throw some stuff in a bag."

"I'm glad you're not going to be staying alone. Will you want anything to eat?"

"Tea, maybe. Soup. Will you open some soup?"

"Chicken soup?"

"Fine. Any simple soup. My stomach is an unknown quantity."

"You'll get a cab on the corner? You sure you don't want me to come up for you?"

"I'll be all right. I'll walk up to Ninety-sixth Street. I'll take a bus if it comes first. Nobody's going to mug me tonight. I'll see you in a little while."

"I'll be here." He hung up. A widow. Betsy a widow. It

189

didn't feel like good news. He stood up, stood for a moment with his hands on the table, to see if he was all right himself. He walked slowly into the bedroom, panic making him queasy. He turned on the bedroom light. He took off his black blazer and hung it on the silent valet. He undid his necktie. He moved as if he had been pummeled. He opened the closet door, standing away while he examined the interior for a burglar with a knife. He hung the scarlet tie in its place on the tie rack. He went into the kitchen. It was as if someone vital to him had died, as if Manners had died, as if he had just returned to his house from Manners's funeral. He found chicken consommé among his soup cans. He put the can on the kitchen table and, gripping the can, started to sob. Throwing an arm to his eyes, he turned to the sink. He washed his face and dried it with a paper towel, and sighed. *Ohimè. Corragio.* Phew! He opened the soup can and poured the soup into a pot, following it with two thirds of a can of water (normally, he did not measure), and tossed the can into the garbage pail. He put some Ritz crackers on a plate and got out two soup bowls and two spoons. He folded two paper napkins and placed them under the spoons. Lifting off the spoons, then, this being the wrong occasion for bothering to set the table properly, he unfolded the napkins and placed them beside the spoons. He walked about the apartment, turning off the bedroom light, the dining-room light, turning on the living-room light. He returned to the bedroom, finding the day's stubs in his blazer pocket; returned to the dining room and dropped the stubs in the tank. He waited in the living room, drifting near the foyer, lining up his words, refining them, cautioning himself to be calm with her, to be generous, to be natural, graceful, to be whatever degree of embracing or unemotional that she would indicate she needed him to be. Above all, not to be graver than she. It was too soon to be waiting by the foyer, so he sat on the couch, as though dead. He was not looking forward to her arrival. It made him angry to know it. He returned to the kitchen, supposing she would want the soup ready. He turned on the flame beneath the pot, as low as it could be made, and watched the soup.

When the doorbell rang, it sounded unexpected, a Sunday-morning doorbell, a wrong doorbell. He hurried to the door, not wanting to reach it but relieved that she was here and something would happen—he would be expelled, he would comfort her. In any case, he would be given something to do. He undid the door and swung it open with an irrevocable heartiness, as, anxiously, you swing open the door to someone you have never met or haven't seen for years. Betsy's eyes were on him. "Come in," he said. "You got here fast." She raised her eyebrows. He kissed her on the cheek. She entered the foyer. He closed the door. He held her for a moment without looking at her, then looked at her. She blinked. "Let's go in," she said. He followed her through the living room. She wore her Russian coat, jeans. She carried a pouched and buckled leather bag, a birthday gift last April from Curtis. "The soup is on," he said. "Chicken consommé."

In the kitchen, she removed her coat and dropped it over the back of her chair. It draped on the floor like a train to the chair, but Alan said nothing about hanging it up for her. He did not want her to feel that he was fussing over her or that he was hoping to extend her visit. She sat. He stood by the chair and took her hand. In this chair, she had sometimes sat naked, or half-clothed, after bed, or before. She was wearing a long-sleeved blue-and-white-print shirt he had never told her he didn't like, and a short-sleeved navy-blue sweater. "So," he said. He hoped he looked no more somber than a doctor about to take a pulse.

"Things are very sudden, as you once pithily observed."

He wanted to squat by her and warm her, but any gesture of tenderness would lead him to tears, and tears were out of the question. "Are you all right?" he asked.

"I'm not dead."

"Do you want to try the soup?"

"Yes, please. Thanks."

He went to the stove and turned the flame up. His soup, he thought; none of the others would know, Monroes, Simonsons, *et al.* She had come to his house for his nourishment. When she peed at the Monroes' later, before going to sleep, it would be his soup. He served them and sat down. "Tell me what you can," he said.

"I still haven't called Andrea."

"Eat your soup and then use my phone."

"I'm not a murderer, am I?" Her eyes filled. She shuddered, and her face was squirming in the crook of her arm.

"Come on, Betsy, come on." He dropped beside her, his cheek against her sleeve, his arms over her back. "How can you talk that way?" He didn't know anything yet, but she wasn't a murderer. "You said he felt sick and he died. This happens all the time. It happened to our publisher, four years ago. Kyle McCabe left his doctor's office after a perfect checkup, fifty years old, and, and dropped dead in the lobby." A consoling story.

"We had a bad talk," she said, concealed by her arm. "A real live confrontation. Now I'm tired."

Meaning that she should be sleeping here, where she was able to let go, with him to watch over her. "Why don't you eat your soup?"

She sat up, wiping her eyes with the base of her palms, and began to nibble a cracker. She stared at the table. She looked like a little girl coming out of a nap.

He took his seat. "A confrontation."

"He was furious at Roberts. Ready to kill. He had just come from Antoinette and Roberts. Roberts told him that little Curtis's problems were Curtis's fault because Curtis had left the marriage. Curtis asked me if I would move with him if he got a bigger apartment, with a full-fledged bedroom for his son. I said what amounted to no. I couldn't say I would."

"If he had to ask you in the first place, he couldn't have been too surprised at your answer."

She looked at him and nodded, but it was as if she hadn't heard what he said. "Then he asked me if I had a boyfriend, and I said no. He asked if I was telling the truth, and I said yes. Then he called himself a loser. He went into the bathroom and came out and sat down on the bed. He said he had terrible pain. He looked it. I helped him lie down. He vomited on my jacket. That's what makes me think he must have known. Then he was dead, like that. He was dead before I knew it."

Alan bowed his head and took a deep breath. He said the only thing he could see he had a right to say. "Do you want to be responsible?"

She gave him a surprising little smile. "Maybe. Don't you? At all?"

"If I thought you were responsible, I would think I was responsible. Or each of us in part. I'll stop trying to take it away from you, for now, but I just want to say I think it's too easy for you to want to be guilty. It could have happened to him on his way up the stoop coming home. It's entirely understandable, but you are forgetting that your marriage was already bad when you and I first met, and his first marriage was *still* bad. You forget that it was he who arranged his life, not you. And he tried to arrange yours, too. That was the problem, in fact. You cannot make someone else a 'loser.' That's something people do to themselves. It's not like him to say that, anyway—'loser'—is it?"

"No, it isn't. And I told him he wasn't. But then, he was." She finally took a spoonful of soup.

He felt the chill of her flatness. "Did Dr. Kay ask you questions?"

"About what had happened?"

Alan nodded.

"He asked me. I told him Curtis had come home upset, and roughly why. It was left at that. But how do I know Curtis didn't tell him we were having trouble? They're quite good friends. The thought I have had most frequently since five o'clock this afternoon is that Curtis has staged all this, that he overheard me delivering my censored account to Dr. Kay, pretending to be dead"—her expression seemed to acknowledge that she was being ridiculous, while daring him to shut her up—"and has since told the truth to the authorities, who will be clapping me on the shoulder any minute and saying, 'Please come along with us, Miss.' "

He took hold of her wrists. "You have got to stop this, Betsy."

She looked at her watch as if he were forcing her to look at her watch. "I'm going to. And I'm going to go. If I'm sounding hysterical, I don't mean to. I won't need a slap in the face. These are simply my thoughts."

He slid his hands off her. "You should say whatever you want. But the excessiveness is not like you. All these fantasies."

She looked at him with calm impatience. "I don't have any idea how I'm supposed to be. I came here not knowing how I'd be. That's why I came here."

"Yes." It was not the first time she had reminded him she loved him in words it took him a moment to add up. But she was leaving. He had to let her be. "I just want you to be all right."

"I suppose it's true that I want to be guilty. But it seems inevitable that I should. Perhaps my trying to be guilty means I'm actually not. So that works out nicely." She stood up.

He stood, too. "I just want you to take it easy on yourself."

"What I really feel, I think, is foolish, or frivolous. He has so much more stature than I do, and everyone's paying attention to me."

His head bulged painfully. She was closed to him. "You haven't called Andrea."

"I'll do it at the Monroes'."

"Shall I take you?"

"Thanks. If you'd walk me to a taxi, I'd appreciate it. There's no sense in your coming. Okay?"

He felt the sting of the thought's vulgarity as he imagined she was jilting him. "Of course." He noticed her blue-jeaned hips. He remembered the many paths that began at her hips. He reached for her hand, and she gave it to him. "Betsy."

"Please, above all, don't cry right now."

He cleared his throat. "I speak with you tomorrow?"

"I'll speak with you as soon as I can."

They were six inches from an embrace. "If you don't, I'll worry about you." The wrong thing to say.

"I don't want to worry about you, though. I have to pay attention to all the attention. To Curtis's parents. I have to try to be some sort of widow. I'm a widow."

"There's no need to worry about me. But why can't you let me—you can't let me give you the attention."

"I would despise both of us if I hid out with you here now. And I would want you to despise both of us, too."

"I understand what you have to do. But why can't you take whatever you need from me and deal with the world as you need to?"

"It can't be in that order."

"I meant simultaneously, or alternately." He smiled gently.

"It sounds reasonable. I don't know yet. I'm not going to mislay you, if that's what's worrying you."

"Hardly. Come. I'll take you down."

She swung his hand and let go of it. She put on her coat and took her bag from the floor. She preceded him out of the kitchen, her love, their future, hidden under her hair. Did she blame him for the death? For not being dead? Now that Curtis was no longer the heavy, was he the heavy instead? For having bullied her into going to the opera with him this afternoon, going in such a half-assed way? Was that part of what she meant by frivolous? Did she feel a taint of opera on the death? On herself? That she had been at the opera while her husband was going to die?

He asked himself questions through the night, over the next day. Was she so cold to him because if she had not insisted, against his intense pique, on leaving at intermission, Curtis would have beaten her home by more than an hour, and possibly found her out? But it had been her own idea, not his, to wear the opera suit she had worn the first night they'd met. Wouldn't she, though, have found Curtis dead already had she arrived

195

home after him? Did she resent it, then, that Alan had nearly caused her to miss her husband's death? Or was she cold solely because the death itself had turned her cold, he having nothing to do with the coldness at all?

Had Curtis aimed at the jacket when he vomited, knowing she had worn it to the opera with her boyfriend (more or less with her boyfriend)? Had she taken it off or was she wearing it? When would it ever be appropriate to ask her such a question? He had not had the opportunity to share enough of the weight with her, to be her friend. Or she had not allowed him to. When would she be able to turn warm again? How could he help her turn warm again? Only by keeping a tactful distance? Allowing her her distance? How could he sneak her back to her condition of contented need for him, which he regarded every day as a miracle, as a lengthening shock of luck? Would they ever go to bed again? Would she marry him now? Why not?

There could not have been a day since they had known each other when he hadn't asked her at least two new questions, or asked her again in expanded ways questions he'd already asked, about her life or her most extremely personal thoughts and habits, or her opinions. His questioning, his questions, their range, pleased her while sometimes embarrassing her a little. Often she laughed at their unexpectedness or intimacy. She called the kinds of questions she preferred, or that impressed her even if she did not prefer them, "literary"—the most specific questions helped make fictional characters. He had learned things about her from his questions that another man would never have learned or noticed, or not for years of close living. He learned things before she could demonstrate them. Her answers only increased her poignancy and the colors of her intelligence. She was inimitable. She was literally the woman he had always been waiting for, the only woman in his adult life he had wanted to claim. The ways in which she was difficult made her more necessary to him. The ways in which she was different from him, and superior to him, had not prevented her from being his. She grew more and more unusual to him the more familiar she became; the more possessed, the more desirable. He must tell her this. He had never formulated the feeling before because he had never felt it. Possession in the past, when it had not made him nervous, had at best kept him stiffly serious for a while, "mature."

Although he talked to Betsy about himself down to his dregs, she knew him more informally than he knew her. Not that she didn't ask him questions. Not that she didn't understand him. She had undertaken to understand him from the very beginning; that was part of the point. She was not, however, a student of his life, and he was decidedly a student of hers, a Betsician, a Betsologist. But when she made an observation about him, or connected an old piece of information to a new one, it was as if she had been thinking about him all the time.

Once Sunday afternoon had passed without his hearing from her, he thought of going up to her house, with the possibility of running into her as she arrived to pick up some belongings, or to phone him from there. But if he left his own phone, he gave up being as near to her as she would let him be at the moment, short of his appearing at the Monroes', which he couldn't imagine a way of doing that wouldn't be like throwing a rock through their window, he himself the rock. Would she want him, not want him, at the memorial service on Tuesday, or would she leave it to him, meaning she didn't want him?

Poisoned by Betsy's silence, Alan took himself to his office the next morning. Walking carefully, as if ill, he nodded to Mrs. Hawthorne, irritably typing, and said an inaudible good morning. In the attaché case under his arm, *The Times* with Curtis's death notice and medium-sized obituary. Memorial service tomorrow morning at eleven, the Riverside. There was no one in the world for him to tell, without betraying Betsy, or looking as if he were showing off, that the Curtis Ring who had died was the husband of the woman he loved as he had never loved anyone, that she had been abducted by her husband's death, that he was in mourning for her disappearance. No one to make it easier for him—to tell him he was being ridiculous and why, to

197

ask him what he expected of her a day and a half after her thirty-eight-year-old husband had dropped dead. He could not tell himself he was being foolish, because he feared he was not being foolish. He walked carefully for fear that she was pulling away, even if she didn't know it, or wouldn't say it.

But in fact, if Curtis hadn't died, and Betsy half-died, Alan would not have been coming in to work today at the peak of zest. The previous week, former Governor Love of Colorado had quit as Nixon's Energy "Czar," because Nixon had named Deputy Treasury Secretary Simon to head up the new Federal Energy Administration. Alan had written the main part of the story on the new energy office, having succeeded in reaching Simon by phone just in time to get the interview into the magazine. *Newsworthy* was devoting most of this week's issue to the worldwide implications of the energy shortage. Bob Manners had assigned Alan to find out what was happening to the Emergency Petroleum Allocation Act, and to see how much of a story he could get out of the truckers' protest against the reduction in highway speed limits and the rise in fuel costs. Alan had learned near the beginning of his magazine career, through a blithe and humiliating mistake, that it was a very good idea not to ask for an assignment to replace an assignment one disliked. And, over the years, he had gained and solidified his value at *Newsworthy* by his willingness not to specialize. He had become a subordinate star, prized in the company, and known in the trade, above all for his dependability.

With most stories that didn't interest him, he found angles from which to gain himself interest—a skulduggery angle, a personality angle. Nothing about the energy problem interested him (except the headline of the week before, "Love Quits in Energy Shake-Up," which he had been so pleased to bring to Betsy). The subject took away his appetite, as if it were offering him gasoline to drink. Occupying his office this morning with sluggish, night-time motions, he recalled a time of superlative misery during his sophomore year at Columbia. Dot Wadleigh, across campus, her period two weeks late. His paper on *Pilgrim's Progress* overdue, and *Pilgrim's Progress* unread.

198

Before he could poke at the files he'd had home all weekend without ever removing them from his attaché case, Mrs. Hawthorne buzzed him. "Mrs. Pursey calling."

"Okay."

"Good morning to you!"

"Hello, Madeline, what can I do for you?" He made a curve of the "you," hoping to soften the impatience in his greeting.

"Hi. What you could do for me is let me do you a big favor."

"I apologize for not returning your call. It's been horrendous around here."

"You're forgiven. Notice you didn't stop me from calling you again?"

"What's up?"

"I have a wonderful friend I'd like you to meet."

"What is this, vengeance?"

"Hardly!" Her laugh—he remembered it—had absolutely nothing sardonic in it. "I assure you, I have no hard feelings. Anyway, I like my friend. She's this very nice, attractive, arty girl, a real music-lover for you. Her name is Renee. She works over at Arthur Mullmann Associates as a gal Friday. We have lunch sometimes. I thought of her for you, I thought of you for her, she was interested. She's frankly having a hard time finding decent men to date. Chet and I would love to have you both to dinner, or you could take her to something, get her out of the singles' bars. She says it's so unbelievable it's bizarre. Are you dating anyone?"

"Yes and no. Sure, I see people."

"Same old Alan?"

"I guess so." He felt a flare-up of lustful curiosity: "What's her name?"

"Renee Engel. Shall I tell her you'll call?"

He wrote the name down on a piece of memo paper and dropped the memo paper into the wastebasket. "No, thanks, you'd better not. I'm way over my head with work. But you're nice to think of me, so thank you. How's married life?"

"The greatest. I thank my lucky stars for Chet every day.

199

He's much too good for me. But I'm sorry I struck out on this good deed. I think you'd like her.''

"I don't understand, to tell you the truth, why you want to fix me up with a friend of yours.''

"Well''—she laughed again, the same straightforward laugh —''no ulterior motives or anything. I said before, she's your type, arty, serious. You don't have to go falling in love with her. Just take her out. She says she likes operatic music a whole lot and would love to learn more about it. I don't think you can do her any harm, if that's what you're worrying about. I don't think you're as evil as you might like to think. Somewhat kooky, yes. Evil, no. I hope that doesn't bother you.''

"Not at all.'' He remembered that both times Madeline Meltzer had stood undressed, she had proclaimed her nakedness: "Dah-dah!,'' holding her brassiere over her head. Did she do that nightly with Chet?

"I suggested you, frankly, because you're a human being. She says they're all so shallow, or, you know, kinky, or just plain oafs.''

"I'm very sorry I can't oblige. But thanks. I must be off.''

"I'm disappointed, I must say. Stay well and happy, Alan.''

"You, too, Renee.'' His heart flattened. "I mean, my God, excuse me, Madeline. Believe me, I know who you are. I'm just distracted. There are twelve people in my doorway, all beckoning.''

"You are silly. Call me if you change your mind, all right?''

"Will do.''

"Chet and I would love to feed you, anyway, and hear all about the glamorous reporter.''

"Thanks. I'll call, Madeline.''

"Bye-bye, then.''

He hung up. He wanted a week off, that's what he wanted, so he could monitor his life. Otherwise, it was going to slip away from him. Just say to Bob, gone stale, eyes numb. No need to bring Betsy into it. Be a man. Maybe Stu Sprague could fill in for a week. Two weeks. He was definitely going to ask. Two weeks against vacation time. He had to be free to watch out for Betsy, watch for her, watch her. Be free to be nervous. To think. To be his best. He dialed Manners's extension, asked Ellie Antonelli, "Can he see me for a sec'?"

"I'll ask. His morning's getting torn to pieces."

"Thirty seconds is all I ask."

"He's on the phone to Riyadh. I'll call you."

While Alan waited, he reminded himself that not once in ten years had he forced Bob's editorship into their friendship. Bob, behind his wide, pale, deadpan face, needed him as a friend more than he needed Bob. In office, opera seat, restaurant, bar, Bob appeared moodless, his extreme signs of emotion a frown or a chuckle. But Bob requested Alan's evening time all the time. Bob needed someone to talk to him while he tucked in his three nightly scotches and delivered his witty observations and responses, his mouth as restrained as a ventriloquist's. Bob never called him by his name; only, sometimes, Don José, or José, in the French pronunciation.

He opened the top file on his desk, and closed it as if he were prying. Maybe he'd suggest to Betsy that next week, after she'd done her duty, he take her away for a week, ten days, Nassau, Puerto Rico, St. Thomas. Or would she reject such a trip as a conventional after-death self-indulgence? He was always worried that she would suddenly find him ordinary, or too content with the cushy life, and was relieved each time he rediscovered that she thought him odd or categorized herself as bourgeois. His phone rang, and he picked it up as Mrs. Hawthorne picked it up, saying "I've got it" while Mrs. Hawthorne was saying "Alan Hoffman's wire." There was no voice at the other end, namely, Betsy. Alan called, "Hello," feeling as if he were standing in the middle of a black tunnel, and virtually praying that Betsy had not hung up along with Mrs. Hawthorne.

"Hi," she said tightly. "Can you meet me at your house at lunchtime?"

"Sure. Are you all right?"

"Yes. I had no chance to call you yesterday."

"It's all right." His phone rang and 3133 lighted up. "Stay right there. Be right back." He put Betsy on hold and pressed 3133. "Hoffman."

"Bob can see you for a minute if you hurry right down."

"I don't want to bother him. If I change my mind, I'm supposed to be seeing him this evening anyway. Thanks just the same."

"You're nice."

"Got to go." He pressed Betsy back. "Where are you?"

"At home. Andrea's making coffee in the kitchen. I'll see you about one?"

"Fine. How's Andrea?"

"I'll tell you later." She hung up.

He ordered coffee, opened up the trucking file in earnest, made preliminary notes, telephoned the Public Affairs Secretary in the Department of Transportation, the Teamsters, the National Association of Truck Stop Operators, and the American Trucking Association. Through Teamsters' locals, he arranged to speak to particular truckers who had struck in Pennsylvania, Ohio, West Virginia, Delaware, and Connecticut last week. He left the office at noon. In his neighborhood, he picked up two roast-beef heroes, cole slaw and potato salad, and went home to wait for Betsy.

When she arrived, shortly after one, in pea coat, jeans, black turtleneck, she dangled a tiny paper bag containing, as it turned out, her lunch of apricot yogurt—she wanted nothing more. "I can only stay about an hour," she said, in the kitchen. "I need badly to go to the movies, and Andrea insists on seeing *Aparajito* and *Pather Panchali,* so I'm compromising. At the Carnegie Hall Cinema. Would you like to join us? Meet Andrea?"

"I can't. I've got to interview some truckers on the telephone."

"I'd rather do that than *Aparajito* and *Pather Panchali.*"

Alan spread Dijon mustard on his roast beef. "When did Andrea arrive?"

"Last night. She stayed at my house."

"With you?"

"With me."

"In the same bed?"

"Yes. But no sex."

"How did yesterday go?"

"Well, the Rings couldn't make it in. So I went out to see them in Woodmere. Dwight and Sheila drove me out. The Rings both looked like wrecked ships. Caved in, capsizing. They walked and sat tipped sideways. It was impossible to tell them any background, or anything about the talk. Their pain was sufficient, you'd have to say. Then the Monroes and I went to pick up Andrea at JFK." Betsy looked at Alan, a little bit lightened. "And she has been a help. Some of the time, she's her most solemn, severe, dominating self, but she becomes funny without any warning. She can be funny carrying a tray. It's the dancer in her. She makes us both laugh. It hasn't changed a bit since college."

He tugged, doglike, at his stiff sandwich, chewed longer than was necessary, hoping to swallow his rage with the food. "So it's good for you she's here. That's very good." He drank some tomato juice. "How were you able to get away? I mean for lunch."

"Because I told her about you last night, and I told her I was coming to see you today, that's how." She smiled quickly, giving out her bashful nasal breath.

"How was that received?"

"I think she's still receiving it. She hasn't said much. A few questions. No condemnation."

"Do I get to meet her?"

Betsy's forehead wrinkled. "If there's time."

"Tonight?"

"I have to see the Rings again, at their friends'. They're coming in tonight, to their friends', for tomorrow."

"That's another thing. Do you want me at the service?"

"What would the point be? No one there is going to notice your absence."

"True."

"After the service, the Monroes are going to serve lunch." She gulped. "Tomorrow night, I'm going to Toronto with Andrea." She gulped again, keeping her eyes on him.

He slowly rubbed the edge of his left hand back and forth across the right side of his chin. He lowered his eyes, to avoid appearing too lyrically wounded, or too gloomily loving. He stopped rubbing and concentrated on the edge of his white plate. He had no idea what to say. Each second that passed in silence showed him as further wounded, whether he looked at her or not. Wounded meant weak, and it meant selfish. He wasn't sure what it meant. Whatever it meant, it meant something not lovable, something discreditable. "For how long?" He looked at her. Despite himself, he was exhibiting an aggrieved gaze, he knew.

"Two weeks? Not long. Whatever it is, I'll be back."

He should be saying, You should not go. You may not go. You must not go. You must go. She put out her hand and covered his. He let his hand lie beneath hers, playing dead. He watched her stand. She sat in his lap, one hand at the top of his belly, the other on his shoulder. "Let's go to bed," she said, looking, from just above him, cross with sadness.

His fingers touched her waist, but he did not grasp her. "There's not enough time."

"There is if we hurry." Her unhappy smile was accompanied by another nasal puff, a breathed shrug which sometimes meant, tactfully, Don't you know that's the way it is, Mac? or sometimes, I love you, or, Forgive me, or, I was right so why did you have to waste so much time arguing? At the moment, he thought he heard suggestions of all four meanings.

"Is bed for me or for you?"

"Both, I would hope."

"I'm digesting. I don't mean my lunch. I mean your news."

"I know." She looked at him, stubbornly sorrowful.

He exhaled a heavy breath and raised her sweater. She pressed her bra down off her breasts.

At *La Bohème,* when Manners asked him what he had wanted that morning, he told him he thought he might like to take the next week off, if possible, to recharge. (He imagined, now, a visit to Betsy in Toronto instead of a trip with her to Nassau.) Manners said he thought it could probably be managed, but he couldn't know for sure until next week began, which might prove inconvenient to Alan. Not a problem, Alan said. After the opera, they sat in The Ginger Man for a while. When Alan went to bed, he couldn't sleep, so he got up and drank two bottles of Molson ale and listened to the first-act love duet from *Otello,* Tebaldi and Del Monaco. He nearly started getting dressed. With no Curtis on Ninety-fifth Street, he could go up there, wake Betsy (and Andrea), and have it out with her in the living room. But how could he spoil her sleep? She was going to her husband's memorial service tomorrow. He could not afford to act like a hothead, a ranting sobber, a third-rate tenor. But he was going to have to see her before she left for Toronto. They were leaving tomorrow because Andrea had to get back to her dance classes, her two boys, Malcolm and David, Jr., and her husband, the pediatrician, who, according to Andrea (Betsy had reported, while dressing after bed), was overdue for the Nobel Prize. Maybe he could persuade Betsy not to leave until Wednesday, so they could talk rationally about her going, or not going. She had put him in a position that left him unable to love her—either to help her or to ask for her—without running the risk of being unfair to her. They had agreed that she would call him from home in the afternoon, between the Monroes' lunch and her departure for the airport, to say goodbye. It was to him as if she were leaving on her honeymoon.

In his office the next morning, when it got to be ten-thirty, he began to picture himself at the Riverside, mixing with Curtis's prosperous mourners, those older and those contemporary, first out on the sidewalk, then in one of the larger chapels, Alan, dressed as he was in fact today, in his deeply responsible gray pinstripe suit, a pale-blue shirt, navy-blue tie, a plainclothes lover, anonymous and respectable, sitting toward the rear (a glimpse of Betsy's head now and then), nodding a stranger's greeting here and there to strangers, clients who thought him a client, perhaps to Jack Mansfield, the bereaved pornographer. A rabbi spoke, a friend, probably Dwight Monroe. Perhaps, afterward, he would end up having a drink with Jack Mansfield in a bar on Columbus, he and Mansfield not included among the lunch guests at the Monroes'. Betsy had said she thought she would be back in her apartment by three. He needed no more than half an hour. He would not let her go without reminding her that he was her friend and not her enemy, that even with the most complete and sympathetic understanding of her public obligations and private anguish, he nevertheless had to say that she was treating their love, and him along with it, as if it were an embarrassment, a political liability, at just that point where, through admittedly undesirable, shocking circumstances, their improved access to a free future should, at the least, be acknowledged. He felt as if he were preparing a case for himself, a brief. Imagining their meeting later, he kept warning himself that he would be that much more winning if he "employed" restraint, "exercised" tact, "utilized" detachment, speaking on his behalf, on their behalf, with irresistible calm and authority, leaving her softened, admitting she had overdone it, grateful to him for providing perspective firmly but lovingly. She might cancel her trip altogether. Or shorten it to a week. If the husband of anyone but Betsy had died, the freed wife would have been putting pressure on him, or would at least have taken a moment to whisper confidently to his cringing heart, "I'll be yours very soon, my darling. I can't wait."

While he ate lunch at his desk, he daydreamed nervously, knowing he didn't belong there, about the lunch at the Monroes', say fifty guests. The senior Rings, rather than Betsy, were the centerpiece of the gathering, crushed together on a couch, or tipped sideways, a niece or sister pleading with them to eat their cold roast beef and their salad, they must keep their strength up. Why should I keep my strength up? Mrs. Ring asks.

The niece or sister is perhaps cutting up the roast beef into bite-sized pieces for Mrs. Ring. Alan felt a twinge of connection with Curtis's parents, partly just because he knew of them and they had absolutely no idea of his existence. Did they, in fact, know of his existence? Had he been subjected, unknowingly, to an obscure, tremendously expensive electronic test, available only to suffering next-of-kin, and commissioned by Curtis's parents, that determined the degree of your culpability for the grief of others? And had he registered significantly high? Such thinking was paranoid, or presumptuous, turning him into a would-be mover in the drama of others. Embarrassing. The fact was that if he and Betsy were at all involved in Curtis's destiny, then it was only through Curtis's destiny affecting theirs. How could they have affected his? You'd have to be able to say that Curtis would still be alive this afternoon if Betsy hadn't lied when asked if she had a "boyfriend." Or that Curtis would still be alive if she didn't have a boyfriend. Curtis had died of terrible luck, which by definition couldn't be anticipated, and he had died of his history and his controlling personality. Whether or not Betsy had a boyfriend had hardly been the main thing on Curtis's mind, in any case. At least as Betsy had described the scene to him, that question had been an afterthought. Unless, of course, Betsy had edited her account of the confrontation, hoping to spare him, the boyfriend, useless guilt. It seemed to him that if there was a villain, other than destiny, it was Roberts, who made Curtis seem the soul of sensitivity. Curtis had arrived home already boiling over with rage. It would be interesting to know what the Rings knew about Roberts.

Antoinette, obviously, was the one who stood by the Monroes' couch, urging the Rings, her ex-in-laws, to eat something. Antoinette was designed to override the delicacy of the circumstances and do what she felt needed to be done. Maybe little Curtis sat between his grandparents, or beside one of them, his favorite. Otherwise, the boy would be playing Monopoly with a Monroe child, or walking up and down the entrance hall, alone, hands in blazer pockets, counting his footsteps, braiding them, teetering, while waiting to be taken home. Roberts, if he had attended the memorial service, for Antoinette's sake, or for form's sake, had certainly not gone to the Monroes' lunch but returned downtown, to Wall Street.

The trucker protest story was turning out flat. And Alan had learned from Secretary Simon's Energy office that Simon would be announcing the new fuel allocation plans tomorrow but that no advance information could be supplied, they were still working on the final details. So Alan's concentration hopped as he waited to hear from Betsy. From three to three-fifteen, he resisted calling her. From three-fifteen to three-thirty, he dialed six times. Then she called.

"I was getting concerned," he said.

"A few of us stayed and talked."

"How was the service?"

"The rabbi was nearly bearable. Dwight gave a perfect speech about Curtis as his friend. His voice kept breaking, which is so out of character that it got to me. There were a lot of people there."

"Was Jack Mansfield there?"

"I've never actually met him, so I can't tell you."

"I need to see you before you go."

"I would like that, but can you make it? We can't leave here much later than five-thirty, because of the traffic, and getting a taxi."

"I'll have to make do with that, unless you could possibly leave by yourself, tomorrow morning."

"I don't see how, at this point."

"Is Andrea with you now?"

"That's right."

"I'll be there as fast as I can get a cab. Can we talk alone for fifteen minutes?"

"I think so, yes. What's the subject?"

"It's a big surprise, Betsy."

"I really love surprises these days."

"I was joking. It's about you and me."

"In fifteen minutes?"

"What do you want me to do?"

"Come and say goodbye, unpeevishly."

"Do you think you love me?"

"I'm not thinking. But yes. Do you think I've stopped? Not thinking—the other."

"I'll be right there. Just wait there."

She answered the door, evidently cheerful. She was wearing green corduroy pants and a brown turtleneck. She kissed him. "I changed," she said.

He nodded. "Where's Andrea?" He took off his coat. Would he be led toward living room or bedroom?

"This way, please. She's supervising my packing. I've never had the chance to hang up your coat."

"My pleasure." He gave it to her.

"Heavy."

"I'll be glad to do it."

"Ugh. Done. Follow me."

Turning toward him as he walked into the bedroom behind Betsy was a confusingly substantial woman wearing a plain gray suit. Her graying black hair was in a bun. She did not smile, but stuck out her hand and laid her head sideways as Alan approached her. The open suitcase on the bed was large, too.

"Andrea Marshall Douglas, Alan Hoffman," Betsy said. "A historic meeting."

He shook Andrea's hand, saying, "Pleased to meet you," and smiling his most complimentary smile.

"And I you, sir." Her voice was husky and hearty. She looked to Alan like a large white squaw. Betsy had not prepared him. He stepped back.

"I've put in five sweaters, my dear. That should do, don't you think?"

"Five is more than enough. Alan and I will talk down the hall for a few minutes. I leave everything in your hands."

"I'm almost finished, I do believe. You'll want to check to see if I've left anything out."

"I'll be back," Alan said to Andrea. He was visualizing her in a leotard, with a weight-lifter's thighs, demonstrating strenuously, severely, to her students.

In the living room, Betsy sat on a green couch between the windows—little Curtis's former guest bed, Alan supposed—above her, a chilly painting of cherries on a blue plate on a white-enamel table. Curtis's discovery, for sure.

"So?" she said.

"She was your classmate?"

"Shh. Yes. My roommate."

"She looks fifteen years older than you. She's a dancer?"

"A choreographer, partly, and a dance historian. She's put on a lot of weight, no question about it. She loves to cook. But she's talented. She teaches at York University. She's famous up there."

"That's fine. More power to her. Are you surviving?"

"I seem to be. A bit giddy this afternoon. Sometimes I actually forget what all the fuss is about. Tell me about you and me."

She made it sound as if it were a minor problem to which he would have a ready answer, when it was a huge problem to which only she had the answer. He thought of her, beneath the painting, as Mrs. Ring at Home. She was leaning forward a little, politely alert, with her hands like a package on her knees. Put off, he began. "You said to me, when we first talked, at the very beginning, that you thought I wanted to be generous. Remember?"

"Sure." She looked as though she were relaxing into seriousness. "And you are."

"Okay. Be that as it may. I took your judgment as a loving insight, and a kind of cue. I took *you* as a cue. You presented yourself as my first opportunity to love someone in a grown-up way. I'm here to say to you that I still want to be generous, and I'm not being allowed to."

She leaned back in the couch, crossing her legs, keeping her eyes to herself. "Since Curtis has died, almost exactly three days ago to the hour, I've seen you three times, once in bed, and I wanted that part more than you."

"Bed has absolutely nothing to do with this."

She looked at him either rebuked or rebukingly. "Then, what? My going away?"

"Maybe, yes."

"Do you think I'm going to move to Toronto?"

"Who knows?"

"Well, I'm not planning to move to Toronto."

"Okay. I didn't think you were. That's not the point."

"Then what's bothering you? Did you expect me to move right in with you?"

"Of course not. But I want to know what you plan to do."

"I don't know yet. Why do you expect me to know? When I'm away, I'll feel my way back. You jump to conclusions so. You move so fast. I don't understand your perspective. We've known each other less than two months. You think that because Curtis has died, I'm free. You think because I'm going away with an old and dear friend for ten days that I've stopped loving you. The truth of it is that I'm hardly feeling anything."

If she was hardly feeling anything, then why had she wanted to go to bed yesterday? He sighed. "I guess I'm being unfair. It's just that if I were in your shoes, and my wife had died, I'd be running straight to you, straight for your arms, your house. Why am I not your receiver, your recipient? That's what I mean."

"How do you know how you'd be feeling if your wife died?"

"Why is it necessary for you to go away? I can take you away myself. To a warm place, an island. Going to Toronto in mid-December is like adding to the punishment."

"When I come back, that would be generous, certainly, if you still wanted to. I just—I suppose I'm uncomfortable in the city. I feel as if everyone is watching everything I do on closed-circuit television to their heart's content. I think I feel safer at the moment unsettled. All I know is, I don't want to be here, even though you're here. So I'm doing as I'm told."

"What do you mean, you're doing as you're told? Not by me."

"You haven't told."

"But Jesus, Betsy! If I told, you wouldn't *do*. I don't want to dictate, for God's sake. You don't dictate to someone you love. At least I don't. What terrifies me—" He snapped his head away, and immediately faced her again. "Shit."

"What?"

"The point is that here's our chance, and it's somehow not going to be taken." He felt as though, having said it, he'd proved it.

"Why? You have no patience. None."

"Then you have to give me a little hope. I have the feeling that I'm all right for you as long as I'm not final. I'm not husband material, or live-with material. I was only good as long as Curtis was alive. Is that a ridiculous thing to say?"

"My God. What's 'husband material'? Was Curtis husband material?"

"I don't know what you *think,* Betsy."

"Perhaps I'm scared that if I move in with you, you'll die."

"You're being truly silly. Die is the last thing I'd do. How much have you thought about it—moving in?"

"Over the last three days, I have not thought about the mechanics or dynamics of sharing your house."

"And when you return from balmy Toronto, where are you planning to live? Here?"

"Of course not. I dislike this place, as you know."

"Where, do you think?"

"I'm not sure. Half by myself, possibly, and half with you. I'd like a place of my own again, actually."

"Before, when Curtis was alive, what did you think in your own head about it? Did you visualize living with me?"

"Of course, all the time. I visualized many things, many versions. Who says it's stopped?"

"Any of them without me?"

"Not that I recall. I doubt it. Not with anyone other than you, certainly. Or not happily with anyone other than you. Doesn't my being free scare you at all?''

"No, not at all. You just said before that you *weren't* free."

"You know what I mean. In the last three days you haven't had a moment's panic that your life is suddenly in danger of being decided for you, with the responsibility for this bitchy widow you hardly know on your hands?''

"All I've thought about since I've known you was being with you all the time and forever and, most of all, making you glad you had married me. That's almost all I ever think about. That's what scares me, if anything.''

"Did you ever think, in your life at any point, that you could do without love? That it was better left alone, done without?'' She had smiled on Saturday night with a similar mixture of defiance and embarrassment.

"I haven't thought of it that way, no. I may have lived that way, but not intentionally. Why on earth would you want to think about such a thing at this particular moment? Just to put me more at ease about your departure?''

She laughed. "Andrea being here, most likely. We used to talk about it in college. And it's occurred to me at various times since then that it's possible love should be limited to fucking between friendly strangers. Everyone should sign a pact agreeing to do without the commitment stuff, that eventually all it did was make for trouble.''

He looked at her, feeling weary, as if he had never loved her. "And you really knew all about it in college, didn't you?''

"We took things hard.''

"But no longer, tra-la-la?''

"Come on. Now things actually are hard. They take you instead.''

"So you want to try doing without?''

"I only mentioned it as an old theory.''

He wanted to leave her there on the couch, get out before she could see him out. He was already home, waiting for her phone call of love and apology.

"What time's your flight?"

"Seven-forty. And I think I'd better get back inside."

"You're leaving me completely high and dry. Completely. Do you want to do that?"

"No."

"What do we do?"

"I'll be back."

He went to the couch and took her hand. "Maybe you're right. Love isn't worth the trouble."

"You're not supposed to agree." She stood and embraced him.

He rested his chin on her amazingly smooth hair, as he had done a hundred times, and then he enfolded her, lightly. "You mean it's all right for you to be a pessimist, but not for me?"

"Your not being a pessimist is important to me."

"And that will save us?"

"Assuming we need saving. It's good for me. I know that."

"I can't say goodbye."

"You don't need to. Just say goodbye. Temporarily."

He wiped his eyes on his jacket sleeve and looked at her with a minimal smile. "One of us shouldn't say it. That keeps the door unlocked."

"I'm silent."

"So now I have to say it?"

She nodded.

"Goodbye."

"I'll call you when I can."

"Will you work up there?"

"I'm going to try hard."

"Remember me to your novel."

"It remembers you. It knows you're the father."

"When will you call?"

"In a few days. It may have to be collect. Are you going to give me a kiss?"

He kissed her reservedly. Her lips had little give to them. He and Betsy had never parted for a matter of hours without three times the devotion that seemed available at the moment. He would have liked to start the whole talk over again, so he could arrange a goodbye of sufficient length and tenderness. From the hall, pulling on his coat, he called goodbye to Andrea.

"Goodbye, sir!" She appeared in the bedroom doorway long enough to wave at him.

"Goodbye, madam," he whispered to Betsy, with a shallow bow.

Betsy smiled and made a kiss at him, her frown questioning his face for omens of patience and forgiveness. "Please take care," she said.

7

"Yes. This is Alan Hoffman? Madeline Pursey gave me your name."

"She did? My, my. I thought I wasn't expecting to hear from Alan Hoffman."

"I'm sorry it's such short notice, but it happens that I have tickets for *The Magic Flute* this Friday. It's the last of the season."

"*The Magic Flute*. I could make a perfectly obscene joke, but I won't."

"Madeline said you liked opera?"

"Oh, I love it. I'm a total ignoramus about it, but I love it. I like the singing. Now, this Friday is the twenty-first. Hmmmm. I'm sure I can make it if you'll let me get back to you later this morning. I just have to check something out with my roomie, and I have our Tuesday-morning meeting in with Mr. Mullmann at ten-thirty, but I can be back to you before lunch."

"That's fine. But I don't want you to go to any trouble about this."

"Trouble! Will you reveal your office number to me? You're at a magazine, aren't you?"

"*Newsworthy*." He gave her the number.

"Got it. What's your sign, Alan Hoffman? May I ask?"

"My sign? Virgo. That's what they tell me."

"Hey! You're talking to a Gemini! Very in-teresting."

"Oh-kay. You'll call me, then?"

"You bet. Bye-bye."

Hanging up, he felt error clanging through his guts. When she called back, he would tell her it had developed he was going to have to leave town on assignment, he would offer her both tickets, she could take Madeline, or anyone she chose. On the other hand, if he was going to go out with someone, it was best to be going out with a twerpola. Then he could tell Betsy about her. Anything for Betsy. Betsy had called him last Friday, three days after her arrival, to say she was safe and sound, had visited York University to watch Andrea rehearse a new dance, was liking the Douglas boys and David, they were all so polite that it was like reclining on a bed of politeness. He'd asked her, wanting inconspicuously to test the depth of her indefiniteness about her return, if she was being given a party on January eighth, her publication day. Not that she knew of; probably just another lunch with Turnbull-Bore. He asked her if she was doing any work. She told him she'd written a long passage, maybe the beginning of the novel, on the night she'd arrived, stimulated by the flight. And he? What was happening with him? The usual. A *Simon Boccanegra*. A *Rigoletto*. Tonight, Britten's *The Prodigal Son* at St. Stephen's Church. Tomorrow night, a Milstein recital at Grace Rainey Rogers. "Same old grind?" she'd asked. Same old grind. He'd asked her if it would make any sense, supposing he could get away next week, for him to come up to Toronto for a few days, stay at a hotel.

"It would be nice."

"Shall I?"

"I don't think we'd better."

"Why?"

"I don't know. It doesn't feel like the appropriate business of

217

the moment. Doesn't that make sense? What am I doing in a hotel room in Toronto with you when my husband's been dead a week.''

"Then it would have been better if you'd stayed here. I don't live in a hotel.''

"I expect to feel much braver when I come back.''

"If you start seeing me publicly when you come back, how do you plan to explain who I am? And where did you meet me? On the plane coming down from Toronto?''

"Or I'll say you came to interview me for *Newsworthy*. I'll say you picked me up in the movies. People aren't going to expect me to give up living, after all.''

"Andrea already knows I exist. You don't have to lie to her.''

"Come up, then.''

"Oh, for God's sake, Betsy. You don't want me to. I'm not going to force myself on you.''

"It's just that I'd prefer being with you when I feel I'm entitled, more entitled. When the circumstances recede.''

He concentrated, hoping to understand her, but he got snagged on "entitled." Her not feeling entitled to him didn't seem to him to increase his value to her. He suspected her of tact, of trying to be tactful, and failing. "Love entitles, Betsy.''

"I have nothing to say to that. Are you saying I don't love you?''

"I'm saying you've gone away. I'm here and you're not.''

"If I were there with you right now, you'd feel I might just as well be in Toronto. You'd wish I were. I don't feel close to anything. Everything's glassy.''

"I'm just sorry I can't help. That's my point.''

"At a time like this, I think it's difficult for people to help unless they're able to be of practical help. Crude basics. Arrangements.''

Was Andrea of practical help? He wouldn't ask. If he asked, Betsy would have an answer that would make him feel like a prick for having asked. "It's very hard just to stand by. You can understand that.'' Tears were dripping into his stomach.

"You'll have your chance. I'll be unbearably burdensome. Have faith."

Reviewing the conversation over the weekend, he was not angry, but he was not hurt, either. It was as if she had persuaded him to borrow some of her distance, or indifference. Numbness. If she was doubting him, declining him, unwilling or unable to take advantage of his love, then it was her loss as well as his. He decided ten times that he would call Renee Engel at Arthur Mullmann Associates from the office on Monday morning. Anyone would say he was a fool not to. Naked Renees, materializing to audition for him, evaporated before they could perform. He had waited until Tuesday to call her.

Renee called back at eleven-thirty to say, "You're on!" He would have to pick her up after dinner, he said, because he had to work late this Friday. He hoped they could have a drink and a bite after the opera.

"Sounds intriguing. Who bites who?"

Could she be a fucked-up virgin? "I don't bite."

"Oh, you're no fun."

"I'll call you Thursday or Friday morning to confirm."

"Hey, I really look forward to meeting you. You sound very manlike, very together."

"Thank you."

"Seriously. You've made my week."

"I'm all tongue-tied."

"We'll fix that. Just you wait."

During the intermission, they stayed in their seats. Renee, nearing the end of her *curriculum vitae,* was telling him how disillusioned she had become in Arthur Mullmann's TV production office, how much of a factory it really was. Mullmann, contrary to what his PR staff wanted you to believe, had really just about completely sold out, she explained. Any even remotely controversial properties got smoothed into complete blandness, so advertisers wouldn't be offended. It was such a shame, when you thought of television's potential as an educa-

219

tional media. But the almighty dollar really ruled, and Mullmann rationalized his greed by thinking of the TV audience as one solid mass of mediocrity. Alan, turned to Renee at an attentive angle, considered her serenely. He had no desire for her, and no responsibility. She wore, beneath a brown suede vest, a boysenberry-colored blouse that looked expensive, unbuttoned so as to display plump slopes. Her hair was photographably goldenred, and long, heavy. But what most interested him about her was her cheekbones. They were high and sharp, and they seemed to him a silly affectation, her very cheekbones an affectation. They twinkled and preened. It might have been her mouth that gave her cheekbones their quality. Her cheekbones were related to her mouth the way eyes usually are (and her eyes were tight, narrow, unripe). Her mouth, when closed, simmered with what seemed to be dirty-mindedness. When she talked, however earnest she was about the subject, she appeared to be confiding something funny or provocative. She interrupted herself and touched his arm. "Hey, I'm having a really good time with you. You're even nicer than I thought you'd be." Her simmering smile expressed pride of expectation. Her meaning was unmistakable. "It's fun, isn't it?" he said.

Naturally, she was having a good time; he provided a veteran pair of ears. Mostly, before Betsy, he had listened much more than he talked. It was a common criticism of him that he didn't play fair conversationally, wasn't "open," avoided introspectiveness, self-analysis, must be "frightened to give." He asked personal questions, gathering all kinds of information, a "brain-gynecologist with magic hands," as Janet Lawrence had called him in her book, but then all he would talk about in return was his job, or a news event, or the opera of the night before compared with a performance of fifteen years before. Those who didn't mind his autobiographical stinginess were themselves too cold to his questions to suit him, too hard-nosed, brisk, too sporty—Antoinette Loesser types. Or else they were those who didn't notice because they were too busy chewing their lives in his ears, unable to stop reciting the saga of their struggle against abuse, exploitation, unfairness, conspiracy. At least he could say he didn't complain. He'd never thought he'd had anything to complain about, other than the complainers, to whose mythology of grievances he was soon added. The question he got asked the most was, Had he ever been married? He would sometimes answer (and if Renee asked, he would say, if he could remember what he'd told Madeline) that he'd been married once, briefly, right after college, to his childhood sweetheart, Roz, but they hadn't been ready for it, they'd expected too much of it and of each other.

A quarter of the way into the second act, he decided he would plead an achy feeling and take her straight home after the opera (one of his twenty favorite operas, being bumped and dragged back and forth across the stage this evening by a cast that was versatilely inferior, as Bob Manners had once defined an ex-colleague).

It had happened to Alan a number of unforgettable times that a clumsy or tired performance suddenly revived toward the end, collecting itself into its intended state of majesty or charm. Sometimes it took that long for singers to warm up, or to reach an aria or scene that was advantageous, or too powerful to damage; sometimes the inadequate singers were pushed aside, in effect, by the music itself, coming in to save the opera, like a heroine. Then everything focused, and the stage seemed to pull in its breath, rising an inch. Tonight, at the moment when Pamina and Tamino embrace, calling one another "mine" in undulatingly loving phrases, before setting out together to endure the test of their love, the fiery cave and the flood, Alan was drawn from his distractedness into perfect absorption, sliding down in his seat, his face soft, his mouth open, his eyes tearful, a fan of love, a rooter, a disciple of the couple on the stage. Pamina and Tamino pass through the fire unharmed, her hand on his shoulder, as he plays the magic flute, whose music protects them. They pause to praise themselves, then pass safely through the flood. They sing their joy again. The chorus welcomes them: the victory is yours, your journey is over. Isis smiles on you. Enter our temple. Pamina and Tamino stand, like love's chosen, in congratulatory sunlight.

The opera had more than ten minutes to go, but Alan wanted to get out, get to a phone, get to Betsy, pass on to her, somehow, the opera's encouragement. They did not have to be apart. If they were going to stay apart for a little while, then they must be friendlier. They were friends, after all. Their separation should seem more of a sacrifice to her. They should be reaching for each other over the distance between them. The instant the applause began, he said to Renee, "I'm afraid I don't feel very well."

She stopped clapping and touched his arm.

"It's some kind of bug, I think. I don't know." He frowned at her.

She touched his forehead. "You don't feel like you have a temperature."

"Let's get out, to start with."

He maintained his frown, not knowing how else to be convincing. In the lobby, she put on her beaver coat and he put on his navy-blue coat. "I'm awfully sorry," he said. "I think I'd just better get you home."

"Listen. Don't worry."

"But did you have anything to eat before? I promised food."

"That's no problem. I can fix us both some tea."

"I think it's probably best if I just drop you and get myself right home. I wouldn't want you to catch anything." He smiled.

"I'm sure I won't. I'm a vitamin C junkie, anyway."

"I think I'd better just take you home and go on home myself."

"I really hate asking you to take me all the way over east, then, but unfortunately I find cabdrivers to be rather insinuating at night."

"Don't be silly. I feel bad enough as it is being such a wet blanket."

"Oh, forget it. You can make up for it as soon as you're better."

In the taxi, he sat in the corner with his coat collar turned up, and looked out the window. He could think of nothing to say. "Hey, you, you're not rid of me yet," she said, hugging his arm.

He could not repeat that he didn't want her to catch his bug. He contributed some opinions on the performance. She listened so contentedly and respectfully, he regretted she wasn't someone else, someone new, from two months or three years ago, when he could have enjoyed her. As they were going up Park Avenue, Renee pointed out the apartment house of Alec Diamond, at whose triplex she had recently attended "a huge publicity blast where one of the biggest authors in the country, yucky drunk—you would know his name, so I'd prefer not to say it"—had lowered his zipper to her, with his wife standing three feet behind him. (Choosy Renee. She didn't like insinuating cabdrivers or drunken writers, who, if the story was true, lowered their zippers to her in public, or even, according to Madeline, oafs who picked her up in singles' bars. She liked *him*.) They reached her building—of the stubby, stale modern kind that made him think of clinics or medical labs—and he asked the cabdriver to wait just one second. "So, I'll see you," he said to Renee before the narrow, metal-framed glass entrance. "I'm sorry to be such a drag. I'm sure I'll shake this in a few days, anyway."

"Last chance to come up," she said. "Tea and sympathy."

"I'll take a raincheck, okay? I'd love to, some other time."

"Will you call me if you need anything?"

"*Lo giuro*. Promise."

"Call me when you're better?"

"I will sure give it my all. Thanks for being understanding."

She touched her forehead to his shoulder, as if she were tipsy. "Hell," she said. "Good night. I'm sorry." She lifted her head.

"Sorry for what? Don't *you* be sorry, of all things." He patted her shoulder. "This cab is going to take off without me. I'd better go."

She stuck her hand into his clump of curls and gave one rough rub. "Don't disappear," she said, turning away, finding her keys in her bag. He waved to her as he stepped into the taxi, but she was entering her door.

By the time he got home, jumpy with energy, he understood that he would gain nothing by calling Betsy at midnight, waking the noted oaken choreographer and the heroically exhausted pediatrician—who strolled among his sick in woolen shirt, plaid woolen necktie, green tweeds—and their two well-brought-up lads. He thought he would write her a dramatically persuasive letter, but she wouldn't get it until the middle of next week. In the morning, he would send her a telegram, so as not to intrude with a phone call. He would call her tomorrow morning. He must be entitled to one phone call. Betsy wasn't married to Andrea. The fact was, he had to see Betsy, if only for an hour, to hold her hand, to remind her how she had lain with him in bed when they talked, her arm across his back, possessively. She must be reminded of her own need. He remembered that he had never returned Roz's call, made when he was in Europe. October! Roz stayed up late, had on occasion called him as late as two or three. He sat down on the bed and dialed Roz, thinking that he had known her for twenty-five years, five-eighths of his life, and if he didn't see her from time to time, he wouldn't recognize her. She was out somewhere, the professional insider, huddling with pols, pollsters, reporters. On the sixth ring, she said, "Yes," as tersely as a frog.

"Roz? Did I disturb?"

"What do you think?"

"Sorry. I'll speak to you another time."

"Whatever." She concluded her end of the conversation by hanging up the phone.

When Andrea summoned Betsy, he heard cheerful talk drop away in the background and resume scattered and subdued.

"How are you?" Betsy said.

"Look, I'm sorry. Can you talk a minute? I've got to tell you something. A nice thing, very important."

"We're all eating breakfast here. May I call you back?"

"Fine. When?"

"Sometime in the next hour. You're home?"

"Yes. In the interim, just give a thought to the possibility of my coming up to see you, just for a short talk. We'll take a walk. That's all I want."

"Okay. I'll speak to you in a little while."

"Enjoy your breakfast."

"It's a feast. Sausages and waffles."

"Enjoy it." He phoned Air Canada and found out that they could put him on standby for a flight to Toronto late that afternoon. He would worry about a hotel later. He had coffee and his customary slice of whole-wheat toast heavily pasted with peanut butter and honey, while reading the paper in the dining room, the phone beside him on the table. In twenty minutes, the phone rang. It was either too early for Betsy or it was Betsy saying no again, so he kept his hello down.

"Is that Alan?"

"Yes. Oh, hi."

"Are you feeling any better?"

"Not really, I'm afraid. What's up?"

"I make a famous concoction of cinnamon tea, honey, whiskey, and a few secret items. Mother Renee's bye-bye-germ brew. Can I bring a batch to you?"

"I can't keep a thing down. But it's extremely thoughtful of you."

"It's just that I plan to be in your neighborhood anyway. I could do your dishes or smooth out your bed."

"Listen. Thank you. But a friend is going to be looking in on me."

"Do you have a doorman? I'll leave it with him, in a jar. Just heat it up. You'll be better before you know it."

"I have no doorman. I make something like it myself. But, as I say, it's not right for whatever ails me right now. I'm trying to reach my doctor."

"I don't even charge for house calls."

"I appreciate it, but I've got to go, Renee. Thank you. I'll call."

He made his bed. He delayed his shower so that he wouldn't miss the phone. If he left for Toronto this afternoon, he thought he might offer tonight's Philharmonic tickets to Roz.

Betsy called at eleven-twenty. "What's the nice thing?"

"This is serious, Betsy. Face-to-face only. I have got to see you. I have something you need. I'm not giving it away on the phone. I can be up there tonight, see you tomorrow, and come right back home and go to work on Monday morning. It will make all the difference. All."

"Can you give me a hint?"

"It's not any revelation. And it's not a marriage proposal. It's just a reminder, to both of us, that we're in love with each other, that we're friends."

"And you don't want to do it on the phone? I'm upstairs alone now. It sounds as if you've said it."

"No, I don't want to do it on the phone, and I haven't said it. I'll hang up, however, if you'd like, and we can forget it."

"That's not necessary. Do you have any idea how extraordinary your persistence is?"

"I can quit. I can't tell if you're being nasty or not."

"I don't think I'm being nasty. It's as if you were an athlete hanging from a bar for an hour by one arm. Most impressive."

"Betsy, forget the whole thing. It's our future, for God's sake."

"Perhaps I should come down to see you, instead."

"Are you joking?"

"Not entirely, no."

"Why bother?"

"It seems like such a grand gesture for you to come up here for a day, for a walk."

"Then I'll stay a few months, haunt you, follow you everywhere. I don't understand what the big deal is."

"When would you be able to come?"

"Tonight, if I can get a hotel room, and a seat on the plane.

226

They said chances are good for the plane. I'm not worried about that. Do you know where I should stay if I come? I haven't been to Toronto for ten years.''

"Let me ask Andrea. Hold on.''

Betsy did not want him, but he was going to go anyway. He was going to go because she had said to him, when she'd left, that his not being a pessimist was important to her. There was something to his going more important than his not being wanted.

"Andrea says the Park Plaza is elegant and right nearby. I can try to get a room for you from up here and save you a phone call. How long do you plan to stay? Seriously.''

"The Park Plaza is where I stayed before, I think. I'm sure. I would stay overnight. Tonight. Will you call me back collect? Will you be able to see me if I come tonight?''

"Of course. Or tomorrow. And tomorrow. It depends how late you're getting in.''

"I think about seven. You'll call me back, then?''

"Yes. As soon as I find something. See you.''

"Okay. Thank you.'' They hung up. She was hurrying to be nice, now that she had succumbed to his persistence, but her cooperativeness was only a friendly version of her distance. After she called him back, he would go and buy her the Beecham recording of *The Magic Flute*. Let Mozart plead for him.

Lofted northward in the fat lap of the plane's hum, Alan felt that he was traveling to the virtuous side of his persistence, leaving embarrassment behind. If his trip, before it had begun, had seemed to Betsy a grand gesture, his presence in Toronto could not possibly be anything but proof that he was ready to do so much more to show his love than complain of her absence that she would have to listen, to soften. Then he saw that he might be thinking like a father pursuing a wayward daughter, expecting her transformation in exchange for his stern loyalty. A happy ending. Betsy hadn't even acknowledged having gone away from him; why should he expect a hero's welcome for flying to her? She might find him far too sober, responsible, virtuous. Sacrificial. She might resent his effort. It might embarrass *her*. If you don't want to worry, he decided, don't think. Betsy had taught him how to worry.

The long cab trip from the airport would have seemed a waste of time even if it hadn't been dull, unforeign, Long Island–like, lined by the lights from ordinary-seeming houses. He wanted to have landed directly in his hotel room, lifted the telephone, summoned Betsy's nearby voice. In the cab, his impatience had nothing to do but mark time. Time, normally, was too fast or too slow. Time was like a snub-nosed beast that bullied your life without paying any attention to you. At the opera, for the most part, slow things happened quickly, fast things slowly. Furthermore, you knew what was coming, and when, but you also knew that if the performance worked, what was coming could clobber you. Anticipation didn't restrain impact, it didn't even prevent you from being surprised. And you knew that the opera would be over, and when it would be over.

As he was driven up a horseshoe drive to the gold-trimmed burgundy canopy of the Park Plaza, Alan entered a scene just completed and revealed for the moment of his arrival. It might have been his first hotel. The lobby's brocadelike brown-and-gold walls glowed in the rose light of sconces. The large sofas and armchairs were red plush, gold plush, his private colors. Room 1004 appeared to him as something more than a hotel room, because of its airy master-bedroom quality, and because it expected an event. An alcove entrance. A flowered quilted spread on the double bed. (The white telephone on the bed table waited tensely for his hand.) Two closets, two wing chairs, coffee table. He could move in. "Old" prints on the pale-yellow walls. The windows, formally draped, held a still deeper scene, all lighted up: that was Queen's Park, the bellhop explained, and the magical, towered, pinkish-brown buildings beyond were the Ontario Parliament. Alan had no luggage other than an old Alitalia flight bag and the *Magic Flute* recording, which he himself carried, but he tipped his guide cordially for having shown him to such a spectacular phone booth. It was five past eight. He sat down on the bed, about to dial, imagining that he had come to the wrong city—that he, or Betsy, was in Montreal. But, in fact, she answered the phone.

"I'm here," he said. "In your neck of the woods."

"Welcome. I can be over within fifteen or twenty minutes."

"I'm in 1004. Very homey here, I must say."

"I don't think I've ever visited anyone in a hotel room."

He hung up his Harris-tweed jacket and his rose-and-gray challis tie and unpacked tomorrow's shirt, underwear, and socks, leaving them on the bed so she could see that he meant to leave the next day. He put the wrapped *Magic Flute* beside them. He brought his shaving kit to the bathroom, off the alcove, where he washed his face and hands. He told himself not to push her, to push her very carefully, to hear her out if she had anything for him to hear. He must delay himself, get the feel, be professional. And then he might have no more effect than he'd had in keeping her from leaving for the city he'd followed her to. Maybe Curtis's death was incurable. His heart prickled. He could lose her. He could lose her. He could lose her to Curtis's death or to whatever she might use Curtis's death to camouflage. When he heard her tiny two-note knock, a whispering drumbeat, he winced with painful relief. Then he exhaled.

He opened the door without flourish and tried not to look too pleased. Smiling at him brightly enough, she marched past him in her Russian coat. He closed the door, and then found that he couldn't turn to face her, so he locked the door. He felt her arms come under his, clasping his chest, her head pressed to his back. He smelled the outdoor air from her coat sleeves. He waited for her to say something, or ease her embrace, but she did neither. He took one of her hands and kissed it, and held it to his face.

"I am so glad to see you," she said.

They were his words, but she had said them. "Glad to hear

229

it." He was empowered to face her, and he did. She looked happy, curious, obliging.

Tears, to his joy, slid from the rims of her eyes. She said, "It's as much of a surprise to see you as if I hadn't known you were coming. No kiss?"

"Kiss." They seized each other. Her thighs and hips were so solidly evident to him it was as if she had taken off her coat. He moved his mouth to her neck, and then he collected the moisture beneath her eyes. "So. You look the same, thank goodness. No tan, even."

"No tan. Dampness is our winter tourist attraction. You look the same, too. Ageless, as always."

"Believe me, I've aged. Are you hungry? Would you like to eat? I'm sort of hungry."

She moved away from him, unbuttoning her coat, and laid it at the bottom of the bed. She wore a russet turtleneck and a brownish-gray wraparound skirt. She took his socks, shirt, and underwear to the highboy and dropped them in the top drawer. "The package is for you," he said. "Is that skirt called taupe?"

"It answers to taupe, yes. You could move in here."

"That's what I was thinking before you came. Because of the coffee table. Maybe I'll steal the coffee table. But there's no record player."

She dawdled by the bed. "What should I do with my coat?"

"How much time do you have?" He gathered up the coat and hung it in the alcove closet.

"An hour. Twelve hours. Until you go."

"I mean now. Tonight."

"That's what I mean."

"You'll stay over?"

"It makes the room a better bargain. If you'll have me."

"Will you open your present while I call room service? Do you want anything?"

"Tea? Cocoa. Tea. I'll have cocoa, please."

"Got it." They sat down together on the bed. Alan ordered a pot of cocoa as well as a pot of tea, and, for himself, coffee, a bottle of ale, two chicken sandwiches, and pastry.

"Cancel my order," Betsy said. She held up the album. "Such a pretty color. Thank you. Why this particular op?"

"I will tell you later." He took her hand. "Shall we stretch out quietly until room service comes?" He kissed her. His hands drifted down the front of her sweater.

She clinched like a prize-fighter. "I'll explode. Let's sit in those nice chairs and look forward to the rest of the night."

"You're not numb or glassy."

She shook her head. "Since yesterday. I liked it that you insisted on coming. You lifted me off a hook. I feel lighter. But I didn't know I was going to be quite this pleased to see you."

"You were sounding so damn stingy, chilly. I decided to have had enough. And I had to tell you something that made me feel entitled to override you."

"I'd like to hear."

"Let's go sit. I have to work up to it." When they occupied the pale-brown plush wing chairs, separated by the coffee table, the illuminated Parliament was to their right for the looking.

"We're the king and queen of Canada," Betsy said.

"I want to know how is Andrea and everything."

"It's cozy, above all. Easy. The boys seem to think I'm the best thing that ever visited anyone's house, and Andrea and David treat me simply as if I belonged there. I'm not an object or representative of grief. It's all matter-of-fact. Andrea and I are on an extended reunion. We're in the present and the past at the same time. We're talking about taking a trip to Cornell."

"It's good you have her."

"I don't even seem to mind that she's such a matriarch. We each know things the other will never know. But she's wiser than I am. And she makes me laugh."

"Does she advise you? Has she been advising you?"

"About you and me?"

"In general. And you and me, yes."

"Not advising, really. She's smarter than that. She certainly understands how we could have happened. She thinks it's a waste of energy for me to feel guilty about Curtis. She thinks it's beside the point."

231

"Do you believe her?"

"I don't know. But it's helped just the same."

Andrea was doing some of his work for him. He didn't mind. He couldn't afford to mind. "What about your book?"

"Which one?"

"Whichever one you want to tell me about. I meant the one you're working on."

"I'm getting somewhere. But I'm writing with reluctance, some distaste. I find that distaste doesn't stimulate productivity. But I've done a dozen or so rough pages. It's like constructing my own nightmare. I don't have my courage yet, my appetite."

"Anything more on *Ecuador?* Are you in touch with Turnbull?"

"Only to let him know I was up here. I try not to think about it. When I think about it, I think of it, or of me, disappearing. Drowning. My hand is sticking out of the water as I go under. As you can see, writing has made me a contented woman."

"Is Toronto the North Pole of Quito?"

"Yes!" She laughed. "The North Toe! Toronto, incidentally, means 'a place of meeting.' How do you like that?"

"How can I not love it? Are you still planning to come back before publication day?"

"I'm undecided. I don't know."

"What's going to make up your mind, do you think? When would you come back, if not by the eighth?"

"A month? Two months? They've invited me to stay indefinitely. They're making it easy for me not to have to decide anything."

She had just said exactly what he had most feared she would say. "How long is indefinitely? What does it mean in practice?"

"The winter, I suppose."

He unfolded his arm to her across the coffee table. She took his hand, looking at him in a calm, unprotected way, as if she were thinking alone. She did not appear to expect him to express disapproval, disappointment, or defeat. "I'd like you to come back," he said, his heart lifting alarmingly.

232

She nodded, raising her eyebrows, earnest.

"I mean I'd like you to come back now, soon, to stay. Spend the winter in New York. Find an apartment for yourself. Stay at your house while you're looking. Stay at mine when you feel like it."

"Suppose I stayed here a few more weeks. Or until the end of January, serenely ignoring pub date, reviews, all the fuss everyone is going to insist on making, or not making, as the case may be."

"That would be fine, as long as I knew you were coming, and when, and that you wanted to come. I'm only thinking that maybe it would be better for you not to ignore your pub date— better to honor it, let it honor you. For one thing, you'll be having other pub dates in the future. I don't think it's good for you to get into the habit of treating them as if they were Judgment Day. Have lunch with Turnbull on the eighth, have lunch with Marilyn, have dinner with me. Look for an apartment. Then come back up here if you want, for a few more weeks. But you can't stay here forever, anyway. I mean, you can, of course, but you shouldn't. I'm very glad you have Andrea, but I'm not going to do you any harm. You can come visit here again, after all. But I want us to make a decision, one way or another, and I would much prefer us to decide that you're going to start picking up your life in New York, more or less with me. Once you decide that, you're going to find me very easy to take, because I'm going to be very happy. We have a lot to look forward to. Morning light, evening light, nighttimes."

She squeezed his hand. "Suppose I'm hard to take, though."

"I'll manage. If you want to be there, you won't be that hard to take, as far as I'm concerned. If you let me love you, and let me leave you alone, and let yourself enjoy me again, and feel your way into your new book, and stop being frightened of reviews, and drowning, and New York, and me, and just let us try, we will succeed. And if we don't succeed, then we won't have succeeded. But we will have tried. We need to try without trying. There's enough money. We both have things to do other than gaze at each other. I'm on your side. I want to associate with you. I can't put it any more informally.''

"You're healthy. Did you know you were healthy?" She left her chair and sat sideways on the floor between his legs, with her head against his thigh. His hand savored the smoothness of her hair. She said, "Perhaps I should fly down with you tomorrow for the week, look for an apartment, come back here for New Year's Eve. They're giving a party New Year's Eve I promised I'd stay for.''

"That's silly. Stay here for the party. Come down the next day, or the next.''

Her head jiggled in agreement. "That's what I'll do.''

"Did you tell Andrea you'd be spending the night here?''

"No. I'll call. In a little while.''

She stayed where she was, nestled, as if she were snoozing, using his thigh for her pillow. Through wet eyes, tears that had appeared so suddenly it was as if they had been tossed at him, he looked at his hand resting on her head. They were way up off the earth, in a room among the stars. Two months ago tomorrow, he had not known her. Now she was his life. Beneath his hand was his life. He started to say, "I cannot be happier," but he couldn't speak. Then he thought better of saying it. And he did not want to interrupt their silence. He leaned down to kiss the top of her head. Her hand came to his cheek. Room service knocked. Sliding his forehead back and forth, he rubbed his tears into her hair.

Promising to pay for the cocoa, she had tea and half an éclair while he ate his sandwiches. He told her about going to *The Magic Flute,* Renee Engel.

"I knew there would be a little someone, in the interim.''

"Do you think anything happened?''

Betsy seemed amused. "I have no idea. Did it?''

"I'm insulted. What happened was that I got so excited at the opera about telling you there was no need for us to be estranged, that it wasn't necessary to be separated or unfriendly, I was so buoyed up, that I was dying to get away to phone you. So I told her I had the flu and I took her home and came home, but I restrained myself from calling you, because it was so late. That's what happened. And she wanted my flu, too. All of it."

"Was she attractive?"

"Yes. Not remotely. The point is, if you'll be serious, that the opera was telling me to be hopeful, was reminding me that love can work, is meant for the benefit of people, if you're lucky enough to find it."

"It's always had a good reputation."

"Come on. I mean that if you're lucky, and you have it, you go through whatever is necessary to keep it, *with* your partner, that's what a partner is, is *for*, right? And then it works for you. All I'm saying is that love is available, to be used, by common citizens. You don't have to be a V.I.P., so to speak. You don't have to be an enchanted character in a Mozart opera to use it. There are people in this world who are meant for each other. And if they get separated in one way or another, they find each other again, and that makes them glad. I can't be altogether wrong about this if you're agreeable to coming back and joining me."

"Because you've put the plan in an unbinding way, a sensible way. If you had flown up here to ask me to marry you, or move in with you immediately and permanently, I wouldn't be agreeable. I'm not that brave. I'm not the happily-ever-after type."

"Will you marry me?"

She laughed. "I might, someday. But it doesn't seem the important issue. What's important is, as you suggest, to take advantage of what we've got. What we've got is friendship. Intimate friendship. The important thing is to remain intimate."

"That's perfect. Do me a favor. Don't decide until tomorrow whether you're coming back right after New Year's or at the end of the month or at the end of the winter. I don't want you to change your mind."

"I won't change my mind."

"How can you be so sure? I thought I was going to have to do a lot of delicate persuading. I visualized lying with you all night, not touching you, or just holding your hand, so you'd thaw, so you'd trust me. So you'd see how patient I can be."

"If you'd like, I can go out and come in again, and we can start over. How easy do you think it will be to find an apartment? The thought of a new apartment excites me."

"You'll find one, in time. You're lucky you have one in the meantime. Two. I can do a little sniffing for you. Maybe there's something in my building."

"Suppose we break up, though?"

"Then I'll move out, as a courtesy. But we won't. You'll see. It's not in the cards."

"Do I wait for you to come home every night from the opera? Like having a husband who works the night shift?"

"First of all, I can cut back at least fifty percent. Secondly, I would hope you'd come with me some of the time, or most of the time. I'll certainly go to the movies with you. I don't care what I do so much if we'll be doing it together most of the time. We have the whole city. We have everywhere. We can travel. What do you plan to do about telling the Monroes?"

"The Monroes? Nothing. When they know, they'll know. We don't have to be retroactive. You're a new friend."

"That's right." No question, her attitude had changed. What had been hard was easy. She was choosing him over anxiety. She was now being realistic in his favor. "Anything else to discuss?"

"Can't think of anything. But there will be. We'll be improvising. I find the whole idea of having choices and love at the same time extraordinarily attractive. Sleeping over, leaving, coming back. Or staying. Times when you're at my house while I'm at your house. We'll each have two keys."

"We'll be a quietly public couple. Everyone will know we're together without being sure what our status is. A mystery team."

"Let us begin. What do we do with these dishes?" She stood.

"I'll call." He raised his coffee cup to her. "By the way, here's to grand gestures."

"Oh, right!" She swooped to kiss him. "Thank you for coming. You'll call room service. I'll go to the bathroom. Then I'll call Andrea. I wish I had a robe."

"You will have a robe. I will be your robe."

He pointed the way to the bathroom on his way to the phone. Room service said they'd be up in fifteen minutes, not to leave the table in the hall. Betsy reappeared and called Andrea. "She says come to breakfast in the morning," Betsy reported.

"I'm in!"

While they waited, they developed a spontaneous game of unprovocative kissing—foreheads, cheeks, chins, shoulders, backs of heads, elbows, shoes, knees, shins—until they were laughing, finally, across the room from one another. When room service arrived, Betsy went again into the bathroom, and when Alan knocked on the bathroom door and told her the room was theirs, she came out naked and said, "May I have my robe, please? I need my robe."

He awakened deep in darkness. One of her hands was attached to his belly, the other touched the bottom of his neck. They lay in the darkness, he thought, like a couple in a sarcophagus, like Aïda and Radames in the tomb. But the way they lay was death-defying. He wanted a photograph, a certificate, of their position. If they could sleep like this on their first night ever asleep together—he was accustomed to nights of thin sleep with women, exhausting, watercolor sleep—they would be sleeping like this for thirty or forty years. Then they would ask for an extension. He wanted tomorrow to be here so that he could leave her to wait for her in New York, begin the waiting so it would be over, welcome her back, start their life. All of his past was women he had been in a hurry to discard, all trial and error for the sake of this achievement. It was not that he deserved it, but he had earned it. Betsy was his. She owned him. She was his because she owned him. Pretending to be asleep, he slipped his arm over her, hoping she would wake. He had to tell her how lucky he was.

"What do you want for Christmas?" she whispered. "Are you sleeping?"

"How long have you been awake?" He moved down a little, so that her breasts spread on his nipples.

"I've been half-awake for a while. Drowsing. Thinking about my new apartment, who will be living in the old apartment. What to get you for Christmas. That I'm grateful to you for being so decisive and so gentle. Discreet. I like our plan, because we can grow into it. Also thinking that you are such a loving lover. You are filled with strong sweetness."

He kissed her. "I wish I could tell you how happy I am without fearing it would scare you."

"Don't worry about it. I want to make you happy. To participate in your being happy. I hope I'll be good at it."

"You can't miss. For Christmas, I would like a sable coat. How long did we sleep? I wonder."

"We started the night quite early."

"Excuse me." He rolled away. "Close your eyes. I'm going to turn on the light for a second." He switched on the bed-table lamp and examined his watch. One-fifty-five. He turned off the lamp and returned to Betsy. "I thought we'd slept for hours. It's about two."

"Let's talk ourselves to sleep. This is not uncomfortable, is it?"

"Lying naked with you, warm in bed, is not uncomfortable."

"Well, then, what shall we discuss?"

It crossed his mind to ask her if her wish for separate apartments meant that she wanted to keep her options open, did not want to cut herself off from the possibility of other men, another man. But to ask her that was not the way to ask her that. In any case, she had said "intimate," that the important thing was to remain intimate. And that they would grow into their plan. "Do you see us living together apart for life?"

"What I see is that living together apart, at least for a while, is a way of giving us a chance for a long life."

238

"What do you mean by a long life?" He might as well say it, they were so comfortable. "Whatever we do, I want to do forever."

"Whatever we do, I hope we'll do for as long as we both want to, and I hope that's forever. How's that? Though I'm told that forever is not the same length for everyone."

"No, I've heard that as well. That'll do, for the time being. Do you worry about getting bored with me, ever?"

"I never think about boredom as a problem. Certainly not with you. You are the opposite of boring. But I don't mind the idea of boredom with someone I know. It's not my goal, exactly, but I think that as long as I can write, I can't really be bored, anyway. I get bored when I can't work. It's what makes me most anxious, that I won't have anything to write, or that I won't be able to finish something, that I'll lose control of it, or that it will disappear on me. You, however, might get bored with me when I'm working well. That's one reason we should try separate apartments. Then you may not notice it so much. I tend to favor my work when I'm working well. I tend to enjoy loneliness then."

"You've warned me of that. I'll just have to let you alone, and let you come to me."

"That's the trick, of course. That's the ticket, as my father used to like to say."

"It's worth it, that's all I know. What worries you the most, other than not being able to work?"

"Daily life."

"Seriously."

"Yes. You know. Losing things, worrying about losing things, worrying about being late, getting lost. Little things are everything."

"I don't worry about them. Funny."

"That's because you're healthy."

"I really meant what big things worry you, about the future, about you and me?"

"The only thing that's always worried me, not about you and

me in particular but about everyone, everyone and me, me and everyone, which is dependency. I'm squeamish about dependency. I sneaked dependency on Curtis and I got furious, more than furious, at his trying to take me over. I think I was drawn to you at the beginning because you seemed undependable. In part. It wasn't your only attraction."

"I'm not undependable."

"On the contrary. Don't be insulted."

"I'm not. But are you worried about my being dependent?"

"Probably. But not at the moment. I like you just the way you are right now."

"How is that? How am I right now?"

"Next to me."

He removed his arm from her back and settled his hand against her crotch. "Then you must like my being a little bit dependent."

"Yes. Also, I like being dependent. I'm hard to please. I feel guilty when I'm needy and I feel guilty when I'm being ungenerous, or resistant. It may not turn out to be a problem with us. But it's always the problem. Dependency is always the problem, for any couple."

"What's so terrible about having a problem from time to time? We're bound to have a problem from time to time. Why not expect it and accept it? We'll work them out. Living apart is not going to prevent problems."

"Is that a clever way of suggesting that we should move in together? We're probably going to be spending weeks together, months, without a break. You're going to be glutted with my presence. All I want is breathing space. And the understanding that if we spend a few nights apart, it doesn't mean I've stopped loving you. It's for your sake, too. You're not used to a steady diet of anyone. You have to go into training."

"If I didn't have you, I wouldn't be interested in anyone. My whole idea is to make this work for the rest of our lives. I'm sick of variety. Variety is what's boring."

"You'll see. You should know that there will be times when

240

you may wish I were there, and times when you probably won't be able to stand the sight of me."

"Whatever it is, whatever happens, I want to do it with you. I want the experience of not liking you. Everything will always come back. I'll be happy for things to change, to change color, but I want to be there with you while the color is changing. I want to be reviewing our life with you thirty-five years from now. I want to have us to look back on. I want to build up an archive."

"Tomorrow is the two-month anniversary of our first meeting."

"*Mmmm!*" he said, as if he were congratulating her nastiness. "Can I help it if I've only known you two months? In addition to thinking me so healthy, do you also think of me as foolish?" He had first realized on the plane that it was to be their two-month anniversary; also that today had been the two-week anniversary of Curtis's death. Did she know?

"Certainly not. If you're foolish, I'm foolish. You're optimistic. Eager and enthusiastic. You should be optimistic for two, and I should be skeptical for two. I share my skepticism with you, you share your optimism with me. You're boyish. It's okay. I'm plenty girlish, in my way. That's one reason I want to make certain we go about this right."

"Fine. I'm all for it. Whatever will make it last."

"Do you know what we have to do?"

"What?"

"We have to stop talking about it. We're not going to build up an archive by wanting to. We'll have to learn on the job."

"I know that."

"Then you mustn't be so worried about setting an endurance record."

"I'm not worried. I don't want you to worry. I want you to know that we'll get there. Maybe I'm talking this way because I started so late. I'm a bachelor in a hurry for respectability."

"I want you to make me a promise."

"Anything."

"That this will not become our subject of difficulty. Permanence will take care of itself. How will we have any pleasure if all you're concerned about is reaching our sunset years? That's not optimism. It's morbidity."

"I do promise. Subject dropped. I'm interested in the entire future, starting at the beginning. You know that. After all, it was my idea."

"That's not fair. Not accurate. I would have wandered back to you, abashedly, sidled back to you. You hadn't seen the last of me. You thought you had, but that's your problem. What you've done is to stimulate an earlier and more dignified return. And I've already thanked you. I expect to continue being thankful, as long as you don't dwell dreamily on our senility, drool in anticipation of drooling."

"I know it will all take care of itself. Say no more." He patted her crotch.

She lifted his hand and held it. "We have to take care of each other. I've never formulated it to myself. It's been like a cloud in my brain that keeps dissolving before it becomes a thought, or it's a thought I had early that got lost, but I think we have an incestuous tang to us. It's as if the ways we're different are a disguise for the ways we're the same. Of course, in one way that's as sexy as can be, that we're relatives, but it means that we have to try to alternate our moods so that only one of us is impetuous or anxious at a given time. I think both of us are impetuous, and we're both worriers, but differently."

It made him happier, more secure, than anything else she could say when she defined the parts of his personality. "Remember, I'm very practical. I'm very good at planning, and getting from here to there, getting things accomplished."

"I'm aware of that. We both check our impetuosity, also in different ways. You by being efficient in the world. Also, you're more cautious than you appear to be. Your life, actually, has been cautious, in a sense."

"That may be true, but if you mean I never take risks, I certainly take a risk with you. I took a huge risk coming up here."

"Well, that must be what I've been waiting to hear you say, now that I hear it. You're taking a risk. So am I. But we're doing it in steps. It doesn't become us to gobble up the future, as if it's all been put on our plates."

"Really, I understand that. But you have to understand that I'm eager to have it all with you. Since I've met you, I feel that I've entered the center of something, that I've climbed onto the world itself, that I'm grown, that I've reached my age. Even though I may lapse. I admire you so much I can still barely believe you exist."

"Shh." She quickly kissed his hand. "Alonzo, I love you. I love it that you're a boy and a man at the same time. I love watching you be. I love you for just what you are. It can't be helped."

"You mean just what I am with *you*. There's a big difference. All the difference. I feel completely composed, completely contented. All my cells. I hope you're lucky enough to feel the same. Or I hope you will."

She kissed his throat. "All I can tell you is that I look forward to everything. You enable me to look forward. Tomorrow, I'm going to stop picking at my book. I'm going to take hold of it and stare it down. I know we're going to learn to handle each other well. It's not going to be all that difficult. We'll love each other much more than we do now. You'll be surprised."

He moved his cheek to her hand, stroked her head, seized by pride, his eyes tightly closed. They talked about the possibility of having breakfast in their room rather than at the Douglases', with Alan dropping Betsy off at the Douglases' on his way to the airport. They talked about whether Betsy should fly down on New Year's Day or the day after, and agreed on the day after. It would be more sensible for Betsy, and certainly friendlier to the Douglases. A week from Wednesday, it would be. Eleven days. She would call him at the office when she reached her house. He would meet her at her house, or at his. Betsy said she was getting sleepy. They fell silent, their hands wrapped between them, Alan thinking—as if memorizing new rules, rules of membership—that from now on, having won her, he must put trust in their future, must trust her love, let her need him. If he did these things, then she would always need him. If he did these things, the future would take good care of them. They belonged together. Fate was on their side. Trust the future, trust her, and trust himself, trust his impulses. He knew, from today, that he had her best interests at heart, or he wouldn't have been able to ask her with such success to return to New York now, resume her life. He would not need to press her in the future. Eventually, she herself would decide that they should live together without interruption. They would move from their separate apartments to an apartment of their own. And then, maybe even better, maybe even more. He understood what he needed to do in order that they should last. It was as if, because he had finally fallen in love, love would reward him with its fidelity.

On Monday, he met his parents (his sister and her family were not up from Washington) for a Christmas-Eve-day lunch at the Russian Tea Room—the annual December 24th lunch, at one or another "good" restaurant, that his father referred to as "the Jews' Christmas," as if it were not his own idea to observe neither Hanukkah nor Christmas, but some hostile tradition according to which Jews who didn't observe Hanukkah were not allowed a real Christmas, either. But Alan enjoyed his father at the lunch; his father insisted that Alan have a second buffalo-grass martini. Alan entertained his parents with an account of Renee Engel's stale diatribe against Arthur Mullmann, and her report of the famous "author" who had allegedly exposed himself to her at Alec Diamond's party. Sometimes it was as if his parents forgot, or didn't care, that he was a forty-year-old bachelor. Like any other couple, they were capable of taking the benefit of his bachelor anecdotes, his freedom. But, he thought, how much he would have preferred to be sobering them with the announcement of Betsy's existence in his life, and he kept imagining telling them about her, and then introducing her to them. He imagined her being irritatingly shy with them, winningly shy, less and less shy, captivating them, multiplying his pride. He did not mention to them that he had been away over the weekend, even though he could have said he'd been in Toronto for the magazine. He would keep her to himself until he could deliver her. On Christmas night, he went alone to a *Barber of Seville* whose star, the enrapturing Flicka von Stade, with a voice and charm far above vanity, embodied and gave out good fortune. Her presence created perfect focus. The stage rose a few inches whenever she came on.

He and Betsy spoke at least every other day throughout the week. She had found a side entrance into her book, a scene she was actually loving to write, and, as a result, much of the rest of the book seemed to be catching fire, in spot after spot, so that she had to make hurried notes to keep up with her thoughts. Her flight, 733, on Wednesday, January 2, left Toronto at noon, arriving at Kennedy at one-twenty. They rearranged three or four times how to spend the evening of her return, where they would have dinner, at his house or out; if out, where; whether she would spend the night at his house or not stay over until the next night. Intending to buy her a nightgown of the same deep and brilliant rose as the *Magic Flute* album, he bought her, on sale at Saks, a silvery raccoon coat, almost nine hundred dollars, with tax. He had never done anything like it. He found *Ecuador* in the Fifty-third Street Doubleday. He bought four copies, and told the clerk they must order more.

Roz called to say she was "pissed" at him for having called so late the previous Friday, especially when he had waited two months to return her call. "It's been unbelievably hectic," he said. She asked him when he wanted to get together. He said he would call her soon and make a date for a drink. Roz said he was a pain in the ass. Her voice had, possibly, one thin streak of friendliness left in it. On New Year's Eve, instead of going to parties—what was the point of parties? He had nothing to seek —he went, again alone, to *A Moon for the Misbegotten* and came home to call Betsy, as they had arranged he would. He and Andrea wished one another a happy New Year, and Alan said he was looking forward to seeing her soon again, and meeting her husband, either in New York or Toronto. Andrea reciprocated. When Betsy came on, he told her about the play, how wonderful it had been, and the performances. He had not minded going alone, he didn't mind doing anything alone, because he was not lonely waiting for her. Her party, she said, was on the smug side, academic-bourgeois, and anyway, she wanted to be with him.

"A day and a half."

"I'm going to have to come Saturday rather than Wednesday —to my regret, you may be sure. Malcolm Douglas is playing in a crucial hockey game in his Little League on Saturday afternoon. I had to promise I'd be there. You can imagine how much the prospect excites me."

"Didn't he know you were leaving Wednesday?"

"I think it's partly a way of keeping me a few more days. It means so much to him that he couldn't ask me himself. He had to ask Andrea to ask me. I am the object of a crush. And he says he didn't know how important the game was going to be."

"I don't blame him for the crush. He's thirteen?"

"Thirteen. So I'm catching the five-o'clock flight Saturday afternoon, even if I have to leave the game early, and I'll be in at six-twenty. I would like, if it's all right with you, to come straight to your house and stay. I don't want to sleep in my old apartment ever again. Will you try to make some closet space for me? Either I'll look for my own place from your house, or I won't look at all, just stay."

"Betsy, I'm not angry with you for postponing your arrival, I swear. I am slightly disappointed. But you don't have to make up for it, I beg of you."

"It has nothing to do with making up for anything. I've thought it through."

"Let's discuss it when you get here. If you mean it, you know it's what I want more than anything."

"I mean it. And I will be a great tenant."

"You're already a great tenant. I've never had a better tenant."

"I look forward to your company. It's only three extra days' wait."

"It's all right. It's you I'm waiting for. That makes everything all right."

"I'd better go back downstairs. Perhaps someone is about to explode a theory."

"What has changed your mind about moving in?"

"Desire and appreciation. Confidence. The wish to make us both happy. You'll be away from the house all day. I'll have plenty of freedom to work. If I'm in a mean mood, I'll stay out of your way. But I don't want to stay out of your way. Now that I'm letting you be so generous, I hope you won't regret it."

"It's not generosity on my part, it's pure greed. Pure, as in loving. I thought I was as happy as I could be. Now I'm happier. The delay is more than worth it. Happy New Year. Happy New Years."

"And many mores."

The conversation seemed less climactic than he would have imagined it to be. He supposed the true climax had taken place between them in Toronto. Tonight was confirmation of what he had privately predicted up there.

On New Year's Day, he stopped in at Bob Manners's open house. He told Bob he would have an announcement to make to him in five days. Bob asked him if he was going to work for *Time*.

"Hardly, no. It's a little surprise. It'll keep."

"What's her name?"

"Betsy. Harris. It's for real. Don't say anything to anyone. I'm not kidding."

"You've been keeping this from me?"

"I've had to."

"How many hours has it been going on?"

"Months. That's not the point."

"Are you getting married?"

"She's moving in."

"Are you holding a moving-in ceremony?"

247

"When you meet her, you will be impressed."

"I'm already impressed."

That evening, he reviewed the clothes in his bedroom closet to see what he might get rid of. He put aside a few suits, a few jackets. But that was not the answer, of course. They would need a new closet, or a wardrobe for her clothes. Or a new apartment. He transferred as many clothes from the foyer closet as he could make room for in the bedroom closet. He took Betsy's raccoon coat from its box and hung it in the foyer closet. He thought of calling her, to tell her what progress he had made, but then he decided not to. The silence between them today was occupied by expectation that began at each end and met halfway. At about ten, he called her after all. "Just checking in. The foyer closet is almost bare. I can't wait for your dresses and pants. We'll have to get your bureau down here. We'll put it in the dining room."

"Don't let me take over."

"You can't. You have. This is the way I want it. Are you all right?"

"Tired. From last night. The party didn't improve, but it didn't end, either."

"Are you ready for bed?"

"Just about."

"Go to sleep."

"I will. Good night."

"Betsy? Are you sad about something?" Curtis?

"A little. Prepublication headache, mostly. I think about things I can't do anything about. What happens to my book is completely out of my control. That's why I worry. I believe it's the feeling known as dread."

"I will talk you out of it, whatever it is."

"I will certainly let you try."

"Sleep well. I love you."

"Thank you."

"Betsy?" He made a telephone kiss. She returned it, and they hung up.

Renee called him at the office early the next morning to ask him if he was better and if he was free for lunch. She'd had a dream about him. He said he was getting better but meeting a deadline for a Terrorism piece and unable to talk. He collected information, some of it fresh and important, on Basques and Palestinians. He went to another *L'Italiana* and another *Simon Boccanegra*. Betsy sounded cheerful again on the phone, was determined to be mature, she said, to ignore her dread and keep her nose in her new book. Alan imagined himself to be a husband whose wife's unhappiness he could cure like a magician. He would always have much more energy and concern for her than she would ever need to draw on. No qualms whatever about her moving in, he noticed, were crossing his mind. And, after all, since it was her reality he treasured, what was there for him to worry about? She gave him nothing he wished to avoid.

Saturday morning, he walked over to the Met and picked up a cancellation for that afternoon's *Bohème,* his third of the season, Corelli singing Rodolfo. The performance would be over shortly after five, and he back home two hours before Betsy reached his house. She had told him not to bother to meet her at the airport, and he hadn't argued, because he wanted to open his door to her. He would buy flowers on the way home, champagne, maybe some caviar. He would dust a little, straighten things, anticipate her pleasure in her raccoon coat. The interim between his arrival and hers would be brief enough and leisurely enough to appreciate. He would hold his excitement to his cheek. They were going out for dinner, to the Café des Artistes, at nine. Then home together.

At *La Bohème,* almost always, Alan's cheeks froze and his eyes filled, at the beginning and at the end—the lingering love at first sight of Rodolfo and Mimi, all promise, all future, and the extended yet sudden death of Mimi, all loss, one event as tense, exciting, and satisfying as the other. And so it was today, at the beginning. The perfect first-act ending, the distant, last high notes of the love duet, Rodolfo and Mimi leaving his garret together for the Café Momus, had Alan staring, for the fiftieth time, tearfully at the empty stage, and then at the curtain, without caring to applaud. But then came the first of the three intermissions. *Bohème*'s intermissions were about as long as its acts. Having decided he would kill the afternoon fastest at the opera, he wondered now how he was going to get through the opera. He left his seat and stood on line for water.

The second act helped out, being especially short, eighteen minutes this afternoon. He and Betsy were dawdling, spectating, in different nations. In four hours, they would be embracing, but four hours, at the moment, might as well have been four more days. He walked and paused here and there around the lobby, ignoring the Lobbyites. He felt as if he were alone in his apartment. He returned to his seat well before the beginning of the third act. He could have gone to the bar, but he wanted to wait until Betsy arrived before he had a drink. His customary impatience with Rodolfo and Mimi in the third act usually got blown away by the music the lovers were lucky enough to be singing. Today, their feuding and reconciling seemed to him contemptibly wasteful and juvenile. They didn't deserve their love if they didn't know how to care for it, as his mother would say of a suit. He decided to meet Betsy at the airport after all. He would underplay his presence there (Don't I know you, Miss?). He would carry her suitcase, escort her into the city. But she might be irked at his showing up. She wasn't a child, as she liked to remind herself. And if he did go out to Kennedy, he would miss the experience of her coming to him all the way by herself. During the final intermission, he relieved his distraction by playing his old game with the lobby crowd, imagining them an opera chorus being a lobby crowd, setting a scene, establishing atmosphere, waiting for Carmen, so to speak. You rarely saw anything eventful happen in lobbies. It was all crowd, no Carmens. The thought of calling Toronto to find out if anyone knew if Betsy had left to catch her plane rose through his mind like a welling of irrelevance. She would now *have* to be on her way to the plane. And in any case, she was going there straight from the hockey game. Anyone who might happen to be home would think it extremely odd that he should be wondering; or it would seem as if he were calling to suggest, for some reason, that she shouldn't come, if it weren't too late to stop her.

In the last act, when Musetta burst into the garret, at the height of the Bohemians' horseplay, to announce that Mimi was outside, ill, Alan was thinking that Betsy would be missing her plane because the hockey game had gone into overtime and she'd had to stay, out of loyalty to Malcolm. Her plane was to take off in exactly fifteen minutes. She'd been hit in the face by a puck. She was stuck in a traffic jam on the highway. Or she was at the Douglases', having an attack of dread, not coming, postponing her coming. Until spring. She would not show. If he didn't meet her at the airport, she wouldn't be there to be met. She was not coming. Her coming was simply too good to be true. If he went home, she would be calling him to say she had changed her mind. She was someone who changed her mind. Colline finished his *Vecchia zimarra* and departed with Schaunard. Mimi and Rodolfo were alone, for the beginning of the end. Alan watched them, trying to pay attention. It was no good. He would miss the heartbreaking death he adored, but he had to get going. He was going to the airport. He reached beneath his seat for his coat and stood up. Excuse me. Sorry. He had never, ever done this. Betsy would be amused. Someone said, "Tch! For God's sake!" Alan had once punched in the hip a man passing in front of him during the last minute of *Aïda*, causing the man to stagger against the shoulders of someone in the row ahead and nearly starting a fistfight. He reached the aisle, feeling as if he had walked onto the stage itself, and lunged up half the length of the orchestra and out the door, into the silent red lobby. He was going to meet her plane, but he had to make sure she would be on it. At this moment, she was absolutely nowhere. He hadn't spoken with her since yesterday. It wouldn't be that odd of him to call. Just checking, he would say, in case the flight had been delayed, some such thing. Betsy

251

would answer. "Oh, there you are," she would say. He ran down the steps of the lobby to the phones. He was alone with the opera, which continued on the TV set beyond him in the lounge, Mimi and Rodolfo still reminiscing. Alan pulled shut the phone-booth door, dropped his coat on the floor, laid a dime on the counter, and grabbed his wallet from the breast pocket of his camel's-hair jacket. He extracted his credit card from the wallet, dialed zero, dialed the Douglases'. The operator came on. He read her his credit card number. He waited. He was being ridiculous. He should hang up, go home, start enjoying the countdown. He tensed to hang up. The phone began to ring in Toronto. He didn't recognize the voice of the woman who answered. Good. Wrong number. "I'm sorry. Is this the Douglases'?"

"This is Ellen Gibson. I'm a neighbor. Is this the hospital?"

"No, ma'am. Not a professional call. I'm a friend of their houseguest, Betsy Ring, in New York. I just wanted to make sure she's caught her plane."

"Well, I doubt if she has. But you'll have to call the hospital."

"I don't understand what you're talking about."

"Mrs. Douglas and Mrs. Ring have been in an accident. I assumed that's why you were calling. Dr. Douglas is with them at the hospital."

"What hospital?"

"Etobicoke General. If you'll give me your name, I can ask Dr. Douglas to call you when he calls."

"No. I'll call. Give me the hospital number. What kind of accident?"

"Automobile."

"Is it serious, do you know?"

"You'd better call Dr. Douglas. Here's the number."

"I don't have a pen, damn it. Give it to me. I'll remember."

She gave him the number and asked him for his name.

"Alan Hoffman. Say the number again."

She said it again.

He hung up, repeating the number to himself, and continuing

to repeat it until he had dialed zero again, and then dialed the hospital. An operator came on. He gave her his credit card number. He held the phone tightly. His chest was like concrete. The phone rang. A switchboard operator answered. Alan said, "I'm calling from New York. There's been an auto accident up there that's come into your hospital. I'm trying to reach a Doctor David Douglas. David Douglas. He's with the people in the accident."

"We'll try emergency."

He punched rapidly at the side of the phone box.

"Emergency."

"Doctor David Douglas there? With an automobile accident? Two women."

"Hold on. He's here."

Alan could now hear nothing at all of the opera outside; it had gone dead.

"Doctor Douglas speaking."

"David? David Douglas?"

"Yes. Who is this?"

Alan was relieved. "Alan Hoffman."

"How did you find out?"

"What has happened?"

"I have extremely bad news, I'm afraid."

"What is it?" Alan put his right hand on his head.

"I have to tell you that Betsy has died."

Alan's scalp went cold. "I don't believe you."

Applause poured from the auditorium as the doors opened and the opera broke.

He twisted away from the noise. "Where is Betsy?"

"Here. At the hospital."

"How do you know she's dead?" Douglas was lying. It might not be Douglas. "What about Andrea?"

"We think Betsy must have died immediately. Andrea has some fractures, a concussion."

"How?" His voice was being squeezed. "How?" he said again.

"Andrea was driving. Someone coming off the access road

evidently skidded into them, hitting Betsy's side of the car. There's a freezing rain up here."

He saw Betsy dead in the car. A roar from upstairs. The curtain calls.

"Are you there?" Douglas asked.

"On their way to the airport?"

"They were on the way to the airport, yes."

Alan's blood had turned white. The roars were getting fuller. While the cheering lasted, the news wasn't true.

"Does Betsy have any immediate family?" Douglas asked him.

"No. None. I'm coming right up there. I'll call you back in twenty minutes from my house. I'm coming tonight if I can get a flight. I can't talk." He hung up the receiver. It bounced off the hook. He hung it up again. A fresh roar above. People appeared, waiting to phone. Alan took hold of his coat and blew out of the booth and up the stairs. In the lobby, he stopped. His heart thudded like feet. He covered his eyes with his hands and breathed. He breathed again. He pressed his wrists hard against his cheekbones. The auditorium din held on. He had said he was going home. He pushed his arms into his coat sleeves. He started through the lobby crowd. His heart was beating outside his chest. He climbed the steps to the upper lobby and stopped again. He stared at the dark beyond the glass doors, the audience bubbling onto the plaza. He buttoned his coat.

ABOUT THE AUTHOR

Richard P. Brickner graduated from Columbia College in 1957. He is the author of two previous novels, *The Broken Year* (1962) and *Bringing Down the House* (1972), and an autobiographical work, *My Second Twenty Years* (1976), as well as numerous articles and reviews. He was a lecturer at City College between 1967 and 1974, and has been a member of the faculty of The New School since 1970.